My Name Isn't Joe

Written by James Thomas

My Name Isn't Joe

Authored by James Thomas
© James Thomas 2022
Cover Asher Fai

Edited by Marcia M Publishing House Editorial Team Published by Marcia M Spence of Marcia M Publishing House, West Bromwich, West Midlands the UNITED KINGDOM B71

FICTION

ISBN 978-1-0686417-8-7

www.marciampublishing.com

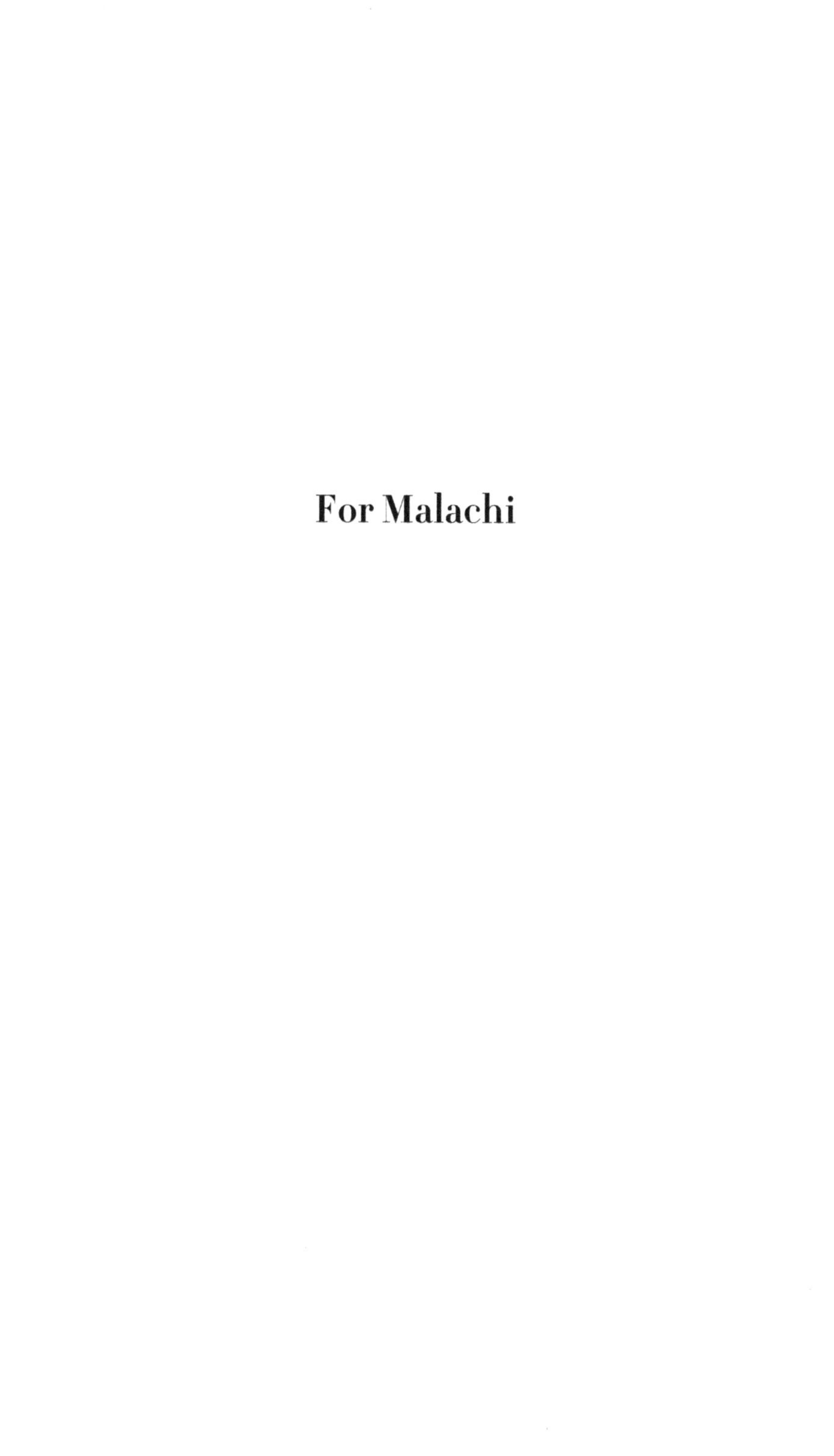

For Malachi

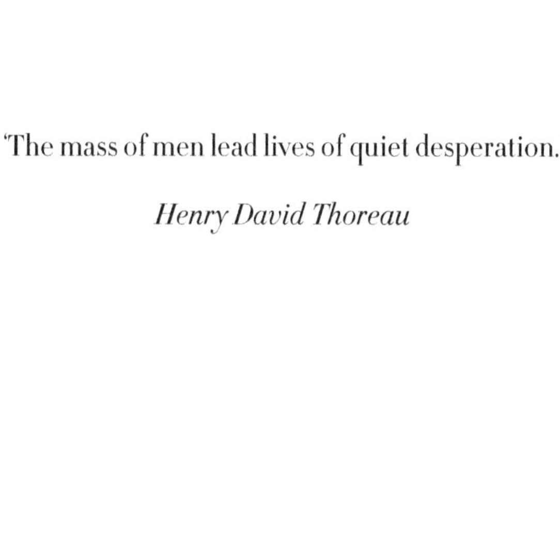

'The mass of men lead lives of quiet desperation.'

Henry David Thoreau

"I think that what made your writing stand out for me is that you demonstrate such a clear and deep understanding of the human condition and are able to convey that through some very elegant writing. Although much of what you write is quite introspective, you never allow the narrative to become ponderous or self-indulgent but maintain a pace which is easy to read but also never hurried. Your writing doesn't merely describe a sequence of events, it is much deeper than that, and it is that which I think really sets it apart from that of so many writers. I feel that you write with honesty, freedom and without fear, as you so clearly depict a young man dealing with his innermost struggles - I really found it extremely moving." **Bill Goodall – Bill Goodall Literary Agency**

Introduction

They say that "you don't know what you've got till it's gone"; well, sometimes, you really do.

<u>**Today**</u> - (Who am I?)

I'm the person you see every day – you sit next to me on the bus, ride beside me on the train and walk past my desk at least twice every afternoon. I'm the person whose witty and well-rehearsed quips go unheard, who prematurely apologises, who smiles too often and regularly mistimes when to laugh. I'm the one who doesn't seem to mind not being thanked and rarely congratulated. I'm the one who makes up the numbers, and at the same time, is never *really* missed. Yet, I'm the reason why there's always milk in the office fridge.

I say it isn't fair – as if I were put in this position, as if those twins of time, fate and destiny, had conspired to make me the person I am. I love passing blame like a naughty kid loves passing wind, but I'm not so naive as to really believe that I had no choice in how I ended up here.

My name is Joseph Bogart, like the famous actor, but for some reason, everyone chooses to call me Joe Bloggs. I work a nine-to-five, earn a decent wage and rent a one-bedroom flat in a reasonable part of London. That's my whole life in a sentence.

I've always been described as a 'pretty average guy', but average in what way? In the mathematical sense of being in the middle, being the mean, that with all things weighed up I'm neither hot nor cold? Great nor terrible? Or is it in terms of perspective, and if so, whose? To a 10 I'm a 2, to a 1 I'm a 7, so to whom am I a 5?

I was too scared to ask myself the more important question - what am I to me? But yesterday, I was forced beyond my comfort zone and pressed hard from within to seek the answer, to what it was I was so afraid of.

<u>Yesterday</u>

I sat in a busy West-London Park during my lunch break, eating a supermarket sandwich and trying not to get any salad cream on my supermarket suit. As I wiped the drop that got away from my chin, I glanced up from my light meal. The sky was a dull, tarnished silver and reminded me of the sparse cutlery in the office kitchen. The grass a few feet away had more patches of brown than green, so most people were looking for a free seat on a bench. A black-cab stuck in traffic was playing *Take the Box* from Amy Winehouse's first album. As I cocked an eyebrow at the aged cab driver's good taste, a couple, after checking the space for bird poop, sat down next to me. I smiled and they smiled back in that genuine 'we don't think you look like a pervert' kind of way.

I guessed they were a little younger than me, maybe mid to late twenties. They talked, held hands and it was clear they had seen *Annie Hall* recently as they made quirky observations about the people walking past; it was cliché but cute.

Then he kissed her.

I glanced over to a great oak in the other direction, but I could feel the kiss lasted a while. I contemplated leaving to give them privacy, but there were no other benches free. When I glanced back, they had finished. They were smiling. She was drinking Coke out of a can with a straw, and he couldn't take his eyes off her.

Usually, when I see couples in love, instead of covetousness, I feel a content envy filled with promise – I don't want what the other person has, as I know one day I'll have the same for myself.

Then, ever so gently, she removed the straw from her lips, brushed the hair from the side of his brow and pressed her cheek against his, whispering in his ear. A look of joy, a stone's throw away from bliss, brightened his face and turned my content envy into the most bitter of jealousies. I didn't want to be with her and I didn't want to be him – I wanted *him* to be *me*. My lips pursed into a grimace, disappointed in myself for feeling this way.

Then, like when a close friend or family member buys a new car and you start to notice that make and model everywhere, I began to notice how many other couples there were around me – in the park, on the street, and when I returned, even in the office. And then, without prejudice, my eyes began to fill with contempt and cold disdain for every single one of them, but I didn't know why.

<u>Later That Evening</u> – (The Moment)

I was on the bus on the way home from work; it was around 7pm. The days had become shorter and the nights colder, so it was already dark and the streets practically empty.

As my bus slowed at a red traffic light, I saw a woman. She looked Eastern European, very pale, thin, her face gaunt and cheekbones sharp and harsh, but her eyes wide, a sea of white surrounding the dark island. She was alone.

All of a sudden, a man dashed across the road in her direction with seeming ill intent. Her slim legs wrapped in skinny jeans shook as her knees collapsed onto each other. A pure, black fear gripped her face and captured her features, holding them tight. Weak and without hope, she clutched her bag. Fragile and feeble she stood; ripe for abuse.

The man slowed, and walked off in the opposite direction, oblivious, focussed on his journey.

Still trapped in shock, her eyes flickered over to me; watching me watching her. In that moment I caught a clear sight of her fear, that overwhelming fear that devastated her, that filled her large eyes, that drowned them and turned her pale skin white. I could taste her fear, the absoluteness of it.

She jolted away as my bus drove down the road, our connection broken, but our thoughts shared. We both knew that if this was another time, another day, another place, that... well, we both knew what could've happened.

Frozen in the fear that gripped her, she wouldn't have been able to scream, her body would've refused to fight back and her eyes, wide with innocent horror, would never close to the atrocity. All she could do was pray that it would be over soon. That picture of fear hung in my mind thick and ominous like a winter mist over a marsh, and I couldn't help but think, in fact I thought against my will, of the other times and days and places around the world where that man's intent was not so innocent, and where that woman would find that the only thing by her side, was her fear.

In that moment, I hated this world. No one should ever know such vulnerability, should ever be so scared. No person's face should ever resemble what I saw.

As the bus continued along a darker road, my eyes refocussed, and I saw my own reflection. There was no potential attacker approaching me, no impending danger about to strike, yet in my face, I saw so much fear.

<u>Nine Months Prior to the Park</u> - (My situation)

My weekdays were differentiated by my favourite TV programmes, and my weekends by the absence of work. I had serious trouble sleeping at night, and without sleep, the days just ran on seamlessly like still frames on a film projector.

On one of these days, during an episode of 'Homeless & Looking for Love', I heard a knock on the door, I had no idea who it could be.

Before I had a chance to lift myself off the sofa, my landlord bowled his way inside with the light from his Bluetooth earpiece flashing as he casually surveyed his land without even a 'hello'. I had completely forgotten he'd booked his biannual home inspection that day.

"How have you been, Perry?" I asked, knowing the flat looked like Oscar the grouch lived there and there was nothing I could do about it at that point.

"Alrigh' mate, alrigh'." His thick cockney accent rolled in tune with each swaying step as he leaned back, offsetting the weight of his capacious paunch.

His phone rang and he answered, switching from cockney to Bengali with a stroke of his beard.

The open-plan kitchen and living room in my flat only makes the place *look* large and worth the rent (over half my salary) ol' Pervindah charges me. The walls are cream and the furniture brown. There's a two-seat felt sofa with dark green cushions I bought to hide the hot chocolate stains.

"Ulta koira gache jhulay dimu!" Perry cursed (I'm assuming he cursed) without breaking stride.

I jumped at his outburst, almost spilling hot chocolate on the carpet. While watching him inspect the flat with such a critical eye, I decided to do the same.

When I moved in, I said "This place will do for now," that was five years ago.

A silence lingered between us.

"You know, I read somewhere," I started, Perry was off the phone, "that due to this area I live in and my wage bracket, I'm part of this new 'lower-middle-class' class."

Perry was looking inside my empty fridge. "That lower-middle-class crap! That's like a homeless guy looking down on another homeless guy because he's moved from crack to crystal meth."

He left the fridge to check the walls. I'd never bothered to put up any pictures or mirrors – there was a mirror in the bathroom but that was there when I moved in. There were a few books piled against the wall waiting for a shelf – *The Great Gatsby*, *King Lear* and *Health & Safety in the Home: A Self-help Guide* – all of which had been stolen from my old school library (well, just not returned). I had a dying plant by the small living room window that my aunty had given to me as a housewarming gift, a DVD and CD stand in the corner beside my bulky TV and a sit-up accessory which had evolved into an elaborate foot-rest and in times of need a laundry drying rail. He checked the bathroom and finished off with the bedroom, the latter not taking long; it was small and mostly filled with boxes of my old stuff.

Before leaving, Perry told me that there was a tenants' meeting on Wednesday if I was interested. I told him I'd try to make it. When I closed the door and gave some actual thought to attending the meeting, I realised that I had no idea what day it was - I think it was one one of the 'T's'

I couldn't sleep at all that night. It's been like this for over five years – now I know how liberals must've felt towards the end of Bush's Presidency, or even two years after Trump's – I'd do anything to see a reality show of those two going head-to-head in a live debate for the made-up role of Master of the Universe, but both being convinced it's a real job. This is one of the many great ideas I come up with during my sleepless nights. I would rarely mull over anything intelligent or interesting. It's either something really silly and inconsequential, or the host heavy, crushing, destructive thoughts and bad memories that daylight and the monotony of work help me fight off during the day.

It's a real kick in the nuts when you hate your job but can't wait for morning to come so you can be there. But it's not all bad, the other night I was cracking up over the joke Mac told at work, about Steve Jobs dying young because God needed help with his iPhone and couldn't get an appointment at an Apple Store.

A couple of weeks ago I dismantled my double bed and put together the single one I'd bought; I found the vacancy in the double made the obvious uncomfortably obvious, and I ended up most nights dozing off on the sofa. I thought the change of bed would help, but it hasn't, not yet at least.

So, now, almost every evening, after I'd watched the headlines on *News at Ten* (I miss Trevor McD), I walk to the furthest corner shop in my area, pick up whatever food and household bits need re-stocking, grab trashiest gossip mag they have (if you're gonna go for garbage, go for the best garbage you can find; they do with rumours and conjecture what a magician does with his hat and a baggy sleeve) then walk back home, hoping that that brief excuse for exercise might help me sleep longer; some nights it worked. This night it didn't.

Without fail, I would find that in the morning, every morning, I would wake up to a pain inside my stomach. It was like something was boiling or burning in there. It was different from acid reflux or heartburn; it felt less like a physical issue and more like... well, I don't know. Some mornings it was like a frothing inside and on others the feeling was more akin to something hard, heavy and cold, cramping my intestines. The pain was at its worst on mornings when *she* had featured in my dreams; all it took was a glimpse of her face and I would wake up in agony. So, in the morning, every morning I would douse that pain with a stream of cool placidity, plaster on a smile and thank goodness that no one notices me long enough to see just what a mess I am.

<u>**A Month Later**</u> – (Appreciation)

It was midnight. There was no moon to be seen but the streetlamps outside were bright and gave my room a golden hue through the large bay windows. I was up on my laptop sifting through emails from Amazon checking out which movies, albums and appliances they recommended for me (Oasis -What's the Story Morning Glory, Nas - Illmatic and Paul Newman in The Sting - these guys know me better than my dad!)

As I put discounted winter socks in my 'maybe' folder I received an email from a girl I'd dated after Uni; she had sent it to everyone in her mailbox. It was a video clip of her and her new boyfriend dancing on the Great Wall of China. I didn't want to but I couldn't help laughing.

We were good together, and very comfortable with each other; we would have conversations in the bathroom while I sat on the toilet – too lazy to stand and pee - and I would shave her legs while she drank white wine in the bathtub and listened to Etta James. She was a child at heart, and the only woman I knew who loved Monty Python sketches and who could make me laugh till I cried.

Five months in, she was diagnosed with Stage 1B ovarian cancer. She wasn't the healthiest person but this was completely out of the blue. Three days after she found out she told me. It was early evening and still light outside – I think it was a Thursday. I knew that something serious was wrong as soon as she answered the door, but I didn't want to push her to tell me what was going on. We sat on the edge of her bed, and, after a short silence, she explained what was happening and ended by telling me that I didn't have to stay, that she would understand if this was too much for me to take on so early in the relationship, that if I didn't really want to stay then she didn't want me to do so out of some misplaced obligation.

I felt the pressure of guilt but reminded myself that she didn't want my pity. I felt a level of responsibility but reminded myself that she was not my wife. With her words, she made it easy for me to leave. In the end, it simply came down to the fact that I wanted to stay, so I did.

Over the following ten months, I stood by her, drew closer to her in fact. I went to every hospital appointment, supported her decision not to have both ovaries removed when her parents and her oncologist disagreed, took turns with her mother to sleep over on nights after her chemo treatment. She suffered – the hair loss, numbness and vomiting were nothing in comparison to the pain she described. I felt helpless but was glad I stayed. I saw a side of her that must've been lying dormant, a strength and tenacity I never knew about. She would shed all her tears the night before a treatment, but on the morning of she was always good to go and took bad news, as she would say, 'as a setback, not a failure.' I'd never seen someone with so much fight for life; as she continued to fight, I began to love her.

In time though, her suffering came to an end. After all the pain, the tears and talks of what we would do if she got through this – she survived.

Then she left me.

"I feel like I have a second chance at life," she explained. "You're a really great guy, Joe, you really are..."

"But not great enough for you to want to stay with?" I replied.

"Don't be like that, Joe."

"Like what? You're dumping me."

"Look, I almost died..."

"I know, I was there!"

"And I appreciated that Joe, I really…"

"'Appreciation', after all I've done? All I get is a handshake and 'appreciation?'"

"So, you did what you did for what? Some kind of payoff?"

"No, I did it because I love you!"

Her gaze fell to the floor, her head following.

"You can't tell me it's just a coincidence," I continued, "that you're moving on three weeks after the doctors give you the all-clear."

She didn't respond.

"Did you love me?" I asked.

Her eyes rose to meet mine. "I still do."

"Then why are you doing this?"

"I've been given a second chance and..."

"You've already said that."

"Let me finish." She stamped her foot in that way she did; at first, I found it annoying, then endearing but this time it worried me. "I feel like I should... no, I... I have to take this second chance with both hands and get everything I can out of it; everything that I want." She held me in her gaze and, with a soft sigh, closed her lips.

I understood.

"Would you want me to stay because I felt guilty for leaving?" she asked. I thought back to what she told me when this all started.

I couldn't hold her look and glanced over at her front door. "What will you do?" My words were spoken so low they were almost mumbled.

Her words though, her reply never left me. "Whatever it takes for me to be happy."

Before leaving, I collected all my things, wanting to be angrier with her than I was. I kissed her as I left. It wasn't a "goodbye peck" or an "I want you back smooch." I wasn't too sure what my intentions were or what she was feeling while we kissed. I do recall, however, that as soon as that kiss ended, I knew it was our last.

That was six years ago now. Her name was Hayley.

With Hayley, I tried. The relationship failed, but I didn't feel that *I* had. I never looked back on that situation with any regret, but struggled to look forward from it with any hope. I know it was the right thing for her to go, but on the rare occasion, like this, that she pops into my mind, I wonder.

"Why was I not enough? Why do they always seem to leave?"

I stayed awake that night, thinking, not of Hayley, but of *her* - the first to leave me. I wanted to sleep but was caught, was afraid of whether dreams of her smile were worse than thoughts of what I had lost. I craved to rummage through the boxes under my bed and find a picture of her. At the same time, nothing scared me more. Caught in this fear, I struggled to see what it was that I wanted to gain, what I desired, and if there really was any point in me trying to get whatever it was, given my track record of losses.

Then I heard his voice, it reverberated in the back of my mind, my dad's voice; not angry but heavy with cold disdain and compounded disappointment.

"You loser."

With his words I saw a glimpse of his face, and knew, that night, there'd be no sleep at all.

<u>**Two Weeks On**</u> - (My 40 hours a week)

That morning in the office, we had all received an email confirming that despite a difficult economic year, there would be no redundancies in our department. Before the message landed in my inbox, I had told myself that I didn't care, that in fact, redundancy would be good for me, that it would force me to make a change and find a role that I could sink my teeth into, something I would actually enjoy. It wasn't that I hated my job or that I didn't like working; I didn't, but that wasn't my main problem. My problem was that I didn't like to be *at work*, in the office, I mean. I despised it. I feigned having irritable bowel syndrome to explain my prolonged and frequent visits to the disabled toilet. I felt like I had to get out, like there was something weighing down on me and I needed to break free, not like in the Queen video but kind of like in the Queen video, I just couldn't stand being there. And when I did get into the larger and much cleaner toilet for the disabled, I would just sit there, no number one or number two, I would just sit there – relieved not to be in that crowded den of dullness. I felt like an old Swedish man, who on stepping out of a packed sauna would take a seat outside on a little wooden bench overlooking a still lake, the crisp air cooling his wrinkled, naked body, the calmness of the water, the freshness of the breeze reviving him from the congested heat he had just left. The disabled toilet was my Swedish lakeside, and although I had to make do with the scent of Mac's lunchtime turd for crisp Nordic air, this was my haven, my porcelain paradise, my skid-marked oasis – there were times I felt so relaxed, I fell asleep. It was on my return from one of these respites that I opened the email regarding the redundancies. As I read it, my relief exposed me for the charlatan I am.

Due to the 'good news' everyone was taking it easy at work and chatting away with a positive buzz which swished around me. Sitting back at the organised mess of my desk, I smiled while listening to the office "dude" re-tell his promiscuous escapades from the weekend. Our office space was an open-plan with identical rows of desks, so it wasn't hard to hear him as his slender frame leaned back in his chair and, anchored by his cockiness, he entertained all. He kind of looked like the guy who played MacGyver, or more like his slimmer, less good-looking younger brother – I could never remember his actual name so in my mind, and sometimes in real life, I just called him Mac.

One of our colleagues a few rows down, Matt, was getting married in a few weeks and he'd celebrated his stag with a few from the office that Saturday. But the way Mac told it you would think it was him having his last hoorah. Something about Matt and his Mrs getting married in spring made me feel that it would last.

Over the past week, everyone had given Matt relationship advice. The longest and most in-depth conversations seemed to be with those who were divorced (I think irony is my favourite form of truth).

I did notice that those who weren't in relationships, and especially those who were older, were giving Matt more life tips than marriage counsel. Matt's desk was opposite the photocopier, so within a few days, almost everybody had put in their two pence worth. I didn't want to be the last person, but then what could I tell him? I wasn't married, or even in a relationship, and as for advice on life, the best tip I had to give was: put your trousers in the oven for five minutes before work during the winter (but use the timer, God help those trousers if you don't use the timer!)

It was after two in the afternoon. Everybody was back from lunch, too full to work but too tired to talk – the office was pretty quiet. I filled my company mug with government juice and glanced over at Matt. He was tall and broad, an ex-rugby player I think, so I couldn't see over his shoulders and glimpse his computer to see if he was busy. But then he clocked me from the corner of his eye, leaned back and gave me his usual friendly nod of recognition, then returned to his screen. I realised in that moment that I had nothing to say; so I made my way back to my desk. Then Matt turned back to me again. He's that 1970s kind of good-looking; he could've played Bond or Superman were it not for his East End accent.

"What about you then, Joe? C'mon, what pearls of wisdom you got for me?"

"Well..." my mind went as blank as a ream of printer paper. I stood there with my mouth wide open. Seconds passed. Matt wanted to look away, but my train wreck hadn't come to its conclusion yet. "You know..." I was firing blanks like a lifelong cyclist.

Matt could've just looked away and waited for me to leave. But he didn't.

"Put my all in...?" he said to get me started. "Ha, 'that's what she said'."

"Well..." I momentarily paused in thought. "Pretty much the same as everybody else. You know, really try your best and her..." my hands started making gestures that had no discernible meaning, "...work. Sorry not her work, *it* work, the, the union, the coming together." I meshed the fingers of both of my hands, then looked down at my gesture. "Not sex, the marriage, you need it in a marriage, sex that is, but what you want is to make happy...ness."

Neither of us were sure that I was finished. Someone else was sure though. From behind me we both heard a slow mocking round of applause. I turned and it was Mac.

'Beautiful, just beautiful. Shakespeare would wet himself with envy.'

"Leave him alone Mac." I could hear Matt holding back laughter in his defence of me.

I quickly retreated to my desk.

I sat down, and funnily enough, I wasn't angry with Mac. Instead, I felt what seemed like a coldness, a liquid-ice seeping into my bowel as if it were being poured in slowly until my insides were filled and the feeling began rising into my chest and I could almost taste its icy bitterness in my throat. And I was caught in thinking that I hadn't prepared and shared my thoughts with Matt, not just because I thought he would ridicule me or question the basis of my advice, but mainly because *I* didn't think that it was worth hearing. Pretty much everyone went for celebratory drinks after work. I treated myself to a Cornetto ice-cream and a small tub of Nutella – no spoon needed; my middle finger did the job just fine.

<u>Two in the Morning</u> - (False Hope)

I'm sure they all had a good time out, and maybe I should've joined them, but then there had been a fairly decent reality show on that night – The Naked Truth (couples were asked probing questions about their partner by their partner's ex's and had to remove clothing with every wrong answer). Plus, it wasn't the last time that the office would go out for drinks, I knew that different groups of people from our office and the office on the floor below went out for drinks pretty much every night, whether it was just for a quick one or till the last train arrived.

I had discovered this when my microwave stopped working and the frozen microwave meals that made up my general diet no longer had a magic box that made them edible in 12-13 minutes. But there was a Pizza Hut around the corner from my work where the strip of local pubs and bars were. While waiting for my cheese encrusted dinner, I looked out at the busy street and considered the fact that most people didn't love the people they work with, they just liked them. But in a weird paradoxical way, they must like them more than they love those at home or others in their lives as they spend all day with people from work and then choose to spend their entire evening with them too, sometimes even Saturday nights as well.

It was during that thought that I noticed, at the traffic lights opposite me between the underground train station and the pub she had just walked out of, stood a pretty woman in her early to mid-twenties. She was a little below average height but her dress and body language exuded a mischievous yet cute promiscuity, as if her stature and demeanour were related. Striding to stand close beside her was a tall man in his forties, a little overweight with heavy grey but only partially receding hair. He took her hand with a gentle touch and held her arm as he gave her an extended "safe journey home" goodbye. She stood comfortably, smiling as he gradually leaned in towards her, careful not to stand too close and break her realm of personal space.

Light rain fell in thin, straight lines; when seen through the window in the light of a nearby street-lamp, it was as if life was being played before me from a 16 mm home video. He wasn't drunk but had probably had too much to drink to notice her patronising smile marred with pity. She held her hand on his waist, slowly stroking it. He kissed her on the cheek to say goodbye but continued talking, not letting her leave. He leaned in a bit closer and kissed her goodbye again. This time as they parted his face was closer to hers than before, and he looked into her eyes as he continued to speak. Her smile remained but became less endowed with pity and drew more towards a sardonic smirk; drink and attraction seemed to have blinded him to the obvious.

He leaned in again for his final kiss and simultaneously her hand moved from his waist and held his hand that was on her arm and squeezed it. She turned her cheek to him fully, whereas before she had stayed quite still allowing him almost to kiss the corner of her mouth. Her face turned sharply to the right. She was now looking in the direction of the Pizza Hut, and for a moment I thought she was looking directly at me. I assumed, hoped, that she only saw her own reflection, as in that moment she looked entirely bored. When eye contact resumed, her expression was brighter than before as she pranced across the street on her way to the train home. The man stood watching, not in a lustful manner but more in longing. He watched her disappear, his left thumb parting the fingers on that hand and, in what seemed like an unconscious action, he rubbed his wedding ring finger where a ring would be.

I wondered if he had taken it off that night and slipped it into his pocket as he met the young woman but was now considering the wife and children he had at home who loved him but whose familiarity wearied him so and compelled him to work late and drink even later in a selfish attempt to avoid the inevitable monotony of home life. That he and the woman were work colleagues, and that her slight flirtations during the day and occasionally in the evenings excited his hope and invited naivety. Or maybe he knew his advances made her nervous, and that she wasn't flirting but was uncomfortable but was trying to be nice as he's a director and she doesn't want to rock the boat. Or maybe he thought she was leading him on and did this in the hope of securing a pay rise or a promotion. Or maybe he didn't know what she felt or what he was really doing, because he didn't care. And he didn't care because either way he knew he was going home alone that night, but at least this way his sleep would be furnished with a smile and that temporary sweetness of false hope. As I paid my bill I wondered if false hope was better than no hope at all.

Even with dairy and gluten doing a number on my insides, I slept a good 4 uninterrupted hours that night.

<u>A Fortnight Following the Email</u> - (Tainted hope)

I'd always thought the Manager for the Accounts team was attractive in a classical kind of way – maybe I was lying to myself and classical was really just a euphemism for old, but she was pleasant, slender and well dressed. She looked like a mannequin that had just stepped out of a Marks & Spencer's window with a twenty-year smoking habit and an artificial tan. Kind of like Kim Cattrall in that movie – not *Mannequin*, ironically, but *Sex in the City 6* or whichever the last one was.

It was the start of winter, but not too cold. I had bought a macchiato but forgot to pick up one of those cardboard cup-holder things as I left. The cup was burning my hands so I took a seat on a park bench and put my drink on the floor. 'Kim' sat beside me and, reaching for her bag, she knocked my coffee over with the pointed toe of her shoe.

She apologised and offered to buy me another cup. I told her it was okay but she insisted and asked what kind of coffee it was. I told her and it turned out she'd just bought a macchiato too and hadn't touched it yet, so she handed me her cup. I looked into her face and this time thought that she was pretty. Then an idea, a stroke of genius struck me. It was a long shot but I had nothing to lose and had been looking for something, and maybe this was it.

I took her cup, turned it upside down and poured her coffee out onto the floor. The problem was I had forgotten to take off the plastic cap so it just kind of dribbled out of the small hole.

"What are you doing?"

"The coffee was supposed to dramatically pour out and I was going to hold up the empty cup and say 'now I owe you a coffee so let's go... and get one together'. But, erm..."

Kim smiled. I liked her smile.

"It was a good idea, getting a coffee together I mean, not the joke. You can stop pouring now."

While sitting in the café we talked about coffee and coffee shops, discussing our preferences and tastes; she was part of team Costa, which didn't upset me too much, as a Starbucks purist.

As people began leaving the coffee shop, we both checked our watches. There was a short silence.

False hope is better than none. I thought.

"Would you like to meet for coffee again tomorrow?" I asked.

She looked at me and visibly thought about her answer. "That would be nice."

We settled on a time and we were about to part ways when she asked me a question that took me by complete surprise.

"So, do you work local?"

I hesitated, partly in embarrassment and partly in disbelief. "I work at the end of *our* office. I'm at the second desk from the last."

"Oh. Oh yes Joe. well... let's keep our little meeting to ourselves then. See you back at the office."

And with that short, shame-tinted reply she was gone.

I fiddled with the half-empty sugar sachet on the table and felt a slow grin slide up the side of my face.

"I just secured a second date,"

A Week Later

A nice Thai restaurant had opened not too far from where we worked that I wanted to try; Kim, though, liked Italian. So over gnocchi that was a little too creamy but still nice, she told me about her job and her friends and family. She asked me about my family, but I didn't want to go there so soon so just told her that they were all fine and busy living life (one of my favourite redundant sayings). We kissed that night. Just as her Uber arrived and stopped abruptly in the middle of the road, she leant towards me, and we kissed. It was pleasant. She had thin lips but they were soft. Kim was eight years my senior. I had clasped her hand while our lips met; her hand was soft. That thought kept me warm while I waiting for the night bus.

The next morning, I sent her an email, asking if she had enjoyed dinner. She asked if I wanted to come over to hers that night for cheese and wine. I didn't allow a second thought and said yes. A night of cheese and wine sounded so very grown up. I sent a message to an old university friend, Pete, who had recently found me and a bunch of others from uni on social media; I explained my triumphs. His reply –

'Get in there son!!!'

The following work hours flew by.

I got to her place on time, freshly showered and wearing the half-decent aftershave I only slap on for weddings. Her hair was different from how it was the night before and she was wearing make-up, which made her eyes darker.

I took off my shoes as I came in and she smiled at the gesture. She had Frank Sinatra playing in the background. We ate, she talked and I liked listening. I noticed an unusual statue above her fireplace – a dark, almost black, wooden hand carved figure of a man with a large nose, large lips and very large 'member'. Before I had a chance to enquire, with a giant smile she greedily went into a detailed story of her first trip to the Bahamas where a guide took them into the 'bush' where a 'village chief' presented her with this carving due to her 'overwhelming sensuality'. She of course felt compelled to pay him for it and was told it held fertility powers.

I couldn't explain why but it all felt a little racist to me, but instead of questioning or commenting I changed the subject and I told her that I had never travelled outside of the UK but wanted to. I explained that I wanted to do Europe first, as it's closer and cheaper, and visit all of its famous sites. Next, I wanted to see all the wonders of the world – I couldn't remember if there were seven or eight; we had a good back and forth trying to name them all.

When I asked what her favourite trip was, she detailed a long weekend getaway that she had made to Rome with her ex-husband; I was amazed when she told me she hadn't had a chance to see the Sistine Chapel, the Colosseum or Trevi Fountain. She explained that it wasn't her top trip because of the activities outside of the hotel, and then gave me a knowing wink. Me being a little thrown and slow on the uptake, didn't respond quick enough which created an awkward silence which she ended with a reproving glance reminding me that I hadn't even seen the inside of a plane let alone the sites of Rome.

The wine wasn't that good so I took sips as we joked about how crazy the fashions were in the 1980s and how we couldn't believe that people were making the same mistake twice. She had a loud laugh and a great smile.

The physical gap between us was diminishing with every chuckle and it all felt very natural. Then she placed her hand on my thigh, quite high up. Her eyes seemed to close in on mine like a fighter pilot's aim.

"You're not the usual type of guy I go for, but you're young and not bad-looking. I don't want anything serious; I'm just looking for a bit of fun."

She kissed me without any invitation. I could taste Brie and what I guessed was a cheap Merlot. I felt that burning in my stomach, and I didn't want to be there anymore.

As I left her bed, she lit a cigarette and searched for the television remote control. I felt that other kind of emptiness; not the type following a moral mistake, but the feeling that you've been hollowed out, that what you just did had scooped something out of you that couldn't be replaced with food and rest. That empty feeling stayed with me all the way to the tube.

It was Friday night and the underground was packed; I hated it. I had to wait four stops to wrestle my way to a free seat. As soon as I was comfortable, I noticed an elderly couple in front of me who had just got on; I was tired and I didn't want to stand. You could tell they weren't from London; the way they checked the tube map, how they had to look around to find the handrails and were unaware that the doors open from both sides. When I noticed the *Les Misérables* programme in the old woman's hand and an anniversary card sticking out of her husband's jacket pocket, I got up and offered my seat. They both refused at first, then he gave it to his wife. I looked down at the teenager slouched in the next seat, waiting for him to get up. He didn't move.

"Mate…" I called to him. But his head remained bowed. I stood closer and called again, then I noticed he had earphones in so I tapped his shoulder. He pulled one earphone out.

"The gentleman wants to sit next to his wife," I said.

The boy, around fourteen, put his earphone back in and flicked his hoody over his head. The old man tapped me on the shoulder saying it was fine, that their stop probably wasn't far.

It was far and this wasn't fine.

I looked down at this kid unsure if he was dressed like a grunger, a hip-hopper, a hipster or just a douchebag.

"Mate!" I said.

He didn't move. This is where my non-confrontational (cowardly) side would usually kick in and I'd look to the old couple and shrug with that "kids today" smirk, and hope that the boy didn't follow me off the train and stab me in a darkened alley. But this time I felt different. This time it *really* wasn't okay, it *really* wasn't fine.

I yanked the earphones out of his ears.

"You need to give up your seat for the old man."

"Oi, what you touchin' my stuff for?"

"I said you need to give up your seat."

"Shut up." He spat the words out the side of his mouth and put his earphones back in.

I felt anxious, angry and belittled, by a fourteen-year-old. I was the boy and he was the man.

I grabbed him by the arm and dragged him off the seat. He tried to tear away from my grip, but he couldn't. When he realised this, I decided to let him go. He barged through to the other end of the train, cursing with every step. The old man shook my hand and took a seat. I caught my breath and held onto the rail as the train took a bend.

Under the jolting noise of the carriage, I said to myself, "I'm not a boy." As the train continued on and those words sunk in, my mind refused to finish the sentence, to affirm what I am, and what on earth I was doing.

All the way home I fought the desire to ridicule my idea of trying, my promise to take on new opportunities. I would like to say I won that internal battle but instead, I consoled myself with the win of one fight that night, as I wedged a chair against the front door before bed, sure that the 14-year-old was just waiting for me to fall asleep before he and his delinquent friends broke in and attacked me with 'shanks' and poor grammar.

The Following Monday – (Black & purple)

Sitting on the train on the way home from work, everything felt quiet. There were office buddies talking, Uni kids arguing, and other commuters on their phones and tablets, yet everything *felt* very quiet.

As the train left Tottenham Court Road and jostled from West to East London, I noticed a new passenger sat across from me. A girl with black and purple hair – the colours complemented each other as bright violet streaked through her natural dark strands. She combed a handful of her strands back with her fingers, revealing the shaved sides of her head. She had two silver studs in her left eyebrow and one large bolt in her right. She had a stud under her bottom lip and one in her right cheek. Both of her ears had six earrings, the right one had a hoop inside the earlobe and the left one had four studs – in the shape of a diamond. She sat there with earphones in, ignoring the looks of shock and even disgust that she received from other passengers. She had an expression on her face, not a petulant one that read "I don't care", but a calm, contented one that said, "I don't mind". Is that what self-worth feels like? I can never work out if it's something you're supposed to be born with or something you work to gain, or if you just have to be from that special "I had a great childhood" club for it to be bestowed upon you. Any which way, I think she has it, and I don't.

As her stop arrived, she glanced up at me, catching me looking at her. I mustered my nerve and held her stare for those few moments. She smiled at me, not alluringly or in that cold but polite British way we have, but knowingly. Her leather trousers hugged her tight as she left the tube, and despite my particular tastes in fashion, I couldn't help but admire her.

A couple of stops later, as I left the train at my station, I was still thinking of the woman with black and purple hair, and the thought of her bravery caused a wry smile to creep up the side of my cheek while the escalator rose to take me above ground. I looked at my reflection in the glass advertisement screens to my left, and was struck by the difference between her and me, both physical and below the surface. As I walked through the barriers and left the station, for the first time in a long time, I was hit with the difference, the dichotomy that existed between the two worlds the underground Tube system had transported me between. The world I left behind was the clinical, suit-clad monotony of glass buildings, tiepins, double expressos shots, black cabs, lunchtime sushi and £10 cheese & watercress sandwiches. Where the air was filled with the bittersweet scent of cigarette smoke intertwining with vaping clouds, and the smell of Columbian hills which wafted from the scores of barista trucks. Where the sky was obscured by construction cranes, the pavements lined with Jehovah's Witness Watchtower carts and the street was full with talk of fiscal growth, the PM's inadequacies and the sight of police officers with firearms. The world my Oyster Travel Card brought me back to was bustling with market stalls selling Jamaican yellow yam, Indian star fruit, Ghanaian cassava and Polish sauerkraut. It was bursting with throngs of multicultural vibrancy, waves of differing languages and music and the savoury aromas of jerk chicken, jollof rice and chapatis. A place that abounded with 99p, 98p & 97p stores, shops where wings, chips and a drink are bought for a £1 and where you'll find homeless people who were doctors in their homelands, and vagrants who are smarter than you - taking your money and leftovers in exchange for their views on Marx, Kant and Dostoyevsky. This is where I live. This place of energy and life is where I call home. Where single parents are rushing to pick up their kids from after-school clubs before being charged money they don't have, where teenagers finally relax as they cross over into a postcode where no one wants to stab them, and where bravery is not a virtue but an aspect of everyday life; for most.

"Be brave, Joseph." A memory of my mum saying those words chimed behind my eyes. She, gently ushering me into junior school on my first day while I clung to her legs and closed my eyes; the soft hands that nudged me forward were the same I didn't want to leave, but I did.

In the dull light of dusk, while I changed out of my work clothes and into my home clothes (clothes that had been relegated from the 'going out' league of clothing because of holes, discolouration and the general embarrassment they would cause if I wore them outside), I was moved by the strength of a feeling, an ache.

Do it!

I didn't know if it was me or a voice in me that spoke the two-worded command, but I grabbed my phone before indecision could morph into cowardice, and I sent her a text. I didn't know if she had the same number and I didn't expect her to reply, it had been almost ten years but it still felt like the right thing to do because it was what I wanted; she, at that moment, was what I desired.

<u>**Two Days from Sending the Text**</u> - (Heart's desire)

Sapphire. Her name chimed in my heart. She texted back at two that morning; I was just dozing off.

You still cross my mind from time to time. I wonder if you're lonely, she wrote.

I looked up at my bedroom mirror adjacent, asking myself how I should reply. The blue light on my mobile phone glowed against my features, lighting my room like scenes from the French films my mum and I used to watch when it was just the two of us.

Are you? I chewed the inside of my cheek in anticipation of her answer.

Not anymore, she replied instantly.

I looked away from my reflection.

I didn't want my disappointment to come across in a delayed reply, so I changed the subject.

How are your joints doing?

Worse, but that's okay. I heard about your aunt Claudine. Wasn't sure whether to call or not so I didn't.

I smiled thinking she still cared about my aunty and sat up, pulling the covers over my chest as I replied: *She's been getting weaker. I'm planning to go and see her soon.*

You were always her favourite. I bet your cousins are still jealous.

I began writing my reply with both hands and a quicker pace.

She'll probably ask how you are. A pulse of impetuousness ran through me and I typed with speed and without caution. *Can I see you?*

There was no reply.

I had pushed too far. I was a fool. Why couldn't I control myself, I'm not fifteen. I stared at my device, willing it to vibrate. Suddenly, the light from the phone vanished and the room was black. In the dark silence, it was as if the conversation had never happened and I had just risen from a dream.

And then there was light.

Okay. I don't know. Why?

My heart beat in time with the thoughts racing in my head. This was the answer I had hoped but was not prepared for. I couldn't allow any break to ensue.

I don't really know. I covered my mouth as the message was sent, my eyes widening in the artificial light.

Let's not meet by the old place, those memories don't make me happy anymore. How about Saturday? Text me the postcode of a Starbucks that's halfway from both of us. I'm still at the same place.

The left side of my cheek curled into a smile; I could already taste my latte.

Night Sapphire.

Nun-night Joseph.

There was a quote from Aristotle I remembered reading in college which slipped into my mind and made me smile before sleep:

'Justice is the loveliest and health is the best, but sweetest to obtain is the heart's desire.'

<u>The Saturday After the Text</u> - (An unfinished chapter)

She was on crutches. Well, one crutch – her left arm was in a cast again.

She was a lot slimmer - I wondered if it was the brittle bone disease or something else. Her hearing was starting to go, but I knew that was to be expected. She had cut her hair short and as usual, wasn't wearing any make-up. Blue Levi's, a short, light-coloured T-shirt and a trendy jacket; her usual attire.

When I first walked towards the Starbucks and saw her, she looked so fragile, so dainty, so delicate; I couldn't believe how beautiful she was.

Simplicity is truly the key to everything.

Before she had even noticed me approaching, I felt like I was falling in love with her all over again.

My first words to her in over eight years:

"Let's sit in the sun."

She brushed her curly caramel fringe to one side. With her bottom two teeth slightly overlapping and her cheeks balling into butterscotch peaches, she smiled with that innocence that blesses the faces of children.

"That sounds like a plan."

We spent ages joking about what I was going to write on her cast, while we both expertly dodged and weaved around our past. Her wit was still quick and her sense of irony sharp; I felt like an overweight and out of practice fencing pro facing the current champion.

"Who wrote the Bible verse on there?" I asked.

"My sister. She goes to church now." When she spoke her body always said more than her words.

"So that's Christianity, Islam... Buddhism and now back to being a Christian again."

"She's not a Christian, going to church doesn't make you a Christian any more than... standing in a garage makes you a car."

I chuckled while she sipped her almond milk Frappuccino.

When she gestured, she moved with the soft precision of a painter applying strokes to an invisible canvas. "Look at all the mess you've made with all those sugar sachets... and who needs so many tissues and stirrers?"

"You never know. First rule of Boy Scouts: always be prepared."

"You never went to Boy Scouts, and this isn't being prepared, this is you being messy; as usual. I bet you still can't find anything in your room."

"Being tidy is overrated. Organised people are just too lazy to look for things."

"So, I'm lazy?"

"... and I'm industrious. I create work."

"Yeah, but for yourself."

"If I had money, I could employ someone to tidy up for me. I'd be creating new jobs..."

"... stimulating the economy?"

"They should invite me to the next G12 meeting."

"Joseph Bogart's amazing solution to the credit crunch – Be Lazy."

"Ooh, ooh, we could get sponsorship from Nike and have them make T-shirts that say, 'Just *Don't* Do It!'"

Laughing together felt like the most natural thing in the world.

I casually watched her, my smile bridging the silence. Her high cheekbones, which made her eyes squint when she laughed, were sprinkled with light freckles; I remembered once trying to count them all. She looked up and I didn't feel compelled to look away.

"I can still see the guilt in your eyes."

My cheeks began to burn. "Saying sorry doesn't change the past."

"Nothing can change the past Joseph, not even God."

I couldn't taste the coffee I sipped. "But I was the one that changed things."

"You always had a problem with letting go. Do you remember when you tripped over that little girl with asthma in primary school?"

I sat up straight, with mock indignance. "That was an accident. I was doing kick-ups with a conker and she ran into my leg."

"Exactly. And what did you do for the rest of that year?"

"I carried her bag every day and sat with her at lunch."

"And made me sit with the two of you as well!"

"I couldn't do it by myself, she hardly spoke."

"That's because she didn't want you there. I never told you this but she changed form group so that you couldn't follow her to class every day."

"Are you serious, why didn't you tell me?"

"What would you have done?"

"I don't know, maybe ask her why she didn't want my help."

"She grazed her knee, Joseph! You acted like you put her in a wheelchair. If I told you then you would've just obsessed over it and pestered her into letting you be her 'carer' again."

"I wasn't that bad."

"Yes, you were. You were worse with me but you were my best friend so it was fine. But she was a stranger."

"I didn't treat you two anything alike, I was nice to her because I felt bad, but you, I loved you."

I wanted to grab those words and stuff them back into my mouth before they reached her. I felt my heart beat harder.

"Yes, you did. And that's why you shouldn't feel guilty." All joviality was sucked from the table.

"But I do."

Sapphire leaned forward, opened her mouth and hesitated, leaning back again.

"If I didn't know you better, Joseph, I would say that you were trying to make me feel bad, for you making *me* feel bad, which... would ultimately make *you* feel bad." She paused with that kind but omniscient expression that left a person with nowhere to hide. "I know you didn't just... jump into this pool of self-pity it's clear that you're in. But I can see, even in the way that you move, that you're doing nothing to stop yourself from drowning in it."

"But I..."

"Joseph... Look at me." Her eyes were confident and strong. There was no sign of malice or pain as she spoke.

"You... you convinced me that you loved me and that I loved you." She rubbed the tips of her fingers with her thumb, a habit she'd had since she was twelve.

"You told me that what we had was so incredibly special. Do you remember the letter you wrote me saying... oh it was something like 'Shakespeare couldn't write sonnets that could describe our love... the gravity that bound planets wasn't stronger than our bond and... and that Romeo and Juliet had nothing on us!' I wanted to believe you so badly."

I remembered the pen I'd used to write that note with. Her eyes widened and she continued. My heart ached and my mind begged her to stop.

"Then, when we were both in a bad place... I came over that night, and your words filled my stomach with butterflies and hope." She paused, stroking her earlobe with her thumb. I knew what was coming next.

"We made love; and when you looked at me afterwards, I knew something had changed." For the briefest moments, her eyes glistened. "Then you told me that you weren't sure if you loved me anymore. But I was. I didn't love you before, but as sure as night follows day, I did after."

I wanted nothing more than to submerge myself in that pool of my own making. Her eyes were the same now as they were then, soft and wanting.

"I had been treated like a charity case my whole life. And I wasn't going to accept that from the one person who made me feel normal." She paused here, smiling with a nostalgic sadness. "You broke my heart. But it's my job to mourn its death, not yours. I love you, Joseph, and I always will. But I told you to stay away because at that time I wasn't strong enough to tell you what I'm telling you now. And as more water passed under that bridge, I didn't see the point, but when you texted me that night, it felt right." Now she smiled, mentally placing the past back in the past. "Joseph Henry Bogart. You're an amazing person. And I know you don't want the pity of others, but your problem is that you're comforted by the pity you have for yourself."

I couldn't look at her. She placed her hand on my cheek and brushed across it until her fingertips trickled from my chin.

"I wish I could fix you, but that's not my job. It never was."

I didn't know what I was feeling, so I didn't trust myself to speak.

"I asked you if you were lonely. It's been almost a decade since I last saw you, but I knew what the answer was before you ignored my question."

My eyes were still staring nowhere. Her index finger led my chin to face her, and my eyes followed. I loved her eyes like I loved the sun – a clear emerald green, like crystal kryptonite. She didn't look on me with pity. She held my gaze without blinking. There was strength in her expression. She was a woman now.

"You're living a self-fulfilling prophecy, Joseph; you'll end up alone and unhappy... because you believe you will."

As it started to get late and the conversation began to come to a natural end, she took my hand and explained, with great simplicity, that she was getting married in a few months. She was so calm, and her calm relaxed my surprise and my pain.

She said that she had really enjoyed the day we spent together and that it gave her the closure she'd thought she already had. Then she told me that she wouldn't be seeing me again. That she wished the best for me, but that this chapter of her life was over and she was going to move forward without looking back, something she hadn't been doing until now. It wasn't a discussion. She shook my hand and made her way to her car. I felt like I would be insulting her if I offered my help, so I didn't.

I so missed having somebody who knew me better than I knew myself.

Sitting on the back of the empty double-decker bus I knew I didn't want that chapter to stop there; I didn't want to stop looking back. But that decision wasn't mine any longer, it hadn't been mine for almost ten years. And when it was, I wasted it.

When I found myself at home, I couldn't remember how I arrived there. I didn't feel lost, just absent of direction.

The Following Week

I sat quietly on a park bench, trying not to get any of my supermarket sandwich on my supermarket suit.

The Next day – (Love in the arms of death)

My dad left a voice-message on my mobile phone while I was at work. He said, very matter-of-factly, that my aunty Claudine, had taken a turn for the worse since her last stroke. The doctors had said that she could go any day now. She'd requested to be released from the hospital.

"She wants to die at home," he stated.

He said I should try to come down that weekend; that she'd asked for me. I got the message while on the bus going home. I made a few calls and passed the stop where I lived and made my way to the nearest car rental company. My aunty lived a two-hour drive away out in the country. I wished I had charged my phone at work.

As I pulled up outside her house, the abundance of greenery surrounding her home calmed me. The large ferns and great cedars overshadowing the rows of trimmed bushes and carpet of thick green grass exuded a heavenly peace. Dew from an early spring shower gave the scene a fresh, glistening finish. But as my rental car rolled along her gravel pathway, the peace that surrounded me made me think of the peace my aunty would soon be resting in; and that thought hurt me.

When I arrived at the front door, my cousin let me into my aunty's beautiful home. Sharp images from my youth pierced my mind. My cousin smiled but looked distinctly indifferent to my presence and why I was present, and simply pointed to my aunty's room. Aunty Claudine was a lot older than my mum. I remember being told that she had pretty much raised her, and so was more like a grandmother than an aunty to me. During my second year at college, she came to live with us for a while; she was a lovely lady, very gentle, incredibly kind.

As I neared, I picked up her familiar scent and smiled inside. In an instant, a flood of warm memories filled me, it felt like drinking a tall glass of smooth, creamy hot chocolate on a cold day. I thought of all the childhood visits, the presents, the stories, the kisses and the hugs – oh, my aunty Claudine gave the best hugs. As I grasped the door handle to her room, a wave of sadness took me.

Be strong for her Joseph.

I filled my lungs, mustered a smile, and opened the door with dull eyes overlayed with joy.

She didn't look as I expected; I thought she would've aged much more and look worn, tired. But she didn't, she looked just as I remembered her: dressed in a self-knitted pink and cream cardigan, hair as white as her blouse, wearing the same black leather round-faced watch my mum bought her as an anniversary gift over twenty years ago, and the engagement ring and wedding band that hadn't left her finger since my uncle placed them there over fifty years ago.

I looked down and saw that she was darning a hole in one of her dead husband's old cardigans, one she had no doubt made for him.

She recognised me straight away. I couldn't help smiling.

"Joseph," she said.

An overwhelming feeling of humility covered me and I knelt by her bedside. A moment passed.

"You were always a quiet boy."

I blushed.

"But you were so sweet, ever so sweet." Her smile moved the wrinkles in her face like soft ripples across a pool of water.

She reached out her weak hand; her bones looked like they were wrapped tight in a brown paper bag, but her touch was so soft. "Your mother would be so proud."

I wanted to ask her then, to discuss the one thing we never spoke about. I wanted to know the truth, and I wanted to know why. But I couldn't, not like this, not now. It would be too much for her. I had left it too late.

Then, for the first time in... well, I don't know how long, I wanted to cry, but I couldn't. Sensing this, *she* held *me* in her dying arms. I felt so loved. I felt so loved.

She mentioned that my dad would be back soon. I needed to get the car back to the rental company that night, as I wouldn't have time to drop it off before work the next day. Well, that was at least the excuse I gave as to why I had to go.

While leaving, I did all I could to subdue all the angry sadness and frustration I felt, for what else could I do? There was nothing I could do for my aunty now. All of my love couldn't save her; a woman who deserved to live a thousand lifetimes. And yet, here I was, worn out before having lived half of one.

The sun was now a scarlet disc framed by the clouds above and the trees below. Its light illuminated the luscious field in front of me.

As I drove away, I thought,

In life-giving earth, we bury our dead.

Reaching into my jacket pocket, I felt the smooth ridge of the wedding band and the diamond edges of the engagement ring my aunty had handed to me. At some point on the way home my phone battery ran out and the music stopped. I didn't notice.

Three Days After Death

I ignored the words of the priest and sat observing the candles around her coffin. When he had finished, family members and friends made their way up to the open casket (my little brother, who was halfway through his trip around Asia, had just landed in Thailand and was unable to make it back in time). They would walk up, pause, and walk away with their heads bowed. I thought it a curious ritual, one I've never understood. As her neighbour passed, his jacket waved near a candle, blowing out its flame. I watched the smoke disperse from the wick and hang in the air; I wondered if that was what had happened to my aunty. Everyone was now standing but me. I joined the end of the queue; the queue to see the dead body.

I remembered her warm embrace, the soft creases in her features. The queue shuffled forward. I held her rings in my palm, remembering her touch. I neared the coffin and eyed the flameless candle.

That is my aunty, I thought. "She is dead."

"Your mother would be so proud," she had told me. What a smile she had. I didn't want to see her like this. I wanted never to remember her as a corpse.

As I neared the open casket, I closed my eyes.

"Your mother would be so proud." Her voice echoed in my mind. I opened my eyes, turning from the dead body behind me, remembering the aunty who still lived in my heart, and thinking of the answers to secrets that may have died with her.

For the Next Three Days

I slept even less and kept dozing off at my desk. Mac spread the rumour that I was moonlighting as a table-top dancer in a bar called the Blue Oyster. They all found it funny until my manager gave me a verbal warning; Mac thought that was the icing on the cake.

To try and stay awake at work I started doing espresso shots, only to find that they kept me awake all night but did little for me during daylight. It was on the third day with no sleep that I sat in Costa Coffee (I'd defected from Starbucks in my delirium) and wrote on a napkin:

What have I given that if it was taken away it would be missed?

My head spun over this thought until I saw a middle-aged woman opposite me breastfeeding. I found myself staring, not perving, just a little dazed and confused. Then I found myself being asked to leave. Then the cleaner found me asleep on the floor of the office's disabled toilet at 10pm.

Tomorrow needs to be a better day.

Today - (formerly 'Tomorrow')

It wasn't.

A Week Later - (Taking it lying down)

The office busybody strode up to my desk and asked me to buy her some cigarettes when I next went out to the shop for the milk run. My eyes didn't rise from my desk as I replied.

"No."

"'No' what? No, you're not going to the shops or no you're not going to buy my cigarettes when you get there?"

I hadn't noticed that her pompous condescension had turned a few heads. I looked up at her face; her sharp nose and thin lips pointed down at me threatening.

"Take your pick." I said.

She stormed off in a huff. The surprised smiles around us were almost audible. Matt, Mac and a couple of the others rolled up to my desk.

"Did you guys see Joe Bloggs go all Michael Douglas on little miss prissy over there?" Mac asked.

Although I hated it when he called me that, I couldn't help smiling at what he'd said.

"Joe," Mac continued, "we're going to a club tonight. Matt's wife's away, my girl's on her reds and my mate's bartending there this weekend. Colin's dropped out, that loser's got the flu, and we need another man to split the cab fare with."

"You guys don't need me."

"It's a recession over here, mate. I heard they caught refugees at Customs trying to sneak back *into* Somalia."

Matt lent forward, "Come on, Joe, you up for it?"

"Why not," I replied.

"And make sure you wear somethin' 'alf decent,' Mac started, "you look like the reduced section of Primark just threw up on you."

I used up all my energy pretending I was enjoying every minute, but the more I drank the easier it got. I started cursing like a sailor and laughing loudly at my own bad jokes. I even jumped on one of the stages and started doing the robot in front of one of the scantily dressed 'dancers'. Everyone thought I was hilarious. No one understood why I kept calling Mac 'Mac'. When I explained why, they all fell about laughing and the name stuck. A woman, who I'm supposing was drunk, grabbed me by the shirt, told me I was sweet and kissed me on the lips. I remember trying to work out if she was hot or not when Mac bet me twenty quid that he could pull her. I remember laughing instead of asking why.

As we stumbled out of the bar, I got into a fight with a hipster who almost knocked me over trying to be cool, swerving through the streets on his motorized scooter. I think I won. Mac called me a hero. A neighbour called the police.

I vomited in the cab on the way home. It must've been a slow night for the driver as he happily charged me an extra fifty quid and chain-smoked in the cold while watching me clean up my own mess.

Stumbling into my bathroom I had to grab and lean onto the sink to steady myself. I looked up into the mirror opposite. My lip was busted and I had what I could only guess were small chunks of kebab on my chin.

I have the face of a worrier.

Not a warrior, but a worrier. I looked like a hypochondriac. I didn't look seriously ill, but I looked like I probably thought I was.

I don't know how much time had passed while I stared at myself but after a while... I couldn't look anymore. I sat down on the toilet seat with my head in my hands. For the first time in my life, the thought of dying flashed through my mind; there were no tears, no real despair, rather a tiredness. "I'm tired of this. I don't want to do this anymore." As if life was a game I no longer wanted to play. With my eyes closed, I felt my head spin. I saw Hayley's face, Sapphire's face, my aunty's face, and then *her* face.

"To lose and keep losing..."

I threw up and passed out on the toilet seat.

That Monday

I came into work shaven and wearing a new supermarket suit. Mac nudged me while I waited by the photocopier.

"You owe me twenty quid. And I've got video evidence if you want proof."

From the way he winked it was obvious he wanted me to watch his video more than he wanted my money, but because I couldn't remember what he was talking about I just smiled, nodded and never brought it up again.

As I slipped back into silent submission like an old pair of tracksuit bottoms, it didn't take long for them to forget my antics that Friday night. By the end of the week they stopped passing my desk to say 'Mornin', and there was milk in the fridge once again.

The Next Day

...Was just another day.

The Next Day

...Was just another day.

The Next Day

...Was just another day.

Three Weeks Following the Funeral – (Magic Hour)

As I jumped on the bus and took a window seat upstairs, I noted how the colours outside had lost their lustre - the blues and greens of the sky and trees were overpowered by the grey concrete and brown bricks that dominated the landscape.

I looked down at my hands, noticing that they had started to wrinkle. I held them out in front of me and examined the creases. I turned them over, studying my palms, tracing the engraved lines with my eyes.

What have my hands accomplished?

As the bus meandered through the early evening city streets, picking up and dropping college kids and working adults, I thought about tomorrow. Not the fact that it will be Tuesday (possibly the worst day in the week – it's not the beginning the middle or anywhere close enough to the end for you to get excited, it's just there, mocking you, laughing, rubbing its well-rounded chubby exterior saying 'I'm here and there's nothing you can do about it for the next 23 hours and 59 minutes, and guess what? Next week, I'll back here again, how ya like that homey!' – I don't know why Tuesday would use Americanisms), I was thinking of tomorrow in terms of what it's supposed to represent, tomorrow – a new opportunity, a fresh start. Maybe tomorrow does exist in that way but I just can't see it. I know I often pass through today while reflecting on the day before, leaving tomorrow to just kind of blend in. It's similar to what photographers and filmmakers (I did courses in both fields during the summer following the end of school – good times) call 'the magic hour' – that window of time between when the sun starts to set and dusk, where the natural light is perfect for capturing life in art the problem is if you don't pay attention and make an effort to catch it, you'll miss it completely. I've missed it so often that night and day, today and tomorrow, rejection and promise have become two sides of the same cheap coin and both sides displaying tails while I continue to bet on heads.

I've got to find my magic hour.

And then it happened.

About 30 Minutes Later

The craving for my great dietary trifactor of fat, salt and sugar hit me harder than a runaway train. I'd had a Mars bar, a packet of crisps and a four sugared coffee for lunch; I was down to my last tenner till payday but hunger was gnawing at my ribs and I was greedy for some real low-grade high-calorie garbage. There was a frozen food supermarket a few stops past my place near the high street, where you could get six burgers for a £1, an extra-large lasagne for £1 and tub of Neapolitan ice-cream for 50p – a heart-attack for half a fiver, you gotta love London!

The streets were sparse as I got off the bus; winter was encroaching. I saw an old lady in a light grey woollen coat struggling with her shopping towards the bus stop across the street from mine. She looked just like my aunt. So much so that I took a step forward wanting to get a closer look, a part of me almost believing it was her. A feeling in my stomach that had nothing to do with food fluttered in my gut.

"Her hair's grey." *My aunty's is... was a startling white.*

I felt like I should've gone to give her a hand with her bags, but watching her made me sad, made me hurt, so I turned towards the shop that would drown my feelings with everything nutritionally unholy but just then a scruffy looking man grabbed the old lady's purse. Its strap however, was hanging on her shoulder and as he pulled at it, the strap was caught by the bags of shopping in her hand and the purse wouldn't come loose. I froze. The thief pulled at the purse again but only succeeded in dragging the old lady towards him. I found my voice and shouted out from across the street:

"Oi, Oi!"

He was startled for a moment, saw a few more heads turn and so he yanked at the purse with all his might, sending the old lady sprawling to the floor. I found my feet and ran towards them. As she hit the floor she let go of her shopping and the scumbag pulled her purse loose and started to run. Already out of breath I gave chase.

People were assisting the old lady on the floor so I sprinted past her and kept my focus on the dirty green bomber jacket that darted past pedestrians, then took a sharp left out of sight at the top of the road. I ran harder and faster fuelled by hate and anger instigated by more than just this mugging. I turned the corner just in time to see him duck down a narrow side street, and I picked up the pace reaching the street's opening in no time – it was a dead end.

This criminal scum was trying to find a way to climb over the security gate used for letting in delivery trucks for the shops on the other side of the road. Giving up, he turned and started pacing into a run back up the narrow way, until he saw me. I was still jogging towards him but stopped when our eyes met – we were only 15 yards away from each other. I was sweating profusely and my heart bashed against my chest like an angry prisoner headbutting the wall of his cell. But I was still able to get my words out, they weren't strong but I meant them.

"Give it up."

His filthy hand tightened on the purse. His shoulders and hunched back rose and fell as he caught his breath. Then he walked towards me. My heart started to beat in a different way. Through the ratty mess of his face, he spoke.

"Get out of my way."

His words fell weaker than my own. I saw that the hand holding the purse was shaking and that his dirty teeth began chewing his dry bottom lip. His face looked emaciated and his stance unsteady.

I stood my ground, and he stopped.

We were only ten feet apart.

Then I stepped forward.

"Give it up."

Although I reasoned that the police would pull up behind us at any minute or at least the small group of people who saw what had happened, I still stepped forward, driven by a compulsion I couldn't name.

I wasn't afraid.

His eyes fell to the floor.

Then, as if by magic, he produced a flick knife in his free hand and had it aimed towards me. He took a step closer. What surprised me more than the blade, was the fact that I still wasn't afraid.

"I'll stick you."

Both of his hands shook as he raised the knife, the tip pointed at my chest.

And then it hit me. It seemed so simple, so simple it felt perfect.

My words came almost as a whisper:

"Do it."

Leaning back, his face contorted in confusion.

I took a step forward.

"Do it."

He looked me up and down with suspicion. A tingling sensation rushed through my body and rested in my bowls. Not from adrenaline or thoughts of dread, but instigated by a feeling of resignation.

No more sleepless nights. No more morning aches. No more emptiness, no more loss, no more pointlessness, no more pain; and no more God-forsaken green-top milk in the fridge.

In my mind's eye, I saw an image of my aunty sleeping.

Just peace.

I didn't know what it was but immediately I felt my sight sharpen and a calm settle in my mind.

Like this, I'll even get to go out as a hero.

A smile began to curl the edge of my lips.

His eyes and mouth twitched in confusion as he leaned back further and asked, "What are you on 'ey? What... what are you talking about, what do you want?"

Smiling, with the golden light of nature's magic hour shining behind me, I replied:

"Nothing, nothing at all."

The man lowered his knife.

I couldn't hold onto the feeling flowing through me long enough to determine whether it was joy or disappointment.

WOOP. WOOP!

The scream of a police siren screeched behind me. I spun my head with a sharp turn and saw a police car speed past the top of the narrow way.

It was so swift. The knife sunk in so quickly I only felt it on its way out. He was gone before I had turned my head to face him. I looked down and saw the thin slit in the woollen material of my coat. I slowly opened it, as if unsure of what I would find. I saw the rich red of my blood pumping out all over my white work shirt. I put my hand to the wound, and fell to my knees. I could feel the warmth of it against my palm. I wasn't breathing. I turned my cupped hand upwards and saw my own blood all over my own hands and felt the searing pain of something so wrong, so terrible and so final. And then, there it was, so brief, and yet so sweet – relief.

I fell forward, and before my life had a chance to flash before my eyes, everything went black

3am The Next Morning

I could see. I opened my eyes wider; I could see. I reasoned that heaven had no need for bad fluorescent lighting, so I guessed I was still alive.

"Ughhh!"

The pain hit and I realised it was the pain that woke me. I looked around and found the nurse alert button on the side of my hospital gurney. I kept pressing it until a nurse paced towards me.

"The pain!"

He showed me how to use the Patient-Controlled Analgesia Pump and the hit of morphine soon calmed me. He told me that my doctor was busy doing rounds but was able to find my surgeon and brought her over.

"I had surgery?"

"You did indeed Mr Bogart. In fact, you're quite the lucky man." The dark brown of her skin and hazel brown of her eyes put me at a measure of ease, though I cocked an eyebrow at her use of the term 'lucky'.

"Relatively speaking. You see, your wound, although subcutaneous, didn't puncture any deep organs or cause any nerve damage but it did pierce a blood vessel, which can be very serious and could've led you to bleeding out. And this is where you're a lucky man. The pedestrian that found you flagged down a passing ambulance on its way here. We were able to bring you straight into the OR where we had just completed a procedure on a Jehovah's Witness, so the cell saver machine was in the room and we were able to retrieve the blood you were losing, then wash and filter it back into your body. This meant that we didn't have to use any external blood, which can come with its own complications. Once we cauterised the artery, we checked that there was no other internal damage and sewed you back up."

My mouth hung open. "Okay."

"It's a lot to take in. The main thing to focus on is resting. Your body needs to heal and you did lose a significant amount of blood so you will feel a bit weak for a little while."

"Will I be okay?"

"As long as there's no infection, you should be just fine." She smiled reassuringly. I tried to smile back. A flash of me smiling and asking him to 'do it' crossed my mind, and my hand moved towards my stomach. With her smile now tinged with concern, she repeated, "You'll be fine Joseph." And then left.

The nurse, who had stood behind her, explained that as part of their protection procedure, they contacted the police whenever they received a stab or gunshot victim.

"The police will be on their way shortly."

They didn't take long and they didn't stay long. I didn't know the time but due to the darkness outside and the surliness of the officers, I presumed we were in the small hours. They took my details and a description of what happened and what he looked like, asking few questions, and giving even less eye contact.

Before they left, I had a question for them:

"How's the old lady?"

"What old lady?" Asked the older of the two who lead the interview.

"The one who got robbed, the one whose purse I was trying to rescue."

The least talkative office looked at me sideways for the use of the word 'rescue'.

"No idea, nothing was reported." They stood ready to leave.

"So, who found me?"

"A lorry driver trying to leave the depot down that road."

"Oh."

"If we find anything on the assailant, we'll be in contact." And then they left.

No one followed me. No one came to help. If I had bled out no one would've known why I'd been stabbed, why I'd died; wow – you gotta love London.

With those thoughts, I fell into a morphine-induced sleep which blessed me with no dream, just silence.

<u>That Morning</u> – (The old man & the clock)

I woke up hours later in pain but a little less than before.

I paused before pressing the PCA pump for a new dose of drugs. It's weird, for six years I've been waking up with a terrible ache in my stomach, but this pain was so different to the one I normally woke with. I paused for a moment, closed my eyes and considered that difference. This new pain was more visceral, more vicious but more surface. The other, with which I was so well acquainted, was quieter, had no definite face to it but ran deeper. I drew in a long breath and eased my thumb from the PCA Pump button, letting this new pain sit with me, seeing how it kept the old one at bay.

I looked around and noted the other patients in my ward, now awake, many of them with friends and relatives. One man, very old, very frail and grey, with pursed lips protruding due to absent dentures, was alone and from his elevated bed, was staring at me, not questioning or inquisitive or friendly. His look was so fixed that I wondered if it would've changed had my bed been empty. A little unnerved I looked around and found a clock, it was lunchtime. And just as I thought of food, a new nurse appeared at my side.

"Good afternoon Mr Bogart, how are you feeling today?" Her light Irish accent and bright freckles brought a kindness to her smile and demeanour.

"Okay, I suppose." Speaking caused me more discomfort than I anticipated.

"Are you in pain? Do you know how to use the morphine pump?"

"I do thanks, the nurse last night showed me."

"Excellent. Now, before we get your lunch order, I wanted to ask you about your emergency contacts." She lifted the top sheet on her clipboard and read from the notes beneath. "We have your aunt down as your emergency contact but her line rang out. And your brother as next of kin but that number is no longer in use. Do you have up-to-date details for them or anyone else you would like to add?"

I didn't know what to say. She looked up at me from her clipboard.

"Erm, can I get back to you on that please?"

"Of course you can. Now, for lunch we have bangers and mash or fish and chips." She smiled as she spoke.

I wasn't hungry but I thought refusal might create more questions. "Fish and chips please."

"Excellent choice." She was trying to be funny, and I felt bad that I was in too much pain to smile. "Would you like a drink? Some water, a cup of tea?"

Her words were sweet to my ears. "I'd kill for cuppa."

"Well, the good news is you don't have to, they come murder-free at this hospital." I had to at least give her a grin for that one. She left and my attention went back to the other patients and their visitors, then I realised:

No one knows that I'm here.

I moved awkwardly in my bed.

No one's coming.

Then, a moment of clarity slapped me, the absence of my TV and all its noise and nonsense became apparent. The sounds and sight of the patients, their loved ones, the nurses and doctors and all the machines irritated me, annoyed me and started to anger me. And the old man who, since I last looked, seemed to have grown greyer in appearance, was still staring, his expression both vacant and yet focussed on me. Then his mouth opened, I thought his jaw had just gone a little slack and that he was about to start drooling but instead it was as if he was trying to speak, his lips moved with purpose but there was no one with him and he didn't look mad, he looked like he was speaking to me. I didn't become inquisitive or intrigued, I felt anxious. I looked up at the clock again and the hands hadn't moved at all. I became hot and sweat pimpled all over my body.

I don't wanna be here anymore.

There was nothing here of my own to distract me, nothing to take hold of my attention, there was just this mass of discomfort and lack of control.

I pressed repeatedly and hard on the morphine pump.

I don't want to be here.

The nurse returned with my tea before the morphine kicked in.

"Here you go Mr Bogart. You know, I used to love your old movies."

"How long do I have to be here?" I leaned up in the bed while holding the button to make it rise. The pain instigated a flash of anger across my face.

She was thrown a little by my abruptness. "Oh, maybe just a day for observation to make sure there's no infection..."

"Where are my clothes and my other stuff?"

She bent down and opened a little cupboard by my bed. "It's all in here. Is everything..."

"Could you pass it for me please?"

"Of course."

All of my belongings fit into one plastic bag which she placed on the empty chair beside me.

"If I wanted to go home today, what would be stopping me?"

"Well, nothing really. We can't stop you; we would just advise against it - you had surgery just last night."

The morphine started to relax the pain but not my mood.

"If all I'm gonna do is lie here, I can do that at home." I gave her a blank stare, almost daring her to refute my words.

"If that's what you would like to do, I can change your dressing now and get you a supply of painkillers." I had brought her mood down with mine.

"Thank you."

She left. I felt bad but not bad enough. Picking up the plastic bag I rifled through my stuff and was relieved to find my phone and wallet, with the little I'd left in it still there. I pulled out my trousers, shoes, and was about to take out my jacket when I noticed my shirt was missing. I checked the bag over and it wasn't there. The nurse arrived wearing gloves and an apron carrying new dressing.

"I can't find my shirt. Where is it... please?

"I think they cut it off of you before surgery."

A flash of me looking down at my blood-stained shirt and blood-stained hands stung my mind. "Oh, of course."

The nurse was very careful and quiet as she changed the dressing on my wound. She said that there was no increased swelling or redness, and that the stitches were very well done. After showing me how to clean the wound, she re-dressed it, took out the cannula from my arm and left.

"I'm sorry."

She turned back.

"I didn't mean to be rude, I erm, this is all just a bit much for me."

She seemed to forgive me with her smile.

"You have been attacked, stabbed and had surgery Joe; it would be a bit much for anyone."

"The doctor said I was lucky; it could've been a lot worse."

"That doesn't stop it from still being really bad." She gave me that look of pity that I'd seen before and never liked, but from her it was different. "There's a number I would like to give you, a helpline where you can talk to someone about how you're feeling."

"I'm not really the talking type, plus this will heal soon enough."

She went to continue with her suggestion but I believe the look in my face dissuaded her.

"If you don't like talking, you can write, put how you feel on paper, in a journal, on your phone…"

"That's not a bad idea. Thank you."

She gave me a little nod. "I'll get a doctor to see to you and arrange your painkillers and discharge." It was just at that point that her kindness touched me that I noticed the engagement ring on her finger.

Lucky man. "Thank you. You've been really kind."

A pink hue flushed behind her freckles as she left.

When she had walked far enough, I took my time to stand and close the curtains. gingerly, I put my clothes on over my hospital gown. My navy-blue woollen coat was dry, but still bore the darkened stain where my blood had soaked it. I thanked goodness that my laziness had taught me how to put on my shoes without bending down, then pocketed my phone and wallet and snuck out of my curtained cubicle, careful not to catch the eye of my 'watcher', who I could feel was still watching me, and crept out of the ward and out of the hospital to where the taxi cabs were parked, and gave my address.

In the car, I remembered that it was Friday and that I should've been at work. I texted my manager to say I was sick: 'stomach trouble'.

<u>**Monday**</u> – (Home or Away)

The agony I woke to on Saturday was incredible. I thought about calling an ambulance but the hospital was the last place I wanted to go, so I called my doctor's surgery and the hospital had already sent over my notes – the wonders of the technological age, it's nice to be reminded that the internet isn't just all porn and cat videos.

My doctor was able to send a prescription of painkillers to my pharmacy who had a delivery service for housebound patients.

After receiving my bag of pills, I made a cup of tea, grabbed a bag of gingersnaps and reasoned that if the dosage of 'two tablets every 4 hours' applied to anyone over 12, that me being in my thirties and in incredible pain meant that I could take 3 tablets every 3 hours or 5 all at once if I knew I was gonna take a long nap and miss my next dose. The pain killers knocked me out but my dosage gave me stomach cramps that pretty much undid the work of the drugs.

While sleeping, I couldn't find a comfy spot on my sofa so I stayed in bed. I wasn't strong enough to carry my TV in with me, so in the silence, I was left at the mercy of my thoughts:

I hated being at the hospital, and now I'm starting to hate being at home.

Sunday was a blur, and on Tuesday morning, I dosed up well on my pills and went into work. On first sight my boss didn't ask me if I was okay, he told me I looked ill and asked me if I want to go home. I told him I was fine.

Matt made me a cuppa and asked if I wasn't better off calling it day, I told him not to worry. Mac shouted from across the office that I looked like a zombie that had bitten an AIDS victim. I went to swear at him and say something horrible about his mum, but the anger caused a sharp pain in my stomach and caused me to hold back tears as well as my words, but Mac caught something dark and just a little menacing in my look so left me alone for the rest of the week.

With every inhalation, I thought that I would faint. But the fear of them finding out that I'd been stabbed, that I was a victim, that I had no emergency contacts or next of kin to call, that they were actually the closest people to me in my life, that was enough to get me through the day, all the way home and back in the day after that, and the day after that and the day after that.

<u>One Month On</u> - (Mac vs Matt PT.1)

"No good dirty, stinking, ugly piece of filthy sweaty monkey throwing donkey swinging..."

It was a bright Tuesday morning. The sun made the few clouds visible shine and glow. I was on my way to work. Then I broke my big toe.

I had just returned from an appointment at the GP where the nurse removed my dressing for good saying that the wound was healing really well. She complimented the surgeon's stitching as if she were looking at a Gucci handbag.

"It will hardly leave a scar." She said, then was surprised to see that I didn't care. Cause I'd used up almost all of my sick days, I had booked this appointment before work, so needed to rush out to make it to my bus stop in time.

I reached the stop just as the bus pulled up. Out of breath, I scrabbled around in my wallet for my Oyster card, and it dropped out, into a mountain of dog poo; the mutt must have had diarrhoea because the card sank right into it. I bent down, getting as close as I dared to see if it could be recovered, but it sat deep in there like a blue wafer in the worst kind of chocolate sundae. The bus was ready to leave and I couldn't be late again, so I checked my pockets for change and was amazed that I had just enough, only for the driver to remind me that buses no longer take money. I knew that the contactless chip in my debit card wasn't working but wasted everyone's time and increased my embarrassment by repeatedly, tapping, pressing and even softly caressing the sensor with my bank card. Eventually, I jumped off and, in my frustration, I kicked what I thought was a loose stone, only to find that it was an excess lump of concrete.

Like a true loser caught in a spiral lose, I chose to hobble to the station, take out money from the cash machine, buy a travel-card (yes, they do still exist) and then get to work only for my manager to send me home suggesting I go to the hospital and get my toe X-rayed.

It had been a while since I had – while conscious - been to a hospital's Accident and Emergency (aka Department for the Drunk and Foolhardy). You meet the most unlikely people in the DDF waiting room; children in football and rugby kits with a limb or two pointing in the wrong direction, a substance abuser comfortably covered in blood, a couple of old ladies on their death bed – the 'well' one differentiated by her ability to still offer those within arm's reach a boiled sweet, and my favourite, a single man nervously standing in a corner, looking well, apart from a face covered with embarrassment and an awkward walk that would be displayed on his way to the reception desk only when no one else was in earshot. But what was most unsettling, was that I fitted in seamlessly with this ragtag group of mishaps.

After 4 hours I was finally seen, only to be told that the hospital doesn't set broken big toes and so don't bother X-raying them either. They said that it had something to do with setting you off balance. They had also run out of mini splints (I didn't realise broken toes were such an epidemic), so after 4 hours in the DDF they told me to go home and that the toe would fix itself. I wanted to swear at the portly nurse and ask if that was the attitude he had taken with his weight problem, but if he chose not to find me funny, I was too weak to fight and in no position to run.

On the way home I decided to treat myself to an ice-lolly on this surprisingly warm day - I thought I deserved it. I ate away looking forward to the joke written on the stick. When I didn't find one (when did that stop?) I snapped the stick in half and was about to throw it away when I was struck with yet another one of my brilliant light bulb moments (I wonder if Thomas Edison coined that term?). I refused to sit back and believe that things would just get better all by themselves, I was going to do something, I was going to fix this. When I got home, I took the two halves of the lolly-stick, placed one under my big toe and the other on top and then got some sticky-tape and wrapped it around my toe and the sticks several times. I looked down at my stroke of genius with childish pride.

With my DIY splint, I adopted a bit of a limp. That whole week the guys at work called me Keyser Soze or Daniel Day-Lewis. Although I didn't get the first reference, I knew they were both meant as insults. Then Thursday morning while making coffee and listening to the 'jokes' about my dodgy foot ("Your pimp walk needs some work," "I didn't know you suffer from toe-rette's syndrome," "You're seriously lack-toes intolerant aren't you," and Mac began chanting "Did you know, Joe lost his toe in a fight with a hoe"), I was smiling and trying my best to be a good sport and roll with the bants, when in an abrupt burst, I swore at them all. Proper hardcore, drunken sailor with Tourrette's swearing. I just lost it, and was as surprised as they all were. Mac looked like he wanted to fight me, Matt laughed and gave me a thumbs up, but everyone else was silent. Though the name-calling stopped then and there, my surprise turned into annoyance. I was upset at the fact that I let them get to me.

Nearing the end of the day, with the attention turned away from me, Mac had a small audience huddled around his desk. He was exchanging emails with a woman he had chatted up that weekend. The buzz around him hummed as he wrote his messages, and broke out in childish "ooooohs" and "aaaaahs" as they read her replies and opened the picture attachments.

Facing the wall, with his back to the laughs and giggles, Matt was on the phone to his wife. Hunched over in his chair with one hand resting on the back of his head, Matt's elbow sank deeper into his thigh as heavy exhalations made his large body rise and fall.

I picked up a few papers from my desk and walked towards the photocopier, blaming reality TV and social media for turning me into an office voyeur.

Approaching Mac's desk, I could see the devilish glee that brightened his face, made his fingers type quicker and the male and female co-workers jostle him with increased excitement.

Matt though, was trying not to be heard, so I didn't do any actual photocopying but just tapped buttons to pick up what I could. I was only able to glean scraps of sentences:

"That's ridiculous ... What do you mean? ... That's not what you said ... I don't understand what you want from me."

There was a moment when he turned away from the receiver, leaving it to face the floor, then returned to the conversation saying, "Okay, okay, okay... you've made your point."

I made my way back to my desk, catching a glimpse of a picture Mac had received.

"John McEnroe!" I exclaimed.

Mac's head spun round bearing the filthiest of grins. "It's been a while, has it Joe?" I laughed along with the rest of the group. I caught Kim's eye as her chuckle died away.

"Mac's way of life won't last forever," I said to myself, "but from the looks of things, Matt's might not either." A line from a Chris Rock special came to mind: *married and bored or single and lonely; ain't no happiness anywhere.*

Looking at those in my office who an hour ago were making fun of my misery but now enjoying pseudo-adult entertainment at some unknown woman's expense, I felt glad that I didn't fit in with them, that I seemed more at home with those in the DDF waiting room.

Matt put his phone down and slumped into his swivel chair. I got up, no papers in my hand, no pretence, and walked over to him. I recognised, with crystal clarity, the look in his face, it wasn't fear or unhappiness but pain; the kind that ran below the surface but could be decerned by one of the initiated. In that instant I wanted to ask him 'how it felt?', and I knew, whatever his reply, I could follow up with – 'I know the feeling'.

I took a step towards him.

He didn't hear me approach.

"Matt,"

He lifted his head as if it were the weight of a bowling ball. "What's up Joe?"

I couldn't do it.

But I could do something.

"You fancy going for a quick coffee, and a chat?"

He looked at me confused, and rightly so, we had never actually spoken one-on-one, apart from my car-crash attempt to give marriage advice.

"You look like you could do with a coffee and a good chat."

Matt sat up a bit straighter and tilted his head while looking at me, then looking over at the mob surrounding Mac.

"You're good people Joe. Thank you, but I need to leave this place a bit early today," he tapped his wedding ring, "there's someone else I need to have a coffee and a chat with."

"No probs."

As I turned away, he continued, "Seriously though, thank you."

We shared a smile and a nod and I walked back to my desk.

Good people.

On the way home I stopped at a charity shop and picked up a handful of books (more so because they were well known and were 15p each than due to any real intention of reading them) and a used DVD of *The Usual Suspects* for 50p. The books made great coasters, and by the end of the movie I realised that the Keyser Soze joke they made at work was actually pretty funny; though still, I didn't laugh.

<u>**The Following Evening**</u> - (He asked how my toe was)

As I hobbled to my flat, I noticed a woman and her child moving their belongings into the place a few doors down from me. I glanced over and then continued about my business.

"What's wrong with your foot?" The innocent little voice sounded somewhat timid. The boy was maybe ten and wearing a bright red jacket and a mis-matched cotton tracksuit.

"I broke my toe." I turned back to my door.

"Which one?"

"The big one." After a moment's silence, I went back to retrieving my keys.

"Does it hurt?"

I wondered if the kid was being facetious, but his expression was a little too sincere and he seemed to lack that annoying maturity that most kids pick up from late-night TV and lazy parenting.

"Yeah, it still kind of hurts."

With his black hair making him look a little paler than he probably was, he frowned. "I hope it gets better," he said.

I smiled in surprise instead of replying.

"Aaron, why did you bring this box of crap with you? None of this junk even works." The boy spun around, almost tripping on the box behind him.

"The Gameboy does."

The boy's mum took the Gameboy out of the box of other old hand-held gaming systems and waved it in his face.

"But it doesn't have a charger!" She seemed like she was in her late twenties but had the look of someone who has smoked and drunk their way into looking late-thirties. She was pretty, definitely attractive, but not my type.

"I might find one in another charity shop."

She shook her head and threw the Gameboy back into the box that sat beside several others.

"The rest of these boxes are yours. Put them by your blow-up bed."

I thought it odd that his mum didn't even acknowledge me, a strange man who'd been chatting with her son, as she strode into the flat.

I put my key in my door.

"Bye... Aaron."

He looked up from his "box of crap" with a wide, happy, innocent smile.

"Bye... sir."

"I'm not your teacher, you can call me Joseph."

"Okay, bye... Mr Joseph."

He smiled again and I didn't know if he was cracking a joke or was really just that cute.

At home, I'd become very proficient at cooking the perfect microwave meal. The elusive secret was, ironically, to cook it in the oven. As my Chinese chicken wings and egg fried rice for two baked, I got changed into my home clothes. While taking off my splint, I considered the little boy's questions. I'd been hobbling about like an arthritic pimp for a whole week and he had been the only person to say he hoped my toe got better.

With my dinner on my lap, I searched the internet looking for the cheapest price for *My Left Foot* on DVD. While getting my debit card I found the Starbucks receipt from when I met up with Sapphie (not throwing it away was one of those silly sentimental things I've done for years – got a whole shoebox full of receipts, cinema stubs and bar mats).

"I wonder how you are."

I hadn't heard anything from Sapphie since we'd met up. I'd been getting used to the idea that I may never see her or even hear from her again. I'm supposing this is what they call growth; a year ago, this admission would've crushed me. Three months ago, I would never have had the courage to spill Kim's coffee. And a week ago I would've been scared shirtless (I'm sure that's a saying) at the idea of offering to take Matt for a coffee and lend him an ear. Maybe my wound wasn't the only thing that was healing.

'Do it.'

The words I had spoken were now whispered behind my thoughts.

"I can't believe I did that." The fear I should've felt finally caught up with me, and I realised that the surgeon was right, I was lucky that it wasn't a lot worse.

I had a beer with my meal and fell asleep watching a pretty ginger lady sell once-in-a-lifetime offers on the shopping channel in sign language. That night I dreamt of Molly Ringwald.

Later That Night - (From dream to nightmare)
The burning pain in my stomach woke me from the sweetest dream.

After Molly and I had a playful argument on the American dislike of the letter 'u' and the British habit of reading a newspaper on public transport to avoid small talk with strangers, we were spirited away to a fun fair (fairground/carnival/amusement park in American English – pretty sure that's a misnomer). As we got into our bumper cars with a bag of candyfloss each, I needed the loo – in real life. When I got back to bed and slipped again into sleep, that was when the dream happened.

Initially, I was more upset about being torn away from my imagination's playground than about the burning in my bowels. The dream felt more than real; I still had a remnant of the smells and tastes clear in my mind – lavender and honey. I couldn't say what the dream was about, I only know that I was tied in so deeply that when the cord to my inner visions was severed, I awoke drained and unsatisfied, teetering on the edge of fulfilment. If I could regain that moment I had been torn from it would only take the slightest breeze to push me over into bliss. Whether the scenario was a kiss to be had or the first mouthful of a new revolutionary ice cream from the genius minds of Ben, Jerry and a certain Mr William Wonka, I wanted to feel it in full, I wanted to indulge. I closed my eyes and tried to pull the broken strands of my thoughts back together, to resurrect the dream and then the feeling. There were greens, sunlight, the breeze... and a touch. But as is always the case in life, it was impossible to get back what was lost; this was one of life's little mysterious cruelties, like ugly babies or bad Spielberg movies. Although immense, my frustration was soon subdued by the pain in my stomach. It wasn't the surface, superficial pain from the wound, but was that 'other pain' I knew only too well.

I got out of bed and hobbled my way into the kitchen and in opening the fridge was almost blinded by the light. I grabbed the anti-acid and downed a mouthful straight from the bottle. The sun was rising; the clock on the microwave read 05:38. I couldn't hear the birds singing. The pain was getting worse, it was stronger than usual. I thought things had been getting better, that I had been feeling better since the incident in the alley. I had assumed that how I felt and the pain in my stomach were connected, but today it was worse. Doubled over and breathing heavily, I looked down at my bare feet, and stared at my makeshift splint.

'It will fix itself.'

As soon as the doctor's opened, I called and made an appointment.

The room felt as cramped as my insides as I sat opposite the female GP, whose starched blouse and measured fringe gave her that clinical look you could imagine toddlers shying away from.

"Do you have trouble passing stools?" she enunciated perfectly.

The chair instantly became uncomfortable.

"Only when I'm drunk," I quipped, squirming a little in my seat.

"Do you drink often?" she asked in earnest, scribbling on her notepad.

"Oh... no, I was joking."

She looked both confused and irritated, her sharp nails resting on her notepad.

"When I'm drunk, I have problems passing the stools... in a bar... because I end up knocking them over."

Her expression read that my witticism hadn't gone over her head but had burrowed its way under her feet. She let the silence continue until she could see that I felt reasonably embarrassed. She adjusted her Armani spectacles and picked up her pen.

"Mr Bogart, can you describe what your stools look like?"

I really had to fight the temptation to say "polished pine wood with a medium honey varnish".

"Brown... sometimes caramel brown, sometimes chocolate brown, and sometimes a little darker than that."

"Have they ever been black?"

"A couple of times, but I think that was because I had a Guinness that night and marmite sandwiches for lunch."

"Black stools can indicate intestinal bleeding."

"Oh." The staff in my joke department suddenly disappeared for a fag break.

"I need to examine you now."

I took a deep breath and began fidgeting with my hands.

"Lie down on the bed over there."

As I rose, my stomach turned. I lay on my back and palmed my lower abdominals with my clammy hands.

"Can you lie on your front, Mr Bogart?"

I wanted to question why people ask questions that are meant as statements or commands, but anxiety kept breaking the links in my chain of thought like a heavy-set bailiff determined to get his job done.

I rolled over onto my front and began wondering how she was going to feel my stomach from my back. As I turned to ask the question, I saw the doctor lubricating *two* of her latex-gloved fingers with quiet precision.

I had heard David Attenborough explain how young antelope can become frozen to the spot when surprised by an approaching lion, but he'd done the feeling quite an injustice.

My words were drunk with nerves as they fell out of my mouth.

"Wha...what's... what, what are you doing... I..."

"I need to conduct an anal examination."

My natural instinct against penetration made me sit up in a snap.

"Ah... I... I don't think so."

"Mr Bogart..."

"I didn't sign up for this. I came in with a problem about my belly not my bum."

"As I'm sure you're aware the two are connected and I need to..."

"Wait a sec. If I hadn't turned around when I did, would you have just put your fingers in my bum?"

"I would've asked you to pull down your trousers and underwear first, but yes."

"What? Isn't there some kind of consent form that I need to sign before you do this type of thing? Isn't there a... a pre-anal counselling session you give to prepare the victim... student... patient... person?"

"Mr Bogart, I didn't want to scare you with this information but your reluctance has left me no choice. Intestinal bleeding is a symptom of prostate cancer."

My body withdrew, my mouth closed and my heart felt like it was beating in my head.

I'd been shocked by the use of a "c" word before, but not this one and not in this way.

My mouth opened, and though my words had been sobered by what they heard they were reluctant to expose themselves.

"Lie on your front, Mr Bogart." I humbly followed her instructions. "Now pull down your trousers and pants." I never imagined that hearing this sentence from a woman would strike me with such cold anxiety.

"Now put your knees into your chest and curl up into a ball." I felt a cold plastic-covered hand lay heavy on my exposed goose-pimpled buttock. Like Attenborough parting the long grass on an African savannah, she slowly but firmly separated my bum cheeks. Cool air washed over my uncharted territory sending a nervous ripple through my body, which notified my tear ducts to prepare for action. I didn't want to be fingered.

"Think happy thoughts." Her tone, icy and Orwellian.

To distract myself, I wondered what it would mean if I liked it, if it felt good. Would that mean that I was gay? I think Beckham is a good-looking man, I mean I understand why women like him. Would he be the type of guy I would go for if I were gay? I don't know, I was confused, I...

"WO, wo, wo, what was that, why was it so wet?"

"That's the lubricant, Mr Bogart." Her words were sharpened with annoyance but I didn't care; it felt like a snail was sniffing for lettuce around my sphincter.

"Do you need so much, how thick are your fingers? You're a doctor, not a bricklayer!"

"Trust me, it's a lot easier with it."

"I'm really not sure about all of this."

"You're being ridiculous, Mr Bogart! This procedure is necessary and routine. Recognise the seriousness of the situation, let me do what I need to do and stop being so childish!"

With contrite obedience, I curled up into a ball with my bottom protruding towards her. With my eyes closed, I thought of what one of my heroes would do in this situation. My mind skipped passed Martin Luther King and went straight to Chuck Norris.

He'd just clench, break her finger and kill the cancer in one swift move.

"You need to relax Mr Bogart, and this will all be over quickly, just... think happy thoughts, and try not to move."

I closed my eyes and tried to think of my dream, then remembered being six and going to my first funfair. I thought about Toffee Apples and the Jolly Rancher ship ride. That was fun. I recalled being on the bumper cars and flying around, skilfully avoiding the other cars, but then out of nowhere, some lady rammed right into the back of me. The bump knocked out my loose front tooth, the one I used to pull on and let hang off of my gum as a party trick during school lunch. It hurt, and I felt sad.

"All done."

I wanted to pull up my trousers quickly but my efforts were somewhat lacklustre.

I sat back down in front of her.

"It's good news, I couldn't feel any irregularities."

I nodded, unable to meet her eyes.

"I'll book you in for an endoscopy where the hospital will use a camera to see what's going on in your bowels."

I heard the syllables 'end-o' and my eyelids and mouth gaped simultaneously. "Where will they put it?"

"Down your throat, Mr Bogart."

I made no attempt to hide my relief.

"My name is Joseph. It feels a little silly you calling me by my last name after we've done... what we've done. I'm sure in some cultures we'd be married now, or at least waiting to be stoned."

She smiled with condescending sympathy.

"Mr Bogart, Joseph, this examination isn't a big deal; in fact, I do it all the time."

She smiled as a short silence ensued.

"Floozy!"

Her jaw hit the desk.

My apology was both sincere and incoherent.

"Your appointment will be in the post." She said, pointing towards the door.

Post Probe

While walking home from the doctor's, ignoring the pain in my big toe and the squelch of lubricant between my cheeks, I noticed a woman in her fifties, black teeth, bedraggled blonde/white, dressed in a tracksuit and smoking a cigarette like she was breathing air, and I was quickly reminded of the relief I hadn't yet digested.

While I waited to be seen by my doctor, I'd picked up a gossip mag and acted like I wasn't excited to see it was one of the issues I had missed. The fourth article was about a man who had just been diagnosed with a neurological disease. He was a fitness instructor in his late thirties with a wife who was a police officer and four children under ten, one of them from a previous relationship. Over the next three months the disease would destroy all of his motor skills and then begin to eat away at his memory. Before the end of the year, he'd be dead.

I felt ashamed. It was an injustice that people like him were dying, while someone like me woke up every morning in good health halfway wishing they hadn't awoken at all. Despite the shame and embarrassment swimming in me, I was happy I wasn't dying. I was glad I had the examination. And I regretted asking that mugger to stab me.

Over the years, I had thought a lot about not living, but had never really considered dying. It's crazy that it took a brief cancer scare and a knife to the belly to really see that I didn't want to die; but I wasn't so crazy that I couldn't see that it took more than this realisation to live.

I thought back to my teenage years, before university, before my natural inclination towards enjoying life dissipated, before things fell apart; it felt so distant, like a lifetime ago, like someone else's life. Back when I would wake up looking forward to the day, when I naturally expected that things wouldn't be easy but would always work out. It was during those days that I got my first real insight to pain. It was during my first year of Uni, and from my douchey roommate, Alistair.

Alistair Cosgrove volunteered twice a week for the Samaritans. He wasn't a great humanitarian or anything, he was just a little dark. His dad owned a funeral company and Alistair worked with him during the holidays. He told me of one instance where they went to pick up a body from a home, a council estate. He said the whole block had come out to see them take their beloved neighbour away. She was a West Indian woman in her late 50's who had died, dropped dead after an asthma attack at home alone.

The four-floor council estate was silent as they carried her out in a body bag from the first floor flat. Almost a hundred people were standing in doorways, looking down from stairwells and filling the corridors as the family followed behind. Alistair and his dad walked with slow and careful precision around the mass of the living, their heavy footsteps echoing throughout the block as all sniffles and talk paused, and no one made a sound. They carried her down the stairs, and outside where they placed her body in the back of their hearse. They had started to drive away, when the youngest son of the deceased broke away from the arms of his siblings and aunts and ran after them banging on top of the car for them to stop. When they did, he threw open the back doors, and embracing his dead mother, burst into tears and began to wail. Like a chain reaction, all of the family followed, rushing to the vehicle, their tears flowing. Then the whole block surrounded the car and above the tears, one voice was heard, that of youngest son crying out, 'don't take my mum away, please don't take my mum away'.

I was on the verge of tears myself but Alistair was smiling, he said that he loved all of that raw emotion, that when in the midst of it you can't help but get swept up in, that it gave him a thrill, a high. He said it was the best job he'd ever done with his dad. On hearing that, instead of fighting back tears I fought back the desire to hit him. But one night after a late shift on the phones at the Samaritans, he came home disturbed; he woke me up but couldn't look me in the eye. He said he had a young female caller that night, which was no surprise as 90% of the calls were from teenage girls who had just had their hearts broken and they felt they couldn't cope.

"I learned this line from Jim, an old-timer there. I would ask them, 'Do you want to kill yourself or do you want the pain to stop.' They would always say 'I want the pain to stop.' Then I would tell them, 'But what if I told you that you could stop the pain without dying?' They would tell me that they have tried everything and that the pain is too much and death is the only answer. I would tell them that I can understand, but if there was a way to stop the pain other than dying, would they take it? They would always say yes. And this was the line Jim drummed into me 'then it's not death that you want, you don't want to kill yourself, you don't want to die, you just want the pain to stop, right?' they always went weak at this question and said yes, and would calm down; at that point I would pass them on. But tonight, this girl wasn't crying, wasn't hysterical. When I asked if it was the pain stopping or death that she wanted, she said both. I was thrown off and I tried to carry on but then she thanked me for my time but said that she needed to go now, then she hung up. We don't trace the calls, they're anonymous, but I thought that was just what they told us. I told my supervisor what happened and she said there's nothing we can do. I have no idea if this girl is still alive, but everything tells me that she isn't. I swear she couldn't have been more than 12.'

The not knowing killed him inside, but he never quit, secretly he hoped to get her call again.

But that line, 'it's not death that you want... you just want the pain to stop?', walking back from the doctors, that line finally sunk into me and more than made sense, it made me want to find a way, a way to make the pain stop.

That Friday

It was Friday evening and the street outside was all abuzz. Winter was coming to an end, the nights were brighter, there were more cars out, more people in them and each one banging the tunes that would soon be this summer's hits.

I had ordered takeaway from that Thai place down the road, my new favourite reality show was about to start – *Celebrity Ninja* – and the *Back to the Future* trilogy I'd ordered arrived in the post that morning (even brand new DVDs cost nearly nothing these days). I had a mug of hot chocolate in my hand, a massive bag of Kettle chips in my lap and I couldn't have been more excited.

As I took the wrapping off the DVD box set and shook my head at the thought that there's a whole generation that doesn't know the genius of Michael J. Fox, I heard a familiar beeping noise.

I got up, following the sound, thinking it was the battery of the fire alarm dying again, and then realised it was coming from the hallway outside. Peeking through the spyhole, I saw the little kid from next door, Aaron, sitting with his legs crossed holding an old brick phone in his hand. Straight away, I recognised the bleeping sound as the Snake game on the old Nokia 6210. The phone, the game and the sound all brought back memories of my college days that made me chuckle. I noticed him glance up towards the stairwell expectantly, sigh, then lean against the wall returning to his game. I looked back at my clock; it was 7:20pm. I felt moved to do something but didn't know what.

During the commercial break of *Celebrity Ninja*, I made another cup of hot chocolate and grabbed a handful of biscuits and thought I'd surprise the kid with a snack. As I walked to the door, the beeping sound stopped. I looked through the spyhole and saw Aaron's mum stroll up to him and put her arm around his shoulders. There were no questions, no words spoken at all; just the silent joy of a little boy seeing his mum. They walked to their door, Aaron holding his mum's hand as she swayed down the hall.

<u>The Following Afternoon</u> – (The rewards of a good book)

It was a cool breezy day; cool enough to wear a jacket but not cold enough for a hat. Leaves carpeted the floor with a golden crunch. I had finally found my sweet spot on this bench and had my elbows nestled in my thighs as I continued to read one of the books I bought. Hearing the Snake game and thinking of my college days reminded me of how much joy I used to get from reading.

One remedy for pain is joy.

And with that thought I grabbed a book, my jacket and headed for the park at the bottom of my road.

There wasn't a pigeon or any pigeon poop in sight, Miles Davis' *Kind of Blue* album played out from a nearby second floor flat and the road surrounding the park was clear; the moment felt golden.

She was as bold as brass the way that she stopped me and said,

"What a great book."

Looking up I replied, "I know, I can't stop."

Completely uninvited, she peered over the book to look at what page I was on. Her hair smelled of summer fruits.

"You won't believe it, but it gets better! Have you seen the film?" Her cheeks rose and her eyes widened with her question.

"No, but now it's on my 'to actually do' list."

She chuckled. "'To actually do list', that's cool. I gave up with 'to do' lists years ago."

I closed the book but kept my palm on my page. "So how do you remember to get things done?"

Her head tilted and there was a wiggle in her hips as she answered. "Well, I've found that important things usually find a way of kicking me up the bum if I forget about them for too long."

"You must like having a sore bum," I said, obviously without thinking.

Her face dropped.

"What are you trying to insinuate? If you're thinking what I think you're thinking..."

I began pleading with my hands; I didn't want to add further insult by interrupting her.

"...then we have a very similar sense of humour."

A delinquent grin burst across her face.

I sighed with a smile.

The long curls in her hair bounced as she seemed to find it difficult to stand still.

"I'm on my way to a little cinema up the road. Want to come?"

"Oh... erm, what are you going to see?"

This was all very random and quick, a bad combination in my book.

"I don't know, they often have a decent selection of foreign films on the go."

Her throwing an extra dash of randomness into the mix didn't make me feel any more comfortable.

"Are you meeting people there?"

"No. Just felt a bit bored. Look, don't worry, I just wanted someone to share popcorn with, a small is always too small and a medium is always too much. Anyways... it was nice meeting you."

And with a smile as bright as her clothing, she waltzed away to the jingle of the bracelets and bangles on her arms and wrists, her handmade scarf fluttering in the breeze.

I would like some popcorn too.

"Wait a sec, hold on." As if by magic the pain in my toe disappeared and I was jogging after her.

Her name was Felicia, and her skin smelled of honey and cocoa-butter.

It turned out that I liked salt and she liked sweet so we both got mediums and ended up throwing almost half of it away. From what I could understand, the film was pretty good. I thought that the acting was a little under-done, but she told me that that was because of all the reality TV I watched. I thought we were going to get into a deep discussion on the negative moral consequences reality TV has on the masses, but instead she proceeded to update me on most of my favourite shows. The discussion floated back to film of the foreign variety when it came up that I'd never left the country. She refused to believe me.

"Why?" she asked, incredulous.

"Well... it's going to sound silly but loads of other people feel the same too so it's not really that weird but I..."

"...got felt up by a flight attendant when you were little?" Her smile was incredible and made my reply start with a chuckle.

"No, I'm... I'm scared of flying."

"What are you scared of?" she asked assuming I had a pre-planned response, when the truth was no one had ever asked.

"I dunno."

"There must be a reason why you're scared, though, right?"

"You would think so."

"Do you get claustrophobic?"

"Not really."

"Are you afraid of crashing?"

"Maybe..."

"You know they say there's more chance of you being in a car crash than a plane crash, right?"

"Yeah, but there's more chance of you surviving a hit on a mini-roundabout than there is of falling from 6000 feet."

She screwed up her face in contemplation - looking like a child having to decide between ice cream and jelly. Then, as if she'd stumbled across the realisation that she could have both, she said in a sing-song way,

"I know what you're scared of."

I felt a little patronised, but that smile of hers...

"Go on then, what am I scared of?"

"Not tellin'."

"Why?"

"'Cause you're smellin'."

My own laughter caught me by surprise. Then she started. She loved to laugh and was unashamed of how loud she did so. At first, it made me uncomfortable but then I didn't care, because she didn't.

Her face bore the remnants of childhood acne but glowed with the soft tone of a caramel latte. The first time she stole popcorn from my box, I noticed that she had slim wrists; they looked as smooth as warm butter. I think she caught me staring.

Her confidence and joviality seemed almost infectious; it was as if you could drink it in. It filled the atmosphere without being overbearing and held your attention without a hint of narcissism.

Over the following weeks, she proceeded to invite and take me to trendy places where I met what I assumed were trendy people. Wherever we went there were always a lot of her friends around and they were always nice to me, but they all seemed to adore her.

The days that we weren't together we spent texting with infrequent phone calls. She would send me the most random of messages in the middle of the day or night asking me questions like:

What happened at the end of Dungeons and Dragons?

Why don't people wear dungarees anymore?

What's Molly Ringwald up to these days? (She's the reason why I fancied every redhead at school.)

The fascinating thing was that she swore these kinds of thoughts had no traceable origin, that they just popped into her head. With that laugh of hers she admitted she didn't care about the answer but just wanted to know whether anybody else was having the same thought.

When she asked me about my past relationships, I only told her about Hayley; I think I was playing for sympathy. She, however, thought Hayley was brave and really respected her decision.

"Did you two ever stay in touch?" she asked over the phone.

"We did for a little while. We would email each other every so often." I was lying in bed trying to wiggle just my little toe.

"What did she end up doing?"

"She did the whole travelling bit. Started in Europe and ended up in the Amazon. She got a decent pay-out on her health insurance."

"Good for her."

"Yeah, she loved it. She err... she met a guy, another traveller from Wales. I was okay about it all, until he started to appear in almost all of her photos."

"What happened?"

"I stopped replying, she stopped sending."

"And what if she emailed you tomorrow?"

"I'd reply and catch up but... I don't think we could be friends."

Felicia was silent on the phone for a while, so long that I had to ask her if she was alright.

"Yeah, just putting on my jacket. There's a Moroccan place that's open till late, they do the best mint tea. I'm taking you there."

"When?"

"Now."

And just like that, we were off to have Moroccan mint tea at midnight.

Before we met up, and this happened pretty much every time we did and sometimes just as I saw her name flash up on my phone, I would get this funny feeling. It was a weird anxiety, not butterflies in my stomach, more like question marks poking my insides with their sharp points.

She was too pretty, too nice, too many others must want her. Why was she texting me?

Every time we went out, I felt like I was just keeping the seat warm for someone better and that the anxiety I felt was like a short, wrinkled, bow-tied attendant who'd every so often tap me on the shoulder to remind me not to get too comfortable.

However, despite how I felt, I *thought* differently.

She's a nice girl and I'm a nice guy. Why not?

I repeated this to myself as we sat watching movie trailers before our film started one evening. She was trying to convince me that the £16.50 we'd each spent on our tickets was worth it.

"Only West End cinemas let you take in a cocktail..." she started.

"Felicia..." I interrupted, in a tone trying for sexy but ending up sounding concerned.

She turned to face me, her mouth still open.

I repeated to myself, *She's a nice girl and I'm a nice guy. Why not?*

She tasted of strawberries; or was it that her lips felt firm yet soft, full and moist and wonderfully sweet? I thought I'd caught her by surprise with my boldness.

"You took your time, didn't you?" was all she said as our lips parted.

Before I had a chance to reply she was on me and we were making out like teenagers bunking off school.

<u>Two to Three Working Days Later</u>

It was about 7pm so I expected them to be home, and knocked again. Aaron answered.

"I've got a present for you."

His wide-eyed face lit up with excitement. I handed him a box and he wasted no time in tearing into it.

"A Gameboy charger!" His eyes and mouth hung open, revealing teeth still trying to find their proper place in the world.

"Yep. You can get pretty much anything on the internet."

"Wow!" His brown eyes glowed with angelic glee, his home-made haircut adding joviality to his look. He couldn't take his eyes off it. I felt kind of proud that I had created this moment.

He held the small, well, comparatively large, device in his hand turning it over and over in excited examination. But then his face dropped. With a slow incline he looked up at me.

"But... why?"

The question threw me and I replied with hesitation, "Because you didn't have one."

"But I don't know you." His small round face wanted to trust me but was unsure.

"I know you don't but..."

"I... I don't think my mum will let me have it. I'm not a charity case or a beggar." His frown gave him little dimples as he handed the gift back with obvious reluctance.

I lowered myself, leaning forward with both eyebrows raised. "I'm sorry, Aaron, I don't understand."

Aaron was about to speak when a voice from inside shouted out.

"Aaron, who is it?"

The shrill sound of his mum made him spin round. "It's the man from next door."

"What does he want?" she called back.

"I..." I began.

She appeared at the door in shorts and a vest, the dark roots of her blonde hair making themselves known.

"What is it?" she asked abruptly.

"I bought your son a Gameboy charger and was just giving it to him."

She snatched the gift from Aaron and ushered her child behind her, pulling in the front door and standing in the small gap in-between. Her brow knotted in suspicion and her hand sat high on her hip as she asked,

"Why?"

"I overheard you say that he didn't have one."

"He doesn't have a Mercedes either." Her reply flew back at me like an arrow.

"Look... I'm not sure what I've done wrong but I just felt like buying him the charger, he seemed like a nice kid and it was only, like, £2.79... plus postage and packaging." (I had no idea why I added that).

"What do you mean he seemed like a nice kid?"

"Look, I'm sorry, I can just take it back, I was just trying to be nice, the kid asked how my toe was and I thought I'd return the gesture with..."

"You mean he didn't ask for it?" Her tone was more inquisitive than distrustful.

"No, no, I haven't seen him since that day you were moving in."

Her green eyes narrowed like a cat's and looked me up and down in silence. Her jawline was sharp and defined, ending at her chin in a "V" shape; she looked like an aged prom queen.

"Okay. But if he asks you for anything don't give it to him. He's not a charity case, he shouldn't go round begging. I look after him just fine. Okay?" She edged out of the doorway waiting for me to reply in the affirmative.

"Okay."

"Aaron, come and thank the nice man."

"My name's Joseph."

Aaron's mum had already left. Aaron's round face poked from behind the door.

"Thank you, Mr Joseph."

I chuckled taking another look at his hair and thought, *She must've just put a soup bowl on his head and cut around it.*

"You don't have to call me Mr. Enjoy your Gameboy Aaron."

He had a wide smile as if we were sharing a private joke. "Thanks, Joseph."

After he closed the door, I heard him say "Yes!" and begin humming the theme tune to Super Mario Brothers.

When I got home, I so badly wanted to call someone and find out if what had just happened was a little weird in anybody else's book. I put on the kettle and rang Felicia. It felt good to have someone to call just like that; it felt real good.

I shouldn't have waited so long to try reading again.

A Week & Two Days On

"Wow, you look tired" was Felicia's greeting as she invited me into her flat.

"Thanks." Straight away I wanted to look in a mirror.

"Come on, you know I find you attractive" (I'd hoped but didn't know) "but you do look tired. How come?" There was something about her genuine concern that made me say what I wasn't ready to say.

"I don't sleep very well."

We walked into her front-room. Her place was nice. It was an old Victorian house that she shared with two other girls and a guy.

"What does that mean?" She picked up a half-empty mug of herbal tea from her coffee table and shook it in a gesture to offer me one.

"Always."

She put on the kettle and we both sat down on her orange sofa and I unzipped my coat.

"Well… I don't really sleep more than three hours at a time." I sank into the soft leather and took in the wooden floors and mauve feature wall; it was very fashionable but felt a little cold.

"Wow. I'm sorry, Joseph."

I didn't know what to say to that. As Felicia had requested, we had planned to go back to the cinema to see that film we'd kissed all the way through, so I was about to suggest I have my cuppa in a take-away cup and that we get going, when she continued.

"What have you tried doing to help?"

"I've tried going for walks before I sleep, I've tried reading, drinking hot chocolate, Horlicks, warm milk. One website said that eating bananas before bedtime helps so I tried that too, but that gave me weird dreams – well, weirder dreams." I noticed a lot of artwork on the walls and flowers around the room but no TV.

"Have you ever thought about trying yoga?"

"Well…" I leaned back and inhaled in an exaggerated way.

"Hey, don't knock it till you try it, that's my philosophy."

"Ah, well, you see my philosophy is the exact opposite."

"What, knock it till you try it?" She was poised, ready to mock me.

"Exactly."

"You're such a fool," she said trying not to laugh, but she was falling for my brand of humour.

"Hey, it's your way of thinking that probably got farmers to look at their sheep the wrong way." I quipped.

"Oh, that's just disgusting."

Yeah, she loved it!

"I'm just saying."

"Okay, no yoga. What about trying to find somewhere where you feel comfortable?" She leaned in towards me, her chin in her palm; she reminded me of my Uni counsellor.

"I feel comfortable at home."

"Somewhere *more* comfortable." Her free hand opened out invitingly, her tone was patient.

"Like where?" I shrugged my shoulders having no idea where she was going with this.

"Your mate's house, your gran's house... your childhood home... where did you last sleep well?"

"In my bed... about six years ago." I leaned back into the sofa.

"And before then?"

"At uni..."

"So, you went straight from uni to your flat?"

"Well, I went back home, my childhood home, for a couple of weeks first, then..."

Felicia leaned closer and interjected, "And how did you sleep there?"

"Fine."

"So, as you can't go back to university why don't you go back home and see if you can kick start a good sleeping routine from there?"

I sat up straighter as I replied, "I can't. It's gone. My dad sold it." I leaned off the back of the sofa, my hands together.

"Oh, well then, you'll just have to sneak back into your old uni and see if you can get a good night's sleep there." There was no smile or smirk with her comment.

"This isn't *Porky's 4 – Joseph's Return*. I'm not a kid, I can't go breaking into universities to get a decent kip." I fell back onto the sofa on the verge of laughing.

"Why not?" Felicia's eyebrows knitted and her head tilted to the side as her palms opened in front of me.

"Because that's bananas!"

She relaxed in her seat, her tone more critical. "It's because you're scared."

"Yeah, scared of getting caught, going to jail and then dropping the soap."

"All that shower business is just a myth. You're scared!"

"Myth or not it's definitely one I'm willing to knock until I try." We were both slouched on the sofa tickled by my comment.

"Oh, so it's something you can see yourself trying one day?"

"You know what I meant."

"And there I was wondering why it took you so long to kiss me. I'd put it down to you being scared there too, but now that I know the real reason..."

"May I remind you that it was *I* who did the kissing first?" I raised my chin and eyebrows in mock condescension.

Felicia looked at me, her face straight, her eyes calm. There was a sombre tone to her retort. "Yeah, I remember the kissing. I also remember that happening a week ago, and nothing else since..."

My features froze and a cat, a big cat, maybe a lion, caught my tongue.

Her look was sure, her stance firm. I knew what I was supposed to do here, but I couldn't move, I couldn't even get that stupid look off my face. Her hazel eyes were enticing and she seemed to have somehow moved closer to me without moving. I was seriously punching above my weight here. I wasn't even good at rounders and yet there I was about to bat at Lord's. (I tried to get out of my own head before I fell over another sports analogy).

I'm not that guy.

That guy who can take a girl's hand – a girl he likes, hardly knows and has only kissed once before, look her in the eyes, brush the curls from her face, lean across the small space between them and kiss her in a way that will make her want him, kiss her in a way that says "I want to be more than just friends", in a way that makes her feel that she would be missing out on something special if all they had shared was a first kiss and nothing more. I wished, if just for a moment, I could be that guy, that person who could do the right thing at the right time, in the right way.

But little did I know I *was* that guy. And I knocked that ball clean into the crowd!

<u>Two Weeks On</u> – (Exposed brick)

I had annual leave I needed to take or lose and she worked for a mental health charity that pretty much let her do what she wanted, so we decided to spend the day together while I was off.

We met at a high street bus-stop in a newly gentrified area where exposed-brick eateries had pretentious names like *Dialogue* and *Notes in Black* (Although I did think coffeeshop *GrindHouse* was pretty smart – the walls were covered with Grindhouse movies posters) and where you can spend a developing country's GDP on a coffee and a French almond croissant, and where estate agencies were trying so hard be trendy they looked like a cross between an Apple Tech Store and a Whole Foods grocery; but I couldn't complain, I got a free jar of local honey for inquiring about a £400,000 studio flat, while I waited.

Felicia was late, but her aura (only the words of hers that I dislike keep slipping into my diction) was radiant and her brown eyes excitable. She wore a retro puffer jacket and rainbow-coloured cotton gloves. She looked too adorable to be cross with.

We went to a bar in the middle of the day, which I thought was a little unorthodox but then I'm not trendy. There, we met some more of her friends for drinks. I wasn't sure what to have; a pint didn't seem suitable in that kind of place and it felt too early for anything stronger, so I played it safe, had a Coke and pretended that I didn't mind the small glass it came in or the large price that accompanied it.

As day turned to evening, the place lightened up and I started to add rum to my Coke. She was far from drunk so where she got the confidence from, I'll never know, but when "Say a Little Prayer for You" came on, she started to sing along loudly and out of tune; but nobody minded. When the chorus arrived, she jumped up on the table knocking drinks everywhere. She sang louder, yet worse, while performing the most unprovocative of dances. And everyone applauded.

When she finally finished, some of the crowd even gave her a standing ovation and shouted "Encore". I felt embarrassed for her but she stood there like she was looking in her bathroom mirror, caught in a daydream and waving at invisible fans. She was so comfortable. Then just as she started to get down from the table,

"I Love You Baby" (I think that's the name of the song, I'm sure it's the chorus) started playing and she jumped right back up. I slipped out of the bar, got on the bus and went home.

All the way to my flat I couldn't work out why she was the way she was. When she wasn't funny, people still laughed with her, when she wasn't looking her best, people couldn't take their eyes off her, and she wasn't incredibly intelligent but she was always speaking, regardless of the topic, but never sounded like a fool.

<u>The Following Day</u> - (Who do you love?)

She called and asked what had happened to me; she wasn't angry or worried, just inquisitive. I threw microwave popcorn at the stupid guy playing Deal or No Deal on the TV and explained that it wasn't my kind of scene. There must have been something in my tone that I didn't notice because for the first time she didn't have a bubbly retort.

"Okay. Hey Joseph, maybe it's best if we just gave this friendship a rest for now."

I sat up, taken aback and a little angered by her reply.

"What do you mean?"

"I'm not blind. It's been subtle till now, you have some kind of problem with me when I'm with my friends so maybe it's best that we just leave things here."

I muted the TV and put the bowl of popcorn on the floor.

"Just because I'm not jumping up on tables and embarrassing myself doesn't mean I have a problem with anyone." My brow knitted, and I found myself shrugging as I waited in silence for her to reply.

"You have a problem with someone, Joseph."

My shoulders hunched over as I leaned into the phone, my voice rising.

"Who? Who do I have a problem with?"

"Who do you love, Joseph?"

"What?"

"Who do you love?"

"That's a ridiculous question and has nothing to do with what we we're talking about."

"If it's that ridiculous it should be easy to answer."

"I love my family, my friends..."

"No, you don't."

I threw my free arm up and gave the volume in my voice free rein.

"What! How would you know?"

"You never mention them. I never hear that you've been to visit them or have spoken to them, and I've never noticed them call you. So, who do you love?"

I wanted to say something but was silent.

"That's my point. And to answer your question, the person you have a problem with is you; sometimes you don't even look comfortable in your own skin, and you don't have anything or anyone pushing you to be. It's like there's nothing you really care about losing, including me; and only desperate people have nothing to lose."

"I'm not desperate."

"I'm sure that's what you think, but what I know, is that you taking your issues out on me ain't fair, at all."

I hung up. It was a reaction I couldn't explain. I wanted to swear, I wanted to call her back and shout "How dare you", I wanted to ask her who she thought she was.

Stupid curly-haired loser, telling me who I do and don't love, telling me she 'knows' what I'm scared of, she knows nothing about me!'.

"Actually, I am scared, scared of being in a relationship with you, you crazy table-top dancing fool!" I shouted at the phone, but didn't call her back.

After a cuppa and some good old-fashioned pacing up and down, I calmed myself and sat on the edge of my bed, and realised that I couldn't call her back. I fell onto the cold mattress, thinking over our dates, trying to find where exactly she had gathered the gall to speak to me the way she did. Flicking through the encounters and conversations in my mind, like a handful of photographs, I was slapped with the realisation that since I had met her, from that very first day in the park, I had been jealous of who she was; it was first masked as admiration, but in truth it was jealousy and soon grew to become envy. But this revelation worked adversely. It didn't clear my vision; rather it clouded my thoughts. I was left in a haze of reflection and with a mouth full of shame.

<u>**That Afternoon**</u> – (Recognitions)

Walking up the carpeted, damp smelling stairs in my block with a packet of Hobnobs and a magazine alleging that Keanu Reeves and Nicholas Cage don't seem to age because they're actually time travellers, I couldn't figure out why I didn't miss Felicia more.

Did it have something to do with the fact that what we had didn't affect my sleep issues or morning pain?

I reached and heard an electronic musical beeping that I would've recognised anytime, anywhere - Tetris on the Gameboy; I could even tell what level he was on. I stopped, turned around and left.

Ten minutes later I returned with a carton of Ribena and two packets of prawn cocktail crisps.

When his mum came back an hour later, she found us sitting on the floor in the hallway, excited as we tried to beat the previous owner's high score.

"Mum, we're on level 10." Aaron's voice almost shrieked as his eyes dashed back to the little green screen.

I heard her footsteps cease and on not hearing a reply I paused the game. Standing up, I said, "I haven't played this game in years, I couldn't resist."

She didn't respond.

"I hope you don't mind, I bought Aaron a drink and some crisps."

She nodded in reply as a kind of thank you, but didn't smile. "Come on, Aaron." Sounding more than just tired, she began walking away.

Aaron, oblivious to her cold air, tugged at my jacket. "Shall I keep it paused until we play again?"

"Nah," I replied, "you go for the high score."

His little face beamed; that was exactly what he had hoped to hear. "Are you sure?"

"Aaron." His mum, looking dreary, stood by their open door.

"I'm sure," I told him.

Aaron sprinted into their home. As the door closed his mum's eyes met mine for a moment, and there was something there I couldn't quite read, but that I distinctly recognised.

<u>That Evening</u>

I opened my door coming in from work and a single white envelope on the floor caught my attention. I opened it, and straight away I knew it was from Sapphie – a hand-written letter, she was just that kind of person.

The first two lines read:

> 'Dear Joseph,
>
> I'm three months pregnant.'

My heart skipped a beat; I felt happy and empty at the same time. I put the letter down for a moment.

Since Felicia's words I realised that I'm just as susceptible to jealousy, envy and every other vice I believed was everyone else's problem.

I know that I've never believed in a soul mate, but as soon as I read those words and acknowledged the feelings that followed, I saw that I not only compared every girl I had met to Sapphire, but that I wanted *her* and not a girl *like* her. I suppose that when she said she was getting married, somewhere inside of me I still believed that there was a chance for us. But when I read that she was pregnant...

"She'll make a great mother," I thought, and imagined how beautiful her child will be, and how happy that child will make her.

In my mind I pictured a girl, and that thought made me glow from within.

I picked up the letter and continued reading.

'He should be born in August, I hope it will be a sunny day; he'll need it if he's anything like his mother. My child's middle name will be Joseph. Now you'll always be a part of my life.

Sapphire.'

It was weird. I could never have predicted my response to her words. I sat, and thought, and felt freed.

"She's gone,"

She's gone, and now I have no choice but to move on.

She's happy now and I no longer have to feel guilty for making her sad. She's happy, it isn't with me, but she's happy and that's all I really wanted for her.

It wasn't so long ago that I woke up to the words "Today is a new day" etched in my brain and on the tip of my tongue. There aren't new days, just ones that make a difference.

<u>**The Next Day**</u> - (The first night)

It was about 7:30 in the evening, cold outside and cold indoors. I hadn't changed out of my work clothes and the thick yet invisible film of apathy and lassitude still clung to me from a day spent drenched in idle boredom; but *Celebrity Ninja* was about to begin!

There's a sweet comfort found in living vicariously through TV, a warm numbing of the mind and senses, like a dull narcotic delivered through the eyes. One day I'm a handsome but troubled doctor in the emergency unit, the next I'm married to a hot domineering wife with three cute kids and a few degenerate friends, and today, today I'm a celebrity ninja.

I get to live such a varied and exciting life from the comfort of my sofa, only having to get up when I need to pee. And in this world, there's no 24-hour stream of violent crimes, natural disasters and terrorist attacks, instead, my chefs scream abuse at contestants for their incompetence, not at me for being addicted to sugar and processed carbs, and the sight of children in this world make you laugh and exclaim 'That's so cute' and ask 'how on earth did they do that?', you don't wince and cringe in pain and horror and say 'that's not right' or ask 'how on earth could someone one do that?'; Reality TV feels so good, because so often reality is only portrayed as being so bad.

You can ignore your dreadful decisions by indulging in those of others; their failings leave you not just entertained, but disturbingly satisfied. It's the pinnacle of "feel-good TV" because these people actually exist, and because what they do and say is watched by millions, that invisible bar of what is acceptable in life just keeps getting lower and lower, and with every dip, every episode, you're left feeling a little better about the hole you're in and the mistakes you make; its genius, pure genius. We've yet to find a cure for the common cold and flu, but by George, we've found one for everyday guilt and shame.

The continuous knocking started as the channel's TV voice with the regional accent (I don't know what that job title is) began to introduce the next show, *Love Hypotenuse* – "we follow the lives of a bisexual Maths teacher and her two partners". I opened the door and Aaron and his mum were standing outside. She looked like she was upset with me and sounded like it too.

"The babysitter has cancelled last minute and I have no one else to ask. I've got to go out for work. I'll only be a few hours."

"Err..."

Aaron was curtly ushered into my home.

"He's already eaten." She stated this fact as if she had done me a favour. "Behave. And don't ask the man too many questions." She kissed him on the forehead. Then looked up at me. "Thanks."

Then she was off, and I was left feeling like I had agreed to something without having agreed to anything at all. I closed the door, looked down at the child and was instantly unhappy with the situation. I was more than used to having the whole of my evening to myself again; it doesn't take any effort to be alone. But it wasn't the kid's fault, he didn't ask for this either. So I split my supermarket Thai Green Curry for two with him, and we watched TV in silence. During the shows he laughed when I did and played his Gameboy during the commercial breaks; I'd never considered the possible joy of silent company.

10:30pm came and I noticed that Aaron was dozing off when the gay man and gay woman on the show had a fight when one called the other "so gay" and I laughed but Aaron didn't. I went into my room to get him a cover. By the time I came back he was fast asleep on the sofa. I covered him with the blanket, glanced at the door as if my look would make his mum magically appear, and then made myself a cup of tea. I stayed up waiting for her all night. Nodding off now and then, getting up to look through the spyhole every time I heard a noise.

"6:30?"

I was sure the small clock at the bottom right-hand corner of the screen was wrong. I rubbed the gunk out of my eyes and realised it was wrong.

"8:30! Monkey-nuts!"

Aaron was still fast asleep on the other end of the sofa.

"Okay, erm..."

I got up and shook him awake. He jumped up in a fright when he saw my face but calmed as soon as he realised where he was.

"You're late for school. I've got to take you home."

He simply nodded, slipped into his trainers and with a drowsy stroll followed me out.

I knocked on his door several times until we heard some sort of movement inside.

The door was flung open, she stood there in a tight pair of jeans and her bra and exuding a waft of alcohol so strong it almost burned my eyes. She stared straight through me.

"You left Aaron at mine all night."

Her eyes dropped down to her son and she ordered him inside.

"Look..." I began.

She walked away as she started to take off her bra and left me standing there, and the door open. I stood confused until she threw one of her shoes, the bang of it hitting the door and closing it in the process. The loud noise made me jump and reminded me about the job I was now late for, and broke me off from the long gaze I found myself in, wondering what it was about her that kept capturing my attention.

<u>**That Night**</u> - (I dream of Molly)

I was at dinner with a woman. We sat at a small table in a decadent restaurant, her eyes facing mine but her body positioned so that when she crossed her legs they glided above the horizon of the table. Her shoes were scarlet and their long heels almost pierced the marble floor beneath. She had high cheekbones, slender ankles and her sculpted calves were divine.

The bow-tied waiter approached her with a suave, indecent stride to his step. Before he had the opportunity to inquire her wants and needs, she batted his attentions away with a casual wave of her hand. Her eyes focused on me with a smile as alluring as it was nerve-wracking. Then mid-gaze, she rose from her seat to powder her nose. I watched her slender figure move with grace in a dress that dipped to the lowest point of her back and clung audaciously to the curve of her hips. I paused for a moment and considered the fact that I was going to spend the whole night with this sweet stranger. And at that point, I was filled with the most wonderful of feelings, something more than just infatuation and akin to excitement.

She returned, her face freshly decorated, and took a sip from her glass; her lips shimmered in the candlelight. Then they parted and I waited to hear her voice. She began to complain that her 1974 Chablis mustn't have enough grapes in it... because "It's just not that sweet." And just like that, her intoxicating mystique dissipated like an enchanting mist over a field, revealing the baron wasteland beneath it.

The waitress who brought us our food was Molly Ringwald. I asked her to take a seat. The chair opposite me was now vacant and I felt it always had been. She smiled that golden smile of hers and her eyes glowed with joyful optimism. She said she liked my tie. I said I liked her teeth; we both broke out in laughter.

I picked up my chair and placed it beside her. As I sat down, Molly was gone; *she* was there now. I curled in her arms and she held me. I felt the strongest sense of belonging, I felt at home. I was at home. We were in our old living room, on our old sofa. She held me close and took in deep breaths – each one telling me how she missed me. I felt overwhelmed with joy and sadness.

I awoke to an eerie sense of being alone. I needed someone. That was the difference. Being with anyone is nice, wanting someone is normal. But need? The word alone made me feel both inadequate and vulnerable all at once. But I couldn't deny what I felt.

<u>Three Nights Later</u> - (Night 2)

When a tame knock at the door came at 7:40 I half knew who it was and was half inclined not to open up.

"My mum asked if it was okay for me to stay here for a couple of hours?"

"I'm really sorry, Aaron, but I can't do it this evening."

"Oh. Okay."

"Tell your mum that I'm sorry."

"She's already gone, and she's locked the door."

I glanced down the empty hallway.

"Have you eaten?"

Aaron shook his head.

"Well, at least this might help me lose some weight."

"Huh?"

"Come on in."

Love Hypotenuse was on but it had got a little too racy so I turned it over; the shows on the other channels were rubbish, that truly unwatchable kind of rubbish you can't even laugh at. As we ate, our silence was no longer that comfortable.

"So... you enjoying the new school?"

Aaron shrugged his shoulders in reply. Why do kids do this to questions that can't be answered by "I don't know"?

"Well, I'm sure you'll settle in soon."

He shrugged again, but this time with a slight frown.

"Don't you think so?"

"Maybe if we stay for long this time."

"What do you mean 'this time'?"

"I've never spent two Christmases at the same school before. We always leave."

"Why?"

He shrugged his shoulders – with correct usage.

"Don't you ever go back?"

He looked up at me and shook his head.

The silence returned.

Aaron started on his Gameboy, but the noise kind of irritated us both.

"Have you ever played Mario Kart?" I asked with a wry smile.

"A few times on the Wii with my cousin in Manchester."

I dipped into my old boxes and pulled out a 1996 Nintendo 64. I dusted it off, blew inside the cartridge and started up a Grand Prix on the "Mushroom cup". It was great – nothing will ever top the original.

At 10pm I got the spare blanket ready and set my alarm for 7am. We had to force ourselves from the game when I noticed it was two in the morning.

<u>The Following Day</u> - (The folly of Eve)

As I stepped into the office a wall of anxious tension hit me; the atmosphere was thick enough to set off the smoke alarm. There was very little chatter amongst the women in the office but the men were silent. Then I noticed that they were not all sitting in their usual positions. I looked behind and saw that the manager's door was closed, which was unusual as there was no one in there with him.

As the day went on, the silent friction only grew. At lunchtime, all of the women rose, gathered their things and left together and all of the men left by themselves. The only two left in my side of the office were Matt and me.

I walked over to the water machine for the first time that day; I thought I'd choke on the tension if I'd gone any earlier.

"What you up to for lunch, Joe?"

"Probably Starbucks for a sandwich and coffee."

"Can I come with you?"

I paused. "Sure. Yeah. Of course."

"I'll grab my jacket."

I tried not to act too surprised but couldn't help but feel a little suspicious.

We walked over in silence under heavy clouds. We ordered and Matt paid.

As we sat and I started on lunch, part of me was expecting him not to speak at all.

"It's weird how you always think 'not me', you know, 'that kind of stuff always happens to someone else', never someone that's too close to you, you know... it's always a friend of a friend and then you hear all about it."

He sipped from his coffee and I followed suit.

"Three months. She's been with him for three months. We've only been married a little over a year. That's a quarter of our marriage!" His eyes rose to the wall opposite and then fell to the floor.

I didn't know what to say, so I said nothing.

"They were sleeping together. They were having sex, Joe. They would have sex and then she would come home and get into *our* bed, next to *me* and say... she's got a headache... or that her period started early and she doesn't feel up for it."

He stared off, probably reconstructing her bedside excuses in his mind. Because of his build, I expected him to bang the table in a burst of anger, but there was no gritting of teeth or narrowing of eyes. Instead, his features softened and his cheeks sagged.

"They took me for a mug. Her and... and 'Mac', they took me for such a mug."

My expression of surprise was so strong I swear Matt could hear it as he turned and faced me for the first time since we sat down.

"Yeah, Mac from the office. My mate Mac. Everybody's mate Mac."

He poured more sugar into his coffee and stirred it with slowing effort, staring at it while not looking at it at all.

"I don't know what I did wrong. We argued but..." He stopped stirring. "Three months, Joe. That's not a mistake, that's a habit. That's intentional."

At that moment he didn't seem able to look up from his cup. This six-foot-plus, sixteen-stone geezer looked too weak even to raise his eyes.

"My name's Joseph."

Matt broke away from his soliloquy.

"What?"

"My name's Joseph, not Joe. I don't like it when people call me Joe or Joe Bloggs. It's not my name."

Matt stared at me for a moment and I stared back. Then he nodded with a smile.

"Fair enough." He kind of chuckled before continuing. "So... Joseph, what do you think I should do?"

I went to speak and then stopped as Matt continued.

"I found out on Friday. My mind's... I just couldn't take it all in. I still can't."

There was a long pause. I thought about saying something but I realised that Matt wanted to speak and not be spoken to.

"I thought I was doing a decent job. We had some problems at the start but worked through that. Things were going well again. Yeah, sometimes she would complain about being bored, but I didn't know what that meant; I'm not her Court Jester."

I was wondering why Matt hadn't mentioned how he felt about Mac and how he was able to spend the whole morning in the same office as him and not have beaten him to a pulp. He drank more of his coffee and ignored his sandwich.

"I really tried, you know, Joe... Joseph." He lent in on the table with his forearms, his back and shoulders rising like a mountain. "I know I was mucking about a bit on that night we went to the strip club but that was a one-off, and I only danced with that bird we met. I put in real effort, it wasn't a half-hearted job, I can honestly say I was trying my best. But I guess it wasn't enough for her." Matt went silent for a few moments. "What does that say about me? Even my best wasn't good enough." He looked like he wanted to swear or cry, but after a moment he conjured a sardonic smile.

"Forever ain't what it used to be."

It felt like the right thing to do, so I spoke up.

"Do you still love her?"

Matt looked up at me, energised by the anger my question roused. I broke into a sweat and my mouth opened to speak but fear held onto my breath. Matt stared.

"Yes."

His expression didn't change as he spoke. Which made it even more difficult for me to continue, but I did.

"It might be a good idea to let her know that."

Matt physically turned his nose up at the suggestion, then sat up and leaned back. My words were the last we spoke there.

We spent an hour and a half out at lunch. Neither of us thought anything of it and neither did anyone back at work. Before we entered our building, Matt stopped me.

"Joseph, that day when you asked me to go get a coffee... you and I weren't friends like that. What made you ask me?"

I paused, wanting to say because it felt like the right thing to do. But instead, I considered my words again before speaking. "Because I could see it was what you needed."

Matt looked at me as if for the first time, assessing me, seeing me.

"Thank you." It was clear that he wasn't just talking about the coffee offer.

He walked on into the office, but I stopped and watched him. For a moment I thought about what it took for him to walk back in there, finish the day, get on the train and go home or wherever it is that he's staying and sit down alone with that morass of problems facing him, and not be completely overwhelmed. I didn't know Matt well at all, but I knew I would see him back at work again tomorrow. And with that thought, I stood in awe.

That Evening - (Episode IV)

As I walked towards my front door, a free newspaper under my arm to clean up the broken drinking glass I knocked over rushing to work, I looked two doors passed my own and saw a toppled black binbag laying out front. The liberty that Aaron's mum had been taking finally struck me.

"I didn't even get a thank you."

I decided I'd have a word with her.

She opened the door quicker than I expected and looked at me with a blank expression. I believed that she was going to ask me what I wanted if I hadn't spoken first.

"Look, I don't mind watching Aaron from time to time, he's a good kid, but you can't just leave him on my doorstep with no explanation, no number to contact you with and no idea what time you'll be back to pick him up. It's not right, it's pretty ru—"

I heard swear words that I didn't even know existed. The venom in her voice even made normal words sound vulgar. A large vein across her forehead began pulsating as saliva flew and her face scorched red. I took defensive steps back as she threw adjectives like right hooks and ended her Hitler-esque tirade by telling me to never knock at her home or speak to her son again. She stormed back inside and slammed the door behind her.

I glanced around me to check for any witnesses or teenagers uploading the event onto the internet, but luckily, I was alone. I shook my head in disbelief and began thinking of what titles someone would upload the rant under:

> After work verbal beating
> Shouting champion starts training
> Babysitter asks for a raise. Epic Fail!

Again, I wanted to talk to somebody about how random this woman's behaviour was. But this time there was no one to call.

At 8:05pm I could hear someone talking in the hallway outside my front door. Being the nosey parker I was, I peeped through the spyhole to see who it was. Standing there with an old jam jar filled with flowers and a single bumblebee buzzing around inside it, was Aaron. He was pointing at the jar repeating in a songlike melody, "Make me honey. Make me honey."

I opened the door and Aaron came inside.

"What are you up to?"

With eyes fixed on his contraption, he replied, "We found out at school today that bees make honey. And that they make honey out of flowers. So, I found an empty jam jar in a skip, got some flowers and then trapped a bee inside it."

"How did you catch the bee?"

He looked up with the intensity of Indiana Jones retelling how he found the lost Ark. "I had to be reeeeally careful. I waited until it landed on a flower, then I had the lid in this hand and the jar in this one and the bee and the flower in the middle. Then I quickly clapped them both together and got the bee and the flower. I thought it would be good to get the flower too because he had already started having sex with it."

I didn't know where to start. I began thinking about how to explain pollination and beehives, then realised I knew nothing about it either.

"Okay. But why do you want to make honey?"

"Well, if I can make jars of honey and sell them, then my mum doesn't have to work so much and we can buy some nice stuff."

I was filled with wonder at how this little boy's mind worked.

"We're going to have to poke some holes in the lid so that the bee can get some fresh air, and we can put it by the window so that it gets some sunlight during the day too."

"Ah, that's a good idea!"

Pretty much every day this kid was being let down by his mum, and yet every day there was a joy, a renewed hope in his step and in his smile. Sapphire had found new joy and had moved on and is having a baby. Sooner or later, I'll have to do like my doctor and pull my finger out.

I couldn't help but smile, watching him bounding around full of energy and optimism as he got on with his task. I sat and watched a reality show that followed two female best friends who had fallen in love with the same gay man, while he spent the whole evening leaning on the window sill watching what he thought was a bumble bee making love to a flower and waiting for it to give birth to a jar full of honey.

Two Days Later - (Loneliness is all the same)

It was a warm, bright Saturday afternoon; the barbershop was almost empty. I usually came in later on Sundays for my haircut but my brother said that he was going to call me from New Zealand that night; night for him, but early afternoon for me.

It was one of those not-so-old-fashioned but definitely-not-so-new barber's that still had those black and white pictures of hairstyles that were taken in the '90s when it was cool to stare intensely into a camera and show a bit of chest hair. The shop was clean and had a decent collection of magazines stacked by the leather sofa for those in waiting. I took a seat and a recent issue of Empire magazine – looking through the movie reviews I thought of Felicia, and still found it odd that I missed how she made me feel but didn't miss her. I started to think of the questions she had put to me over the phone, then put down the magazine and decided to peruse the barber's more modern photos of hairstyles - which pretty much looked like the cast portfolio for Kid & Play's House Party (great movie).

In the barber's chair was the butcher from next door. The barber, who'd taken over his father's business, was about fifteen years younger than his customer. The radio was on and the DJ felt he had to remind us all what season it was, despite the heat, so he played Will Smith's "Summertime" for the third time since I'd sat down. I picked up yesterday's newspaper and eavesdropped.

"So did she get the house with the divorce?" the barber asked.

"She didn't want it."

"What about all the stuff inside?"

"She said that she was bored of it all."

"It's a big house to have all to yourself."

"I'm hardly there. It feels too empty."

"Yeah, I know what you mean, I don't like to spend too much time in my place alone."

"You don't know what I mean," the butcher said with a sombre laugh.

"Mate, bar a bit here and there, I've been single for two years so I know what you're talking about."

The scissors did their work in silence for a little while.

"The difference is..." started the butcher, "well, apart from the fact that you get married with the idea that you'll die with that person and you get a girlfriend with the hope that she'll at least see you through the winter, it's the mindset. When you switch onto being married it's not a switch that can be turned back off just like that. You don't go from single to married and then back to single again. It goes single, married, divorcee! You're in a new bracket, a totally different mindset. You're never really 'single' ever again."

"Yeah, but after that's all said and done, we're still in the same situation; you haven't got a missus and neither do I. Loneliness is loneliness."

I unwrapped the emergency Mars Bar I kept hidden in my inside jacket pocket (always be prepared), whilst thinking that the barber made a good point.

"All right, let's say you're a guy laying in bed," the butcher began, "and you're lying there thinking, 'I wish I had a million quid.' And you lay there thinking about all the things you would buy and how happy you would be and you go to sleep smiling because tomorrow's a new day and you never know what might happen. I'm a guy laying in bed and I'm thinking, 'I had a million quid... and now I've got nothing.' And that thought keeps me up all night."

The scissors stopped and the butcher continued.

"Yeah, we're in the same situation, but it's totally different."

My brother didn't call that afternoon or night, and I laid in bed thinking about what the butcher and the barber were saying.

I thought of another option. Instead of wishing I had a million quid or thinking about the million I'd lost, I could be sat up planning how I was going to be a millionaire. With both the other options, you lay there night after night without a penny in your pocket and no plan.

I've done that for too long. I'm either mourning the loss of what was or just dreaming of what could be. All the while, I'm emotionally broke!

I found the rings my aunty gave me, and thought of what she and my uncle had. Even when he was dead and she was dying, she was still fixing his old clothes, still finding ways to give to him. I thought of the kind of love that could create that kind of self-sacrifice. Then wondered if it was the willingness to sacrifice that created that love. I couldn't help but think of the absence of that kind of love between my parents. It seemed like my mum did all the sacrificing and my dad all the taking. And I feared how much of him was in me, his selfishness, his detachment, his comfortability with being alone. A pang of anger struck me. I sat up straight.

Forty-Five Minutes Later

A comedian once said that his little brother told their dad that he was going to travel the world to "find himself". The father replied, "Well, what are you gonna do when you find him and he's a plonker as well?"

Felicia was right, I need to be better but I can't make a better me on my own.

I need to find a girlfriend – not necessarily love or "The One" – I'm not trying to be Laurence Fishburne – I just want, need, someone to help me be a better me. And I can't wait for them to knock over my coffee or comment on my book. I've got to make it happen.

In college and uni, you could just wander around campus or ask one of your friends to hook you up. I wasn't going to try it with anyone at work again, and the single friends I was in contact with on social media didn't live locally and all the others were married - and married people only know other married people.

I had seen the *Talhotblond* and *Catfish* so had what I thought was a rational fear of crazy people online and steered clear of using social media and internet dating sites to fill my potentials list. But I wasn't to be deterred.

I thought of my Uni mate Pete, not to date, but to be my

wingman out clubbing. He was married but always sent out pictures and videos of him at some amazing clubs and bars.

I logged onto my social media account and asked him what decent bars and clubs there were near me. He listed a few but recommended one in particular – The Lounge. I asked him if he was going there tonight and he said he probably would be. I told him that I'd meet him there and buy him a drink – I didn't want to drop the whole wingman stuff on him straight away, as we hadn't seen each other since Uni. While waiting for him to reply, I looked at the time and it was already nine o'clock. I jumped up and went over to my wardrobe.

"Trousers or jeans, trousers or jeans?" I reached out for my old Levi's. "They still fit." Result!

"Shirt or T-shirt, shirt or T-shirt..." I picked a white shirt; I thought it would make me look grown-up, not old but not like I'm trying to be twenty-one either.

I looked in the mirror and wondered if I should tuck the shirt in or not, then noticed the little crotch tear in the jeans and remembered the last time I went clubbing I'd torn them in our Uni bar when my friends had bet me a round of tequila shots that I couldn't do the splits. Alcohol had told me I could, a groin strain and ripped Levi's had proved otherwise. So I ended up wearing a pair of black trousers and because I wasn't sure if they allowed trainers or Converse I wore black shoes.

Pete hadn't replied yet, so I went all old school and started drinking at home to save money while out. It was 9:45 when Pete replied writing *Cool.* I nodded to myself, paced around a few steps, took another swig from the Wray & Nephews rum I kept for whenever I had a cold, and grabbed my keys and wallet and bolted through the front door.

<u>Half an Hour Later</u> – (...then what the hell am I?)
I arrived at the bar, happily surprised to see that there wasn't a queue as the weather had turned and it was freezing outside. I sent Pete a message to say I was in. The place wasn't even close to being packed. I checked my watch again and shook my head.

I was happy to see that there were a fair few people there my age and some a little older. They looked like the after-work drinks crew. Or it might have been a leaving do – one of the guys there, in his forties, looked completely smashed.

"Damn, these guys dress good," I thought.

The music wasn't R'n'B, or Pop, or Dance, or Drum & Bass, but You could listen to it without having to dance, and dance to it without breaking conversation, but I had no idea what it was.

The barman didn't look old enough to drink and I picked up a mocking tone as he asked, "What would you like, *sir*?"

"Rum and Coke," I shouted back, overestimating the music's volume.

"Double or single?" He made it sound like a challenge and a double-entendre. I wasn't going to back down.

"Double!"

Apart from looking a bit smug, this young man looked like he threw everything to the wind, caution, worry, his hair; isn't it an oxymoron to style your hair to look messy? I love that word, in fact, that's the bartender's new name: 'Oxymoron' - calling me sir!

I checked my phone, no reply from Pete yet. Oxymoron returned with my drink, I couldn't hear him properly and didn't want to look stupid so I coolly withdrew a £10 note from my obese wallet and waited for my change. But Oxy stood there waiting too; I was confused.

"£11.50," he shouted.

"£11.50? What did you do, squeeze the rum out of a unicorn's teat?"

I gave him a fiver on top and when he returned with my change and a tiny receipt he replied,

"There's a pub down the road that sells cheaper drinks. That's where my *dad* goes."

Then he waltzed off to his next group of customers, flicking open the top button of his shirt and with a smooth ease that made me sick, began flirting with the girls he was serving.

I wanted to shout back that I hoped his mum was at the pub too 'cause tonight I was out on the pull she might get lucky. Then the thought that his mum was probably in my dating range made me sit down on a nearby stool.

I put the change in my wallet, noticing that I only had enough money for one more drink and a cab home, which meant that whatever lady I chose to buy a drink for was going to be the one who got all my attention, so I had to choose wisely; the added pressure excited me.

Looking at my wallet you'd think I had enough here to get George Best drunk, but in truth, my wallet was like a well-endowed man with impotence. It was full of store discount cards for places I'd only visited once and had no definite plans of returning to. But how stupid would I feel, if I did happen to pop into one of these places and missed out on getting a stamp, which after another twenty would reward me with a free espresso shot if I bought a large latte, a muffin and a pastry of *my* choice?

Pete still hadn't replied.

Must be on the underground.

I looked around, only sipping at my unicorn juice and Coke, and asked myself how this was going to work. The place was starting to fill, the crowd getting younger, the skirts getting shorter, the guys' shirts getting tighter and everyone seeming to be vastly better looking than me. If I was going to have any success, I needed my wingman. Pete was great with the girls in college, and married a stunner – she could double for Halle Berry. I sent him another message:

Where are you mate, your beer is getting warm?

When he gets here, I'll tell him that I thought he wasn't coming so I drank it.

I needed to pee and a trip to the toilet was a good excuse to walk around and survey the land.

All the urinals were being used, bar the middle one – aka no man's land – so I went for the second cubicle as the first looked like it had been hit by a diarrhoea grenade (or 'dirty bomb' – boom, boom).

With no reply from Pete, I decided to sit and pee while formulating a plan of action, but my attention was taken by something scribbled on the cubicle wall:

'I had your mum last night'

Followed by someone else's writing:

'Ur drunk dad, go home'

Just as I started laughing the cubicle door burst open – it was the drunk guy from the leaving do.

"Hey, sorry mate, I forgot to lock it," I said.

Oblivious to my words and to me, he continued to stumble in.

"Mate!" I shouted.

The man, his eyes closed and mouth poised for vomiting, pulled down his zipper.

"Johnny Cochran!" I cried, leaping from the seat.

With my trousers tugging round my ankles, I fell to my knees. "What the hell are you doing?" I shouted.

This snapped him out of his daze and he turned to face me but had already started peeing. It was like a scene out of a James Bond or Indiana Jones movie – the deadly urine spewing its way around to me as I dragged my trousers up, and launched into a forward dive through the cubicle door as back-splashes of pee fell all around me. With a quick glance back, I swiped my wallet from under the door just as he slammed it and began throwing up.

I rose, expecting a hero's applause, only to have the towel and aftershave man tell me, "It's not that kind of bar, mate. The Blue Oyster's up the road."

I returned to my stool, unsoiled and emboldened. The music was louder and the dance-floor livelier. Oxymoron was rushed off his feet. A song everyone knew came on and before I knew it, arms and hair were sent flaring around as everyone grabbed their drinks and dashed off their stools to join the vibrating mass in the centre of the bar. The pull of their energy lifted me from my seat. I sent Pete another message, telling him that he was really missing out and needed to hurry up.

The bass of the speakers sent a hypnotic chill through my body. I watched the crowd, a mass of silhouetted expressions, swaying together in some disjointed unison. It was innocent, it was sexy, it was fun, it was intimate and individual and unadulterated; it was giving me Goosebumps just to watch. My phone vibrated.

Finally.

But it was only a reminder I'd set to watch a new BBC comedy. I went back on to my social media account and was baffled more than shocked. Pete hadn't sent a message explaining that he was going to be late. Pete hadn't sent me a message saying that he couldn't make it. His account page was all of a sudden blank, and I couldn't access any of his information, pictures, messages - nothing. I scrolled up and down, and then I realised - Pete had unfriended me.

Then just like that, the smoke cleared. I was a worried-looking man in his thirties, dressed in his black work trousers, black work shoes and white work shirt tucked into his cheap belt, standing at the back of a trendy bar filled with gorgeous people who weren't even alive in the 80s. Now that the smoke had gone, I could see the thin pane of glass that separated them from me. I was a spectator at best.

Just then, I missed my house clothes. I missed my favourite mug full of hot chocolate. I missed my sofa, my TV and my MSG-filled food that would sap the little energy I had left after a week of work and leave me with just enough for one trip to the toilet before a final stroll to bed.

"It's Saturday night," I said aloud. "I should go and enjoy myself." I left my drink unfinished and made my way home.

In the cab, I tried not to think about the night. I counted the change in my pocket and found the miniature receipt. I asked the driver for a pen. He had a thick Irish accent; he was from Dublin. And just like that, I started to try and write a limerick:

If it's said that triers always try

And it's known that liars always lie
Then if I am neither
A liar or trier

...

I couldn't finish the last line.

<u>Monday Evening</u>

Aaron turned up while I was watching a reality weightless/porn addiction group therapy show called *What Fat People <u>Really</u> Want.*

"Mr Joseph, who do you think is prettier, the one that kind of looks like Snow White or the one that looks more like Sleeping Beauty?"

"Erm, I'm little more partial to brunettes these days, so I'd have to say Snow White."

"I like the one with big boobs."

I almost fell off the sofa. He said it as if he had commented on her eyes.

"What do you know about boobs?"

"I saw them on my friend's phone at school. He's got loads of pictures of big boobs; videos too."

I wanted to laugh but I felt an obligation to be responsible.

"Aaron, women who show their bodies like that are bad and you shouldn't look at them."

"Why are they bad?"

"Because they should only show their bodies like that to... to people that they're in love with."

A look of confusion passed over Aaron and I wasn't close to being sure about what I was saying at all.

"Does that mean that my mum is bad? I've seen her show her body to people she doesn't love."

I didn't allow the shock to set in, knowing that a long pause would make this conversation even more difficult.

"How do you know that she doesn't love them?"

"Because she only knew them for a little while. Sometimes a day."

Aaron looked upset.

"Well, sometimes grown-ups make mistakes."

Aaron paused in thought for a moment.

"Have you ever shown your body to a girl you don't love?"

Silence.

"No."

Aaron smiled and continued watching television.

"Are you hungry?"

"A bit."

"Fancy fish and chips?"

His smile seemed to make his freckles shine. "That sounds like a plan, Batman."

On the way back from the chippie we heard music coming from Aaron's home – it sounded like Guns & Roses.

"Did your mum leave music playing when she left?"

Aaron shrugged his shoulders.

I told him to wait by mine as I walked up to their door. I thought that she might go bananas again if she found him with me, so my idea was to knock and if I heard footsteps to run and leave Aaron to go inside.

I put my ear to the door and went to knock, but then stopped just short. I leaned away from the door a little disturbed. I walked over to Aaron and instinctively took his hand and we walked straight into my flat.

"Listen, Aaron. Anytime that your mum needs to go out for work, just come straight here. Don't wait outside."

His smile was full of gratitude.

While Aaron was sleeping, I was up thinking about why I lied when he asked me about women. It bothered me. I think it was an inclination I felt to be different, I wanted to be better, I wanted him to have someone to look up to. But I couldn't fall asleep before asking myself why lying felt like the right thing to do, as if what I had done was wrong. Then I thought back to what I heard at their door and knew that was wrong. Again, I wanted someone to call and confer with – my own phone a friend option. But in lieu of that, I made a plan: right or wrong, I won't lie to Aaron again.

<u>Three Days Later</u> - (Plans v Procrastination)

For the past two days, Aaron's timid knock had increased a bit in confidence. When I opened up that night, his usual look of apology had vanished. He bounded his way to my sofa singing:

"What do you do if you want to do a poo in an English country garden?

Pull down your pants and suffocate the ants, in an English country garden.

Get a leaf and wipe your underneath in an English country garden."

We both started cracking up.

"I've never heard that last one before."

"Me and Nicky were going through all of them today."

"How many did you get?"

"Twelve."

We were in stitches by the time he got to number eight: "with a little squeeze you can kill off all the weeds". His round face was tickled pink. He rolled on the floor holding his belly, giggling himself silly. He made me miss being a kid. Then, after all the talk of poo, he announced he was hungry and asked me if I knew how long I could jump up and down for without stopping.

During an advert break, we sat and ate a well-deserved bowl of spaghetti hoops on toast, following a clean 90 seconds of jumping from him, 10 seconds from me. An ad came on about car insurance for women which was set in Ancient Egypt – they tied in the theme and special offers on no-claims-bonus deals by ending with "all the mummies love it".

"I haven't been to a museum in ages," I said out loud to myself.

"Why?"

I opened my mouth to answer and then realised that I didn't have one. Aaron looked at me puzzled.

"I couldn't tell you," I responded.

"Is it a secret?"

I laughed and Aaron's eyes fell down to his Gameboy. "No, no, I mean I don't know why. There's no real reason."

He was silent as the knockout round of *Celebrity Ninja* started again. I felt a bit bad for laughing at him.

"Can I come too?" he asked in a humble tone.

"What do you mean?"

"Can I come with you when you go to the museum?" Aaron replied.

I did want to go to the museum, but as usual, I was merely stating a fact, not making a plan – I've gotten way too used to talking to myself.

"Yeah, of course you can come with me." I turned my attention back to the TV.

"When?"

"I haven't thought of a day yet."

"Most Saturdays are boring for me. Sometimes there's a birthday party to go to for someone at school, sometimes I don't get invited, but there hasn't been one for ages. What do you do on Saturdays?"

"Not much." The next question kind of asked itself. "Do you want to go this Saturday?"

And there was that smile again. "Sounds like a plan, Batman."

<u>That Sunday</u> - (Saturday, Sunday, Happy Days!)

Our trip to the museum was good; no, it was really good; in fact, it was fun. I can't remember the last time I'd used that word in reference to myself. I had good times with Felicia, but I don't know when I last had fun. I noticed on the back of a passenger's book on the tube a couple of weeks ago, a quote from Ernest Hemingway:

> *Most of the time I don't have much fun. The rest of the time I don't have any fun at all.*

I laughed out loud as I read it (a real laugh, not a "lol" it was kind of funny so I chuckled inside laugh, but an "I got a few dodgy looks as I did it" laugh). I laughed so hard because I thought it was so true to me. I felt like I'd adopted the attitude that fun is for kids, and misery for adults. I no longer expect to have fun. I guess that's what made Saturday so good.

We snuck hamburgers into the museum, and every few minutes one of us would take a bite while the other stood guard. We spent just as much time laughing at the artefacts and sculptures than we did staring in amazement. We covertly joined a paid tour with a group of German tourists whose suspicious eyes didn't leave us for a moment. I tried to remember if I'd ever learnt any German I could use to help us blend in, but I could only come up with that song from *The Sound of Music*, which didn't help at all – I tried. Aaron asked me loads of questions about the Babylonian section while we ate peanuts out of my pocket. I surprised myself with how much I remembered from the Bible studies I'd done when I was a kid. Aaron was so impressed.

As we sauntered through the paintings section and took in everything from portrait to postmodern, I turned to Aaron,

"Which one do you like the most?"

He looked up at me with an excited smile, as if he'd been waiting for me to ask that very question. Then he grabbed my hand and dragged me, almost running, back to the Surrealist segment.

"This one!"

Beaming, he pointed up to a Salvador Dali piece.

"Dream, Caused by the Flight of a Bee Around a Pomegranate a Second before Awakening." I read out.

"For just the title this one should win all kinds of awards." Aaron replied.

Grinning at his excitement I asked, "So, what is it that you like about this painting so much?"

Still staring at it in wonderment, his eyes moved with his words as he spoke with pace, "There are two Tigers flying through the air being gobbled by a giant goldfish that's just been shot out of a piece of fruit I've never seen before, and then there's this random elephant with skinny legs a mile high just walking through the background with a mountain on its back like this is all normal." He paused for a breath, "And let's not forget the random naked lady; this is one of greatest painting of all time!"

Somehow, I'd completely missed the fully naked woman sprawled across the bottom of the piece.

Should I tell him not to look at the naked woman? Is her nakedness a part of the art or is it pornography, it didn't look erotic but...

My thought was cut short by what was maybe the greatest accolade of all time:

"This is the N64 Mario Kart of paintings." Then he blew a kiss to it.

I didn't know what to say. I think even Dali himself would've been lost for words.

Then he looked up at me looking down at him.

"What?"

"It's amazing seeing you so happy."

His joy increased. "What about you, what was your favourite?"

I hesitated, even though I had in mind which one I stood at most. I was kind of worried about what Aaron would think, not of the painting but of me for liking it.

He had been open and honest, so should I.

"It's over here."

We strolled over to the abstract expressionist collection and I stopped in front of Jackson Pollock's *Full Fathom Five.*

Aaron's head tilted to the side and his little nose scrunched up as he took it in. "What's it supposed to be?"

"I'm not entirely sure to be honest."

Still staring, still trying to understand it he asked, "So why do you like it?"

I tried not to overthink and manicure my words, but to tell him how he told me – straight.

"It looks like different things, different creatures almost, all beneath the surface, fighting each other, at war with each other whilst not knowing that they are all part of the same thing. They look lost in confusion, tangled and angry, so they turn on each other and just cause pain, not knowing that they are only hurting themselves, with lots of unnecessary pain. That's what I see in this – a lot of unnecessary pain."

A long moment passed before I realised that Aaron hadn't said anything. I looked away from the painting and down to him staring up at me.

"What?" I asked.

"Why do you like it then?"

"What do you mean?"

"Why do you like the picture if you only see pain in it?"

My lips parted. Words rose to my throat; but went no further. I really wanted to tell him.

There was silence. Then a growing sadness rose on Aaron's face, and then he spoke:

"I saw loads of people going upstairs. Some lady said there's a man in a box who doesn't talk." His head jerked back and eyebrows pointed up in incredulity at the idea.

"Let's go check it out." I replied.

As we walked to the stairs, I couldn't help but think,

Aaron saw in me what I saw in the painting and wanted it to stop. How special does that make him!

When the museum closed, we ended up having to sprint down the high street to catch our bus home. Aaron was lagging behind so I scooped him up and threw him over my shoulder. We missed the bus but I continued running to try and save our embarrassment. The pretence didn't last, though, the only cardiovascular exercise I got was holding my breath on the tube when a sweaty armpit was thrust in my face or an old person decided that public flatulence over the age of seventy was socially acceptable. As I leaned on a bin trying to catch my breath, Aaron thought it was a good idea to take advantage of my weak disposition and poke me in my side and dart off whenever I tried to catch him. His red jacket whipped around as he dodged my grasp, laughing like my feeble attempts to catch him was the funniest thing on earth.

We picked up Chinese for dinner and Aaron found a comedy on one of the free channels we never watch. I think it was called *Spies Like Us*. It was a little rude, but Aaron laughed so hard he shot Sprite out of his nose.

When I woke up the following morning, Aaron was watching repeats of *Ready Steady Cook,* when good ol' Ainsley used to host it.

"Mr Joseph sir?" He thought this was funny.

"Yes, Master Aaron?"

"Can you cook good?"

"Yeah. A little. I can do the basics... bacon and eggs, toast, burgers, chips."

"What about stuff like that?" Aaron said looking impressed with the impressive-looking dish on the TV.

"I've never tried." (Apart from microwave meals my oven was exclusively used for warming up my work clothes on winter mornings and warming the flat when the central heating was playing up.)

Aaron's wide eyes looked up at me.

"Why not?" I responded. "What's the meal called?"

"Chicken Cordan Blue, I think. The guys said it was French."

I jumped on the internet and got the recipe for Chicken Cordon Bleu.

"Have a shower, we're going shopping."

The meal was awful, but I couldn't argue with two consecutive days of fun.

Scraping most of our meal in the bin, I looked over at Aaron slouched on the sofa - his little bloated belly stretching his T-shirt, his index finger halfway up his nose and the broadest smile of contentment sprawled across his face as he watched episodes of *Pinky & The Brain,* I'd found for him on my laptop. As I chuckled, I felt a wave of something ominous pass through me, like a malevolent voice speaking to me, warning me:

'His happiness is real and will continue on, but don't expect the same of yours. Do not get too comfortable *Joe*; like always, this will not last.'

My eyes began to sink.

For the first time in a long time, I internally replied with more than my usual sullen resignation. I mustered strength I didn't know I had, and breathed the single word:

"No."

And dared to believe in more, in fact, I went further, I knew that things had somehow changed, and I told myself they *will* get better. Then the smile I had a few moments earlier, along with the ones I had enjoyed whilst cooking and playing the fool at the museum, were all superseded by the depth of the smile I bore then; I never knew a smile could feel so significant.

The Morning After the Weekend of Fun - (It's just not right...)
My alarm went off at 6:30am. I wasn't happy. I stretched in my bed and stopped immediately in shock. Lying beside me was Aaron, fast asleep. I jumped out of bed.

Leaning over, I shook him awake.

"Okay, okay, I'm getting up," he said with his eyes still closed.

"Aaron, wake up. We need to talk."

He must've recognised the serious tone in my voice as he opened his eyes and sat up straight away.

"Aaron... you're in my bed."

"Yeah. I came in last night while you were sleeping."

"Aaron... it's not right for a man and a young boy who aren't related to sleep in the same bed."

"Why?"

"It... it's just not right. Your mum wouldn't be happy with it."

"But why? It was cold out on the sofa last night."

"Okay, I'll sleep on the sofa tonight and you can have my bed, yeah?"

"But then your bed will be cold."

"We can't sleep in the same bed, Aaron."

"But why, though?"

I had to stop and think.

"Okay, would you sleep in a strange person's bed?" I asked with more conviction.

"No."

"Why not?"

"Because they're strange."

"So?"

"So I don't know what they might do."

"Exactly!"

Aaron looked confused at my triumphant smile, then I was confused with it too.

"Wait a sec..." I started.

"But you're not a stranger. And you wouldn't do anything bad to me, would you?"

"No, no, of course not. Okay... look, I'm going to give you a proper reason later tonight... after I've given this some thought, yeah?"

"Okay."

Aaron left to go home that morning in silence. I was left feeling like I'd done something wrong.

<u>That Night</u>

We ate and watched TV in silence.

At about 1am, Aaron walked into my room with his head down and pillow in hand. He lifted up the covers at the foot of the bed, got in and made himself comfortable.

"I can't sleep." His words were whispered but clear.

"Aaron..."

"When I was little. My mum used to let me sleep in her bed all the time. But when I got older, I got my own room, but she would still let me sleep in her bed with her on nights when it was cold... or when I was scared."

His weak voice hung in the air with such power. I couldn't tell him to go.

"Did you ever sleep in the bed with your mum when you were little, even when you had your own room.?"

"I did."

His little head and bright eyes popped up above the rim of the duvet by my feet. I could feel him smiling and willing me to go on.

"I remember my brother and me sharing the bed with my mum on cold nights when Dad was away; they had the softest sheets. My brother often had nightmares, so my mum would hold him till he slept, while I held her. Then during the night, when my brother started snoring, my mum would let him go, turn over and find me still awake, waiting. She would kiss my forehead, hold me and tell me it's time to sleep. She wasn't upset, she knew I stayed awake so that she would hold me too, but in a funny way it wasn't just for me, I did it more for her and I think she knew it."

"What did..."

"It's bedtime now Aaron."

"Okay. Night Mr Joseph Sir."

"Goodnight Master Aaron."

As he dozed off, I thought of those nights we shared the bed with my mum, and how safe I felt there with her.

I remember it happening a few times, I would wake up from my sleep, in the middle of the night, and I could hear my mum crying. Just sobbing softly into her pillow, trying to stifle the sound. I didn't know what to say, so I said nothing. I kept my eyes closed and I did the only thing I could think of, I held her closer, and I kept her tears my secret.

<u>The Next Day</u> – (Lessons from MacGyver)

I pulled out the remains of my old double bed from under the current single – after two years the vacancy in the double became painful vacant, and I wondered if that was one of the reasons why I couldn't sleep.

It took us five hours to put it together. There were missing nuts, bolts, washers and all sorts, so we went MacGyver style and used string, elastic bands and blue tack to get the job done. The only way we could stop the entire thing from collapsing was to stuff my boxes of old unpacked bits and pieces under the wooden frame.

Before I tested the bed for its structural integrity, I took out from the box underneath it the rings my aunty had given me. I opened the ring box I bought for them - I was just about to ask the cashier in the jewellery shop if she had any spare boxes they were throwing away, when I saw one with a dark emerald velvet cover; green was her favourite colour too.

"They're beautiful."

"They are," I replied.

He stood closer and stared, apprehensive. "They look really expensive."

I nodded, realising I'd never thought of their monetary value.

"Why don't you have them... like, on show so that you can look at them more?" he asked. He didn't take his eyes from their glow, tilting his head to see how the light fractured in the diamonds at different angles.

"With things as precious as these, you don't want them out in the open where something bad could happen to them. You keep them somewhere safe. It's the... the proper way with things that are this... special." I closed the box and placed it with gentle care into my bedside table drawer.

We decided we would sleep head to foot like my brother and I did when we stayed round my aunt's house during the summer holidays. I joked about how I was scared of him dreaming of football and kicking me in the nuts while he was sleeping. Then he made the point that I might repeatedly kick him in the face while dreaming that I'm running from a giant rottweiler with pointy horns, metal teeth and fire shooting from its bum like a rocket; this then turned into an in-depth discussion on what was worse – repeated kicks to the face or one superkick to the crown jewels. He made several valid arguments for the latter but talked himself tired and fell asleep mid-debate and slept without a stir.

During his snores, I considered what Aaron had said about displaying the rings and really wanted to look at them again. So I snuck my hand into my bedside table drawer, feeling like a thief or the Cadbury's Milk Tray Man, and in the dark quietly retrieved my auntie's rings. I switched on the torch on my phone, laid it on my pillow and let the light hit the ceiling. I opened the box and fixed my eyes on the jewel within; the diamond was truly beautiful. Each facet of its face was like a glowing memory of her that shone in my mind's eye.

But somehow, in the face of such beauty and emotional wealth, my awe was overcome by fear. I was so afraid of anything bad happening to this treasure I held so dear, so scared of losing them, damaging them altering them in any way at all, that I was overcome by a compulsion to lock them away and never again let them see the light of day. I had no secret vault or combination safe, so I grabbed an old T-shirt from the floor, wrapped the little green box in it and pushed the bundle right to the back of my bedside drawer and pushed it shut.

Aaron was right.

And yet I couldn't stop thinking of ingenious ways to better hide the rings from everyone.

<u>The Following Week</u> - (A mother's work)

Things had calmed down at work. The tension gradually dissipated every day until Mac was seen no more. There was no leaving do, no present and no card passed around. A week after his departure, Matt came over to my desk to personally invite me out with the rest of the office for drinks after work. I was taken aback by the offer. And Matt was equally surprised when I said that I couldn't make it because I had plans that night. He smiled and said, "That's cool, Joseph. Next time."

That night Aaron and I attempted to make our own popcorn chicken. Hot oil spat out of the pot like bullets from a machine gun sending us both running and ducking for cover. They came out a little burnt but surprisingly nice. We were very proud.

Aaron's mum rarely came to collect him in the evenings and when she did, even though he tried to hide his reluctance to leave – she knew her son – it was clear to her that he wanted to stay and so she left him at mine pretty much every night. So, I was surprised when one chilly Thursday evening, there was a light knocking at the door.

Standing outside was Aaron's mum, but behind her was a man and a small child.

"This is Aaron's dad. He wants to say hello," she stated, void of emotion.

An angry jealousy boiled in my stomach as I digested those words. I looked behind me and Aaron was glued to his seat, eyes full of apprehension.

"Aaron, come and say hello to your dad," his mum commanded with a tired hoarseness.

As Aaron rose, his dad took a step closer to the door, ushering the little girl forward with him. She looked around Aaron's age; her hair was long and oily. There was a sad prettiness about her that I paid little attention to.

Aaron's dad hugged him and introduced him to his sister. The two shook hands without meeting eyes. All but Aaron turned away from me. I felt like I was intruding and so I left them alone outside, closing the door, but pinning my eye to the spyhole and listening intently.

The rugged charm that Aaron's dad exuded seemed to be wasted on his son, as Aaron looked up at him with cautious eyes tinged with fear.

"I haven't seen you in ages, son, you're getting big." His Manchester accent was faint but there. "You must've all the little pre-schoolers chasing you round, hey?"

I didn't think Aaron remained silent because the questions were rhetorical.

"Well..." his dad continued, "I wanted to see ya to let you meet ya little sister. Thinking about it she might be older, you two can compare birthdays," he said with a proud smile. "And the other reason I came by is to let you know I'm going to be coming round to see you more often, keep an eye on you, make sure you're all right and all that."

Aaron gulped and squeezed his hands together as he struggled to maintain eye contact with his dad. He was a tall, well-built man with facial stubble greyer than the hair on his head. He looked mid to late forties, maybe ex-army, like my dad.

"Now you two run along to the off-licence down the road and go buy yourselves some sweets."

He rolled off a £10 note from a thick wad of cash.

"Take your time, I need to have a... a little word with ya mum. And when you get back you can tell me who's older and by how much."

Aaron looked up at his mum with concern when his dad mentioned "having a word" with her. She gestured with a turn of her head for him to go. Before he did, as if he knew I would be watching, Aaron glanced back at my door. The two children trotted along with mutual disinterest.

I felt anxious yet envious. This turd, this douche, this scumbag with amazing stubble had one of the greatest kids on the planet, and all he had to do achieve this little miracle, was not use protection. It made me sick!

What on earth made him worthy?

I couldn't stop wondering what Aaron's dad wanted, but more importantly, how Aaron was feeling and what was going through his mind. An hour and twenty-three minutes passed before there was a knock at my door. Aaron stood in front of his mum looking subdued. I looked up at her; her eyes were red and the left side of her face shone bright pink. Although clearly drained, she stood straight with her head high.

"He won't be coming back again; for a while at least." Her eyelids glistened. "Can Aaron stay here for the night? ...and the weekend?" she asked.

"Yeah, of course, of course. Do you err... do you want to come in for a while, for a cup of tea or something?"

She looked away and shook her head. She placed a gentle hand on Aaron's shoulder and ran her hand up to his cheek. Once he took a step towards me, she walked away. The bulge of a bottle in her back pocket betrayed her plans for that night... and the weekend.

Aaron sat in silence for the rest of that evening, eating a packet of Rolos. I didn't try pushing him for conversation. I had an idea what I would say, but I got the feeling that he did not want to talk, and that the silence might do him some good.

I thought of how Aaron's mum looked when she dropped him off. I wondered what she had done, or put herself through to rid them of his dad. When I thought of how she stood when returning him, there was almost something heroic in her stance, I felt respect for her. It was the first time that I had seen her act more than just his biological parent – her sacrifice had shown her love. His mum, that night, she was his proctor, his guardian, his mother. While Aaron warmed his feet on the rectangular block thingy in the middle of my laptop charging cord, I felt my feelings warm towards his mum, and wondered what it was, that day she found

Aaron and I in the hallway playing Tetris, that I had recognised in her eyes.

<u>That Saturday Morning</u> – (The wind in the willow)

I had ordered the original *Chronicles of Narnia* TV series box set for us to binge watch but it arrived on Friday while I was at work. So, I woke up early the next morning and made my way to the Post Office with my little red reference card to pick it up. I left Aaron asleep; I still hold that Saturday mornings are sacred to children – unless it's to wake up at 7am to watch *Once Upon a Time... Life* and find out that white blood cells are really little people in spaceships flying around your body killing bad guys.

The depot was a distance, and there were no buses along that route that I could get from near my flat. It was really chilly and I didn't fancy the long walk. There was another option, though, a field that lay in between my flat and the depot; it was always muddy and covered in dog poo but this route would halve the travel time, and sharpen my agility - just in case I one day became famous, then said something stupid on social media, got cancelled and then three years later launched a strong comeback on the incredible *Celebrity Ninja*.

Walking through the field on my return, it got a little foggy and I got a little lost. As the sun rose and began to shine through the mist, I found myself in the middle of a small barren patch surrounded by tall pollarded willow trees (I Googled the name when I got home). The cloud-clustered sky was pierced with small openings above this patch; streams of light shone through with a divine glow. A hard wind crashed into the park in heavy waves but as its waters were filtered by the trees surrounding me, its harsh whirls were tamed to soft tones that reached my ears with a refreshing calm. I stared at the trees encircling me. They stood naked and malnourished. Their bony appendages reaching up to the sky, pleading for mercy; an upward gust carrying their mournful cries.

My eyes settled on one tree in particular; it was shorter than most, taller than a few, but was the thickest out of them all. It looked old. I reached out and touched its skin. I had always found it hard to conceive that a tree could be beautiful. But for a moment, I saw more than its beauty, I saw that it was alive.

Once upon a time, this tree was young, then she grew, matured and endured the trials of winter with faith in better days; but even more than this, the tree loved. She was in the most intimate, intense and passionate relationship... with the Sun.

Before he arrives, she begins to adorn herself with the scent of spring and blooms of beauty. On her lover's arrival, she is dressed in the finest garb and fullest colours. Such is their love that even when he leaves at night, she looks just as luscious in the jealous light of the moon. But as he prepares to travel for the year's end, she struggles to conceal her dismay. Their days together become shorter. She discards her bright colours and sweet perfume, and decorates herself in gold and bronze to honour and reflect her king's glory, possibly in a final plea for him to stay. But he never does.

Then, as I witnessed, she dies in his absence. In her anguish, she cries dewdrops. Her appetite disappears and her golden jewellery falls from her meagre frame leaving her exposed, her nakedness now a sight to pity.

But the memory of their six-month love affair feeds her while she waits and endures. It nourishes her during the persecution the envious moon sends nightly. She stands strong awaiting her husband's return, hungering for his caress. Even in this, her most desperate state, love overcomes her desperation.

This idea roused a reverence of nature in me. And as my appreciation deepened, it stirred thoughts and feelings in my mind, of my mum. I soon forgot the bite of the cold and no longer perceived the tree before me. My dad was no King, although my mum made excuses for him, citing the racism he faced in the military as the main reason why he was the way he was:

"He can't reconcile within him how something he loves so, can hate him so much. You have to understand, it's this dichotomy that he lives with every day that makes him so angry."

That day I learned a new word and something new about him. Even with this in mind, my dad was still no King, so I understood why she left him. But as the next question began to form in my mind, I saw the tree in a new way – I was the tree and my mum was the Sun.

I rubbed my face, bringing life back to my cheeks, turned up the collar on my jacket and turned my back on the sight that had moved me, on the beauty that now hurt me, and I walked away.

<u>Saturday Evening</u>

I left my flat to make that most sacred exchange of money for pizza – the love for pineapple and ham still confuses me but Aaron seems to get it. On my way back in I walked past my door, took a cautious look around, then placed my ear against the door of Aaron's flat. What I heard held my attention and drew me closer.

There was no music, no TV, no male voice, only tears. I couldn't hear self-pity or hysterics; just tears. Then silence. Then a loud, hard, long snort. Then silence. Then tears.

That Sunday - (The sin of absent fathers)

I didn't know what to do. It had seemed like he'd enjoyed The Lion, the Witch and the Wardrobe but at the end of each episode his little cheeks would sag and his eyes wander to the floor and his countenance turn greyer than the sky outside. He had remained quiet for the whole weekend. In the evening I felt moved to talk to him. I didn't feel like it would be a good idea for him to face a week of school with his thoughts and feelings bottled up the way I imagined they were.

So, while sitting in the toilet between episodes, I practised my most approachable tone. I thought of how I would've wanted my dad to speak to me.

"Aaron..." I started, sat beside him.

"Do you think that God is real?" he asked.

"Wow. Err..."

I should've kept my mouth shut. I'm sure that school wouldn't have been that tough to handle.

"Yeah, I do believe that he's real," I replied.

"Can he watch everyone all the time?"

"I would think so," I answered gingerly.

"Do you think he does... watch everybody all the time?"

I started to wonder if this was going to turn into an awkward conversation about masturbation.

"I would say that if he can then he would."

A slight anxiety began to build as I waited for his reply, wondering whether my self-righteousness would call on my newfound ability to lie to children with little remorse.

"So, he sees all the bad things that people do to each other?"

"Yes."

Aaron's head rose but his eyes didn't meet mine. "Then why doesn't he do something to stop the bad things before they happen?"

He looked up at me during my silent retort. I was sure he saw not only my sympathy but also my own perplexion. He continued to stare. His eyes looked like they yearned for more than just answers; his cheeks paled, and he chewed the inside of his lip. My heart hurt for him. I reached over and gave him a hug. On contact with my arms, he burst into tears. He sobbed and sobbed and sobbed.

Holding him there, I felt powerless. Then he hugged me tighter, and I hoped to God that at least this was helping.

"It will be okay," I whispered.

As those words left my lips, his tears began to subside. As he rested in my chest sniffing loose snot back up his nostrils, I tried to recall memories of me crying in my dad's arms; but there weren't any. So, I repeated the words that I had once longed to hear from him.

"It will be okay."

Aaron struggled to get to sleep. I thought about different things that might take his mind off all the negativity that must've been buzzing around inside his head. I brought the TV into the bedroom and hoped that that might send him off.

He lay down mindlessly flicking through the channels. I flicked through the pages of my mind to try and think of something that could help. I went to make him a warm cup of milk when I heard the words, "This is English Courage" spoken in a smooth American accent. I dashed back into the bedroom to see Kevin Costner escaping prison in his role as Robin Hood.

"Leave it here, leave it here," I exclaimed. Aaron laid the remote on his pillow and I sat at the foot of the bed. "This is a classic."

Despite his efforts, Aaron only made it halfway through the film before he fell asleep. I stayed up and watched to the end, filled with the same glee and excitement I felt when I first saw it – Morgan Freeman simply has the greatest voice in the world.

An hour after the film ended...

An ancient tower rested on the edge of a cliff, kissed by a sky that had lost the love of the sun. At the peak of this dark fortress, a courtyard protruded and there stood a King; aged not by years, but by disappointment.

His fingers, coarse as rope, ran through his beard, which hung thick, grey and smooth like the feathers of a great eagle. He lifted his listless eyes to the heavens and sighed such depth it seemed that part of his life force escaped his lips.

He turned, heading back towards his kingdom but only a remnant of the vast manifestation of his power still stood, its former glory victim to a disaster suffered long ago.

Like a creature rising from the deep, his tongue crept through his lips, moistening them as it rose and descended, and he whispered, "A Coward dies a thousand deaths, but a King only one..."

Then, he looked over at me.

I was just a teenager. His look intensified. My knees locked and every ligament was pulled taut by the coldness of his stare.

"Coward!" he cried out. I felt scared. Then, as if he could smell my fear, he continued.

"Fool!" His insults stabbed me, and I stumbled back, wanting to cry. "You are no son of mine," he sneered.

This last slur sank deep, touching a nerve that filled me with anger and the impetus to reply:

"This was supposed to be *my* inheritance. It's what I deserved!"

He shook his head as he repeated, "You are no son of mine!" The icy tone with which his exclamation was delivered presented it as a taunt. My shame burned like hot coals upon which the fuel of hatred was heaped.

In a burst of unbridled fury, I leapt forward, drew my weapon and sank the blade deep into his stomach. His cold blood, black as oil, ran out down the sword and over my hands and began to crawl up my arms.

I pushed him away with more strength than intended. He fell backwards through the weak, rocky edge of the tower, his blood reaching out to me as he fell. But some still remained on my hands. I began scraping it off onto the floor, but it fought my efforts. Then the ground began to shake beneath me. As I looked up, I saw the tower crumbling all around, but I couldn't stop trying to get his filth off my hands. I had to; I couldn't let it get inside of me.

Massive stone blocks crashed by my side. The tower swayed violently as its great pillars lost their integrity. The faint sound of my mum's voice rang out high above the destruction; her cries were unclear; I couldn't tell if they were in concern or condemnation. Still, I couldn't get his blood off of me. As I struggled, large, jagged cracks appeared in the stone slabs beneath my feet.

"No..."

I woke up drenched in sweat, my heart bashing against my ribcage. My hands were sore and covered in scratch marks. I got up to change my T-shirt, then decided on a cup of coffee over a return to my pillow, scared of a return of my dream.

I examined the scratches I had made in my sleep, I paused looking closer, dismayed by how my hands had aged. I no longer cared about the scratches but felt troubled by my aging hands, and then it hit me, why I was so troubled by the sight of them – it wasn't just that they were aging, my hands were starting to look like my dad's. I rushed to the bathroom mirror. And there, around my brow, under my eyes, in the developing creases around my mouth, I could see him, and I could see his bitterness, his discontent; and how it had become my own.

The Next Day – (Aristotle is my guy)

Aaron's theological questions didn't stop. Lying at opposite ends of the bed, I asked him if they discussed things like this at Sunday school. He sat up giving me the same look of bewilderment he gave when I made a *Sesame Street* reference about Oscar the Grouch.

"What's Sunday school?"

I sat up. "I forgot you don't have that anymore. What about RE – Religious Education?"

"I don't think we start that until secondary school."

"Don't you have a granny or granddad that you speak to about this kind of stuff?" I asked, clutching at straws.

"We go and see my mum's mummy sometimes but we haven't gone in ages. They had a *really* big fight last time we went. And my mum always says that if her dad was still around then my dad wouldn't be my dad." His eyes glanced away from me. "Then things would be different, better."

I wanted to ask him why things would be better but I saw how painful it was for him to squeeze out that last sentence. "Where's your granddad?"

"He's dead. Mum says he's sleeping." Aaron's reply threw me as I considered his mum for a moment.

"Do you..." I began.

"Do you think God cares about *all* the bad things that happen to people?"

Before I could attempt to stall him for time, he continued.

"I mean, God has all the power in the world... so he should make bad things only happen to bad people, but..." He looked lost.

"I'll be honest with you, Aaron. I don't know the answers to those questions about God, I'm sorry."

"But why?"

"Well..."

"I mean, don't you ever ask these questions?"

I was stumped. "Not in a long time."

He slid back under the covers.

"But not because they're not important questions, they are and it's a good thing that you're asking questions like this, it shows that you're thinking. I suppose I just stopped looking for the answers."

He lay in silence, not stirring. After a minute he sat up on his elbows. "Do you think there are answers?"

I took in a deep breath knowing that my reply could have a major effect on him, but equally, so would my honesty. If I lied to him, about such a big issue, he might never put his trust in me again.

His look was expectant, as if he knew that I knew the answer. He reminded me of my English teacher who always said I never tried hard enough. He said something to me back then that only sank in as I sat there with Aaron, not knowing what to say to him.

We had an assignment to write about our view on the Rwandan civil war between the Hutus and the Tutsis. He gave me a D for mine. I was surprised but didn't complain, that seemed to upset him even more. My teacher, Mr Whittingstall, was smarter than most but not as smart as he thought.

"In Aristotle's book on the Nicomachean ethics" he started, in his 'scholars' tone, "he proposes a philosophical school of thought called Practical Wisdom. In that half of his thesis on Wisdom, he encouraged people to apply the law of the Mean when it comes to matters of morals and virtue. Do you know what the Mean is?"

I was already bored. "No, sir."

"So you're not flying through Maths either, I take it. Well, the Mean is the sum of the values divided by the number of values. Do you understand?"

"I think so, sir." I didn't.

"Take the numbers 10 and 2. Add them together and then divide them by 2."

"Six, sir."

"Good, that is the Mean. Now, Aristotle speaks on the Mean relative to us in the matter of Virtue. For example, Courage and *Cowardice.*" He looked down at me over his glasses as he mentioned the vice. "If a person is too courageous," he continued, "he thus becomes foolhardy. But if he is lacking in courage then he becomes a coward. So, if cowardice is 2 and being foolhardy is 10 then a man must aspire to a Mean level of courage, which is 6."

I hoped his point was made.

"But..."

It wasn't.

"...Aristotle in his wisdom called this process the Relative Mean. So, the level at which the virtue should be practised is determined also by the situation. So, if a man is to save a child from drowning but he is a coward, a courage level of 6 may not be enough, so he leans towards the extreme, the 10, to find the mean level appropriate for the situation."

I used all my strength to fight off yawning.

"Your literary ability is drowning because you write like a coward. Lean towards the extreme. Be courageous, Joseph. Your courage needs to be strong enough to overcome the cowardice you suffer from. Aim for 10 and you'll find your Mean, you'll find your virtue." He leaned back on his desk, his attention focused on me. "Do you understand, Joseph?"

The expression he wore when he asked that question was reflected on Aaron's face as he sat opposite me.

I straightened upand aimed for a 10.

"I believe there are answers, Aaron. I don't know what they are or where to find them. But I do believe they exist and can be found."

Relief washed over his features like a stream over parched land. Reassurance moved him to smile and, satisfied, he slid back under his covers and went to sleep; only stirring to say, "Night, Mr Joseph sir."

"Goodnight, Master Aaron."

My A-Levels proved not to have been a complete waste of time after all.

I rested on my pillow.

Aim for 10 Joseph.

I thought of my dream, of my dad calling me a coward, of how my hands and face began to resemble his vice.

His blood is in me.

I exhaled a deep breath.

Aim for 10 Joseph; and then you'll find your virtue.

That Wednesday – (Blood brothers)

We made lasagne and tidied the flat. It was a lot more enjoyable than it sounds and than I thought it would be. We did a pretty good job with both. "We", I've been using that word a lot.

"Did you used to cook with your dad?" Aaron asked as he stirred the white sauce 'in slow and steady circles', just as instructed. We stood side by side, he with a pot, me with a frying pan. *Mos Def & Talib Kwali's - Blackstar* album played in the background, competing with the hum of my semi-functional extractor fan. I had told Aaron that this was the only Album that my brother and I both loved. Maybe that's what made him think of family.

"Nah," I said with a sardonic laugh. "My dad was a military man. The kitchen was no place for a guy like him."

"What about your mum?"

I hesitated. "She was a busy woman. She supported a few local women's groups and mental health charities, one of her larger charities held their AGMs in different cities around Europe – every few years she would go, by herself, we would stay with my aunty. She was very hard-working; she managed our house and the community pretty much." Then I remembered, "I did make flapjacks with her once for their neighbourhood watch meeting; it was really weird though."

"Weird how?"

"Well, we were having a great time, my father was out and my brother was napping so it was just the two of us; I was her little assistant. She complimented me on everything I did that afternoon, even down to how I sprinkled in the sultanas, it didn't seem to matter that I was making a terrible mess. And in between giving instructions and in the little silences, she would hum tunes, mainly the old soul songs she would play when she was alone in the front room. I had never heard her sing but her humming voice was amazing; that was something I loved." I hadn't realised that I had stopped talking till Aaron poked me with his elbow. "Sorry, yeah, it was while I was stirring and she was preparing the baking tray, I looked over to see why she had gone quiet, there was no 'stir it a little slower' or 'add in a little more brown sugar', and there was no humming either. There was just silence. So I looked over to her and she was watching me, just smiling. Then out of nowhere, tears just started to fall from her eyes. Then she was off, she went to her room and closed the door. I carried on stirring, for a while. Then when I realised she wasn't coming back, I put the flapjack mix in the fridge turned off the oven and switch on the TV. We never cooked together again. But she still made her famous flapjacks, they were her tea time speciality when all the Neighbourhood Watch ladies would come by after school or when her women's group came round to organise their weekend trips to France."

"Maybe she burned herself on the oven. She sounds like a really nice mother though." Aaron smiled to himself with a thoughtful expression.

I poked at the mince absentmindedly. If he had said, "lady" or even "mum" I would've smiled and agreed. I stared through the steam rising from the frying pan, aware that I needed to say something but unsure of what to say without sounding disrespectful.

Aaron looked over at me in the silence. The chorus of *Knowledge Of Self – Determination*, attempted to fill the silence but couldn't.

"She wasn't a good mother, Aaron. She was a good woman, but I can't honestly say that she was a good mother."

Aaron replied with a reassuring smile. "My mum says the same about her mum. She says she was a bad wife too."

Although I wasn't saying anything that I hadn't already thought and believed for years, verbalising those thoughts brought more than a nostalgic feeling. I didn't feel bad, I felt eased; like a bottle of Coke that had had its cap turned. It was a new feeling that compelled me to indulge further.

"All the other mums always talked about how well my mum did; my dad was away a lot so she ran the house most of the time. They thought she was perfect, and for a long time she was."

Aaron looked away from me as he spoke. "I've seen my mum do some really bad things…"

I stopped stirring and even though he couldn't see me I gave him my full attention.

"…but I still love her."

A few moments passed and his eyes rose to meet mine. They were sheepish, as if he was sorry for the reproof he gave, but steady.

"But your mum is still here, Aaron." My gaze fell away. "Mine left."

There was an untimely pause in the music between tracks. His eyes widened in time with his mouth, both about to utter an apology. I tried to reassure him with a warm grin, but it was clear that Aaron felt both bad and intrigued, but I couldn't say anymore, at least not then. Aaron's stirring spoon slipped from his hand and was lost in the sauce.

"Oh, sorry, sorry." He bit his bottom lip and hopped around the pot, tentatively reaching a hand towards the submerged utensil.

I took out another spoon and rescued his, continuing in a lighter tone, "I was a bit of a clumsy kid when I was young." I washed the spoon off in cold water and handed it back to him. "My brother thought I was hilarious. He never listened to the rules; he was the 'rebellious child'. He would sip soup and hot drinks as loud as he could. It would take my mum ages to get him dressed for church and then just as we were about to leave, he would strip off all of his clothes and run around naked taunting my parents; he loved being naked, and peeing in public. If you made him laugh hard enough he'd wet himself and laugh more. The worst was when he was about seven or eight."

The mince began to congeal into little balls and the sauce thickened as I reminisced with glee and Aaron listened on, his head bobbing up and down to the rhythm of the story over the music.

"On days where my parents were having friends over for dinner, he would actually, for the *whole day*, hold in all of his farts."

Covering his mouth, Aaron sniggered.

"His stomach would make all sorts of noises, my parents assumed it was because he was hungry; he used to call them 'belly farts'."

Aaron laughed out loud before his hand could stop him.

"He would sit there with the naughtiest little grin on his face, almost bouncing in his chair. Then his eyes would focus on the guests, on the oldest man around the table. He knew that the oldest person was always the first to get served and first to eat. Now the first time he did this I didn't have a clue what was going on. My brother was sitting opposite me almost shaking with anticipation and staring at my dad's Sergeant Major. I thought that maybe he was excited by the man's high rank and was waiting to ask him a load of embarrassing questions like 'How many headless soldiers have you seen?' and 'Is it fun to kill people?' But then I noticed that his excitement grew as the man began to cut into his beef and I got scared thinking that he'd done something to the food, or the man's cutlery - like rub the spoon on his balls."

Aaron broke out into a fit of laughter, his eyes squeezed shut, his chin buried in his chest.

"It's not funny, he'd done that to me before. So at that point, I was starting to get anxious and thought that I should warn the old man or tell my parents before it was too late. Then the Sergeant Major began to raise his fork. My brother's fists clenched tight as he could barely contain himself. I was starting to break a sweat thinking that I can't stay silent but I didn't know what to do. It's not I could call out to the man and say, 'STOP! I think my little brother has soiled your cutlery with his testicles.' I would end up in more trouble than him."

"So, what did you do? What happened?" he asked in between breaths.

"Just as the slim cut of steak reached his lips and my brother's eyes were about to pop out from the pressure inside his stomach, I screamed out the first thing that came into my head. 'BALLS!'"

Aaron stared at me, his mouth open in shock.

"Everyone turned to me, staring daggers; everyone except my brother, whose eyes were locked onto the Sergeant Major, who shook his head at my outburst and placed the fork into his mouth. Just as he did, my brother's eyes squeezed shut and in a violent burst tensed his whole body. He made an obscene grunting noise and everyone now looked his way, but nothing happened. Then he took a deep breath and squeezed again." My face grimaced. "And then it happened. It was as if Saddam Hussein had hidden the WMDs up his bum; literally, an explosion went off in his pants. And just as a smile was appearing on his face, his fart was followed by something a bit more solid, just as vocal... and a little wet. He fell off his chair with a nasty squelch. One of the younger wives ran from the table holding her mouth, all the men shouted in disgust, my brother broke into hysterics and my mum slapped me around the head, blaming me for planning the stunt; thinking my call of 'balls' was his cue. My dad went to grab the little smelly bundle of laughter, who at that point was trying to un-stick himself from his trousers by taking them off. Then we all heard the young wife chucking up her guts in the kitchen. My brother brought the whole evening to an end when he laughed even harder at the poor woman's vomiting, and in his state of... well, lower body instability, let a torpedo of yellow liquid shoot out of his groin. He had opened his trousers so only his Y-fronts stood in between his willy and my parents' dinner party. The Y-front fabric acted like a shower head and his pee sprayed out everywhere like a golden sprinkler."

Aaron fell to the floor, rolling around and holding his sides and kicking his legs in hysterics. Once he had calmed down he asked me what happened to my brother afterwards. I explained that my parents took him to the doctors to find out if there was something wrong with him because he was so naughty. When he got the all-clear, my mum was always checking on him trying to thwart his juvenile antics.

"It's funny..." I said with a wry smile, "I never really misbehaved and did all I could to listen to my parents, but my brother, 'the rebellious child', was the one who got all the attention." I paused as the haze surrounding my childhood began to gain a bit of clarity. "And he loved it." I went quiet for a moment. As Aaron calmed down, we dished out dinner and ate to the northern accents of the contestants from a new show - Passion Peninsula (hot singles team up into couples and have to complete challenges to get closer to the mainland and win a prize of an all-expenses-paid wedding for the winning two on the peninsula they just escaped from).

After all the laughter and a full belly, Aaron went to bed early.

I was up, staring at my wallpaper. I had muted the TV and continued playing the album my brother and I used to leave on repeat. It was about 1:30am. I was slouched in the chair uncomfortably. Tension, having pulled my face into its centre, now eased its grip, unfurrowing my brow and relaxing my cheeks. I was filled with an angry disappointment that was being diluted with a satisfying realisation. I wondered why it had taken me so long to see something so simple.

The final lines of our favourite song Thieves in the Night played out:

"Hiding like thieves in the night from life

Illusions of oasis making you look twice"

"Jealous of my own little brother." I smiled "Tonight I'll pray that he's okay, and still enjoying himself."

"Hiding like thieves in the night from life

Illusions of oasis making you look twice"

I thought of how much I loved my mum's attention, and how, whenever I had it, he would always play up.

He was just a kid.

And just like that, I let go of the anger I didn't even know I was holding onto.

"Stop hiding, stop hiding, stop hiding yo' face

Stop hiding, stop hiding, cause there ain't no hiding place."

I saw why we weren't as close as we should be, and I missed him; I missed my brother Benjamin.

<u>An Hour Later</u> - (Nothing to hide)

I awoke, mistaking the first knock at the door to be a noise from the TV. But the second was a lot louder and I hoped it hadn't woken Aaron. My mind was too preoccupied to wonder who it was and even bother to look through the spy-hole before opening.

"Can I come in?" Her voice was different, lighter.

Aaron's mum stood in front of me, teary-eyed, partially dressed and either drunk or high or both.

Before I had a chance to answer she walked in past me. I closed the door. Her movement lacked its usual confidence. Her head hung and her shoulders were pulled closer to each other narrowing her frame; even from behind she looked almost scared, a little unsure. She turned to face me. Her hands held her elbows, strands of her hair hung over her eyes and she couldn't stand straight; I could smell her vulnerability.

She looked straight at me.

"Where is he?"

"Aaron's asleep. Are you okay?"

Her eyes started to stream. She pursed her lips shut to stop herself from crying and dropped her head to hide her tears.

Seeing her in this state was like seeing a different person. It was like staring at the Great Wall for weeks and then one day getting close enough to see through its cracks and view a quaint, luscious village behind it. There was a soft prettiness in her fragility, and this drew me towards her.

"I can't. I..." she started.

As I took a step forward, she fell into my arms and sobbed. For a moment I remembered when Aaron had done the same thing only a few days before. I felt like I could help her too.

Appropriate phrases and questions ran through my head as I thought of what she might want to hear. Then, in one swift move, her head snaked up past my neck, and she kissed my lips.

I tasted the heavy scent of tobacco, alcohol and something else that I couldn't immediately identify. Her tongue attempted to invade my mouth, but I retreated, leaning back.

Her face was a canvas of sadness and smeared make-up. She leaned into the light, revealing hues of helplessness and contrived lust. A drop of blood trickled from her left nostril.

"Let me thank you," she whispered.

She lunged at me with her lips. I held her back by her wrists.

"What are you doing?" I said.

She tried to wriggle free. "Please..." Her plea was fraught. I'd never had to use force on a woman before. I felt uncomfortable as I overpowered her, pushing her onto the sofa.

"Look..." I began.

"WHAT'S WRONG WITH YOU?" she shouted, jumping up. "Don't push me. Don't you EVER push me!" She paced around the room taking in deep, angry breaths, staring at the floor and talking as if I wasn't in the room.

"I just wanted to talk. That's all." She wiped her face, coating her forearm with sweat and blood. "But I don't care. It doesn't mean anything anyway. Who cares?"

I don't think I should have said it, but I did:

"I do."

She peered up at me, and it was like I was looking through her. There was a look in her face that caused a transparency in her eyes. As I recognised her expression, I realised that it was the same one I noticed that day in the hallway. My realisation though, must have been too obvious. With an inhalation and a twist of the head, her wall was erected. She boldly strode past me, opened the door and swore before leaving.

I closed the door once I heard her get into her own flat, and walked into the bathroom. I looked in the mirror. It wasn't there. What I had seen in the face, in the eyes of Aaron's mum was no longer visible in me. The change was slight, it was like the absence of a small wrinkle that you had watched grow over the years or the remnant of an injury long forgotten but the scar ever-present until it wasn't. I don't know when it went or why, but the air of desperation that had clung to me for so long seemed to be fading, seemed to be all gone.

<u>Six Days Later</u> – (To be loved)

I was stood by the kettle in the office talking to the new HR rep about her new hairstyle - she'd gone from braids to a natural afro look. Matt strolled up and joined us. He had a broad smile as he asked to speak to me.

"Joseph, I want to invite you round for dinner on Friday."

"Wow, that would be great." Then I remembered that we were going to the cinema to watch a comic book movie that night. "Ah Matt, I'm busy on Friday, I'm, I'm taking my... err, my nephew out."

Matt looked disappointed.

"My wife really wants to meet you. She wants to thank you."

I almost asked 'for what?' but could see in Matt's face, that I would only find out if I accepted.

"Can I bring my nephew with me?"

Matt brightened again. "Course you can. Is eight all right?"

"Should be fine."

"I'll email you my address. And keep this to yourself, you're the only one I've invited."

"Will do. Thanks, Matt."

As he strode back to his desk, I recalled how I'd watched him as we'd come back into the office after our lunch. I knew from that day he would carry that weight. He bore it until it became bearable, then light, now it seemed as though it didn't even exist. He didn't let the burden wear him out, *he* wore out the burden.

Aaron's going to be so excited. I wonder if he has dinner clothes?

It was raining on the way home and I was trying to brush the water out of my hair with my wet hand when I noticed Aaron waiting outside my door. I assumed something bad had happened to his mum.

"What's wrong?"

"Nothing," he said with a smile. "It was raining so I waited inside."

"Doesn't your mum pick you up from school?" I fumbled in my pockets for my door keys as a new worry entered my mind.

He replied with frank nonchalance. "Sometimes. She comes at half-past three when she does. But if she ain't there by then, then she ain't coming.".

I opened the door and we went inside. He grabbed his Gameboy off the sofa and went straight to the radiator rubbing himself against it like a randy pup on his master's leg.

"So, how do you get out of school if she doesn't pick you up?"

"Oh, I just sneak out and wait until one of you comes home. You're usually home first so I just play out until half-six. You're never home later than that."

"So you come home *by yourself* and then wait for three hours *by yourself?*"

"Yeah. If I stay at school, they give Mum a fine for not picking me up on time. One time they called the child services people and they took me to a house somewhere until they got hold of my mum." His expression lost its nonchalance. "I didn't like it there. So when I know she ain't coming I just sneak out and just go."

"Okay... okay, well, if that happens again, I want you to call me on my mobile and I'll leave work early and come and get you. Winter's here and it's getting darker earlier, the weather's bad and just... it's just dangerous. Agreed?"

Aaron smiled. "Mmmmm, Okay."

I wrote my number down on the back of an unnecessarily long Starbucks receipt from my back pocket.

"Here, I want you to memorise this."

"Okay."

"Aaron, I'm serious. I don't want anything bad to happen to you. *I'm* not going to let anything bad happen to you. So memorise my number, and I'm going to give you some spare change every morning so that you can call me from a phone-box in an emergency. Okay?" The seriousness of my tone changed his expression. It wasn't one that I could make out but he seemed to have taken in my words.

"Okay." His reply was sheepish, almost sad, but there was a smile, ever so slight, teetering at the edge of his mouth. Then he dashed over to the sofa.

A show must be about to start on TV.

I walked into my bedroom to change out of my wet clothes but spoke loud enough for him to hear me speak while I did.

"I've got some good news." I paused as I took off my shirt. Aaron didn't say anything. "We've been invited out to dinner by a friend from work. I think I helped save his marriage. Well, I thought we'd better go clothes shopping and get you something nice and new to wear. We can go to the shopping mall by the train station tomorrow, it's open until nine now." I paused again as I looked for my ridiculously warm tracksuit bottoms. In the silence, I was surprised that there was silence. These days, the flat was full of early '90s gaming music, reality show chatter and childish laughter. But there was nothing. I took a break from my search and walked into the living room. Aaron was sitting on the sofa. It looked like he was crying.

"Aaron, what's wrong?"

He was startled, having not heard me approach. "Nothing, nothing." He wiped his face with his forearm.

"Are you sure?"

"Yeah, yeah, I'm okay."

I thought that maybe he felt I had spoken to him harshly. But I wanted him to realise that I was serious and to see that he was putting himself in danger. So I went back to my search, talking loudly over my feelings of guilt.

<u>**That Friday**</u> - (It's normal)

Matt's wife, Julia, was not a good cook. She was a lovely person – smart, affable, talkative – but her skill in the kitchen hit minus figures. But I did the polite thing and finished my food nonetheless. Aaron gave me a look to say:

"I think she cut out the cardboard drawing of the meal, seasoned it with Mr Bland's tasteless herbs and spices and left it in the oven for too long. Honestly, do I have to eat this?" (His look was that long and in-depth.)

Then I looked back to say:

"Although I feel like I've eaten the dry seagull-poo-infested sand from Brighton beach, I finished it so you have to too. It's the polite thing to do."

And with that, he returned to his laborious task under Julia's merciless gaze. He finished it, eventually. Then he glanced over at me, his expression saying:

"You owe me one."

My look said:

"I know."

Then something uncanny happened; he smiled. The whole time I'd been joking in my mind that he could read my expression, but with that slight smile I started to believe that he really could. I smiled so wide that Matt asked what I was thinking about. When I replied, "How good the food was," Aaron had to feign a cough to smother his giggles.

During dessert, thankfully from the supermarket, Julia sipped from her glass of port and then looked at me with a vague grin. There was a jolly voluptuousness about her person, which was tempered by her long black hair, dark intelligent eyes and slim jaw. Due to her tan she could pass for being Mediterranean, South American or Caribbean; but in truth, she couldn't have been more British if she tried.

"I hope you don't mind me talking openly in front of your nephew," she began. Aaron shot a look over at me; I had simply introduced him by name. My eyes told him "I'll tell you later," and we both listened as she continued.

"I owe you so much, Joseph. I thought Matt would never forgive me, he's quite stubborn, especially when he's in the right." Her eyes swayed down towards her glass, but before her gaze reached the pool of sweet burgundy liquid, Matt had gently gathered her fingers and palm into his own, and her eyes rose. "I had given up. I *wanted* to try; I was willing to do anything but I seriously believed our marriage was a lost cause." Julia's words became a whisper and her eyes narrowed. "But when I came to the house to collect my things... and he took me by the hand and told me that he loved me... I just crumbled. What he said, and the way he said it, humbled me. I felt like I didn't deserve him..." Tears stumbled her speech. Matt put his arm around his wife, closing his eyes for a moment and holding her with a tenderness to his touch. "I'm sorry. I... I just really want to thank you, Joseph, for what you did."

A flash of Aaron's mum trying to thank me the week before streaked across my mind.

"It was nothing, I..."

"No, it was and still is everything to me. It might seem like it was a small thing, but that small thing changed my life..." Her free hand grasped Matt's. She pulled his hand down from her shoulder and gave it a tender kiss, leaving a deep purple imprint of her lips like a sweet bruise. "...our lives."

"And because you played such a large part in keeping our marriage together," Matt started while still looking at his wife, "we wanted you to be the first to know... that we've decided to adopt a child."

"Wow!" I said with complete surprise. Aaron had his mouth open ready to ask the obvious but was able to stop just short. The couple smiled at his cute apprehension.

"We're unable to have kids of our own Aaron, but we really want one. We," Matt looked into Julia's eyes. "there's a lot we took for granted and a lot of things we put on the back burner for stuff that isn't half as important."

"And neither of us wants to make that mistake anymore." She gave Matt a quick peck on the lips.

"You're the first person we've told," Matt said looking back at me.

"We haven't even told our parents yet!" Julia added.

"Again, wow! I can't believe it. I feel very honoured; I don't feel worthy. It's a big deal to be the first to know. I really appreciate this. Thank you... and congratulations. It's great news."

We all had another glass of port and Aaron some grape juice so that he didn't feel left out.

The rest of the evening was spent discussing how adoption and guardianship worked, then Matt updated, well, informed me, on all the office gossip and mentioned that he heard the HR Rep had taken a liking to me.

"Aaron, would you like to see the bedroom we're doing up for our family's new addition?" Julia asked.

Aaron didn't respond quick enough to make a plausible excuse. "You can help me pick out colours..." He still wasn't convinced. "We're hoping to get a boy."

"Yes, please."

Julia stood up. She was tall and moved with grace and power. She held out her hand. Aaron walked over and took her open palm as if drawn to her, like it was the most natural thing in the world to do; in that moment I knew she would make a great mother.

I turned back to Matt, whose attention was focused on Aaron and Julia as they entered the room down the hall behind him. He could just about see them moving around in the room and only make out his wife's high tones as she showed Aaron how the room was going to look in her mind.

"There's nothing in this world she wanted more than children." Matt's voice took on a sombre tone as he continued to watch. Then he began to turn back to the table, shaking his head. "When the doctors told her that she couldn't conceive, it devastated her. We tried the hormone injections, artificial insemination - the works. But she had something called endometriosis, and it had gone untreated for a long time and had done a lot of damage." He grimaced and there was a flash of regret across his features. "The thing was it wasn't a big deal to me... I mean, it didn't bother me at all that she couldn't conceive. I told her that I'd always liked the idea of adoption and joked about how I was always worried that my kids would get my family's dodgy nose or my daughter might inherit my hairy back. I told her I didn't have to worry about that anymore. When I said that, she went mad; I mean, completely ballistic – screaming, crying, shouting, swearing. She tried to fight me!" he said shaking his head. "I had tried to be jokey, to lighten the tone, but really I had just dismissed the worst, life-changing news she'd ever had, and tried to make light of the situation. Then on top of that, I handled her outburst all wrong. In my mind, I said I was giving her space, but in reality, I was being cold and just left her to deal with it alone. I'd ask her if she wanted to talk about it and she would look at me like it was my fault that this had happened. So after a while, I stopped asking. It wasn't the best way to start a marriage. In time, though, things started to get better. I tried harder, and we started talking again, talking and listening, and things got good; it felt like we were back on track. Then we started discussing other options for children. When? How? And then... and then she confessed; she told me about her and Mac. And then I spoke to you." His face began to brighten with appreciation.

"You're romanticising my role in all this. I didn't even pay for my own coffee that day. This was all you guys."

"Nah. My head was stuck in a place where I was a hundred percent in the right and had nothing to say to her. But when you told *me* to tell *her* that I loved her, that made me think about my responsibility in all this."

"That was pretty much all I said for the whole time we were there."

"And that's all that was needed. The right words at the right time. You were the right man for the job and you did what was needed. You could've said the easy thing and just sided with my anger like some people did, or say nothing and decide you didn't want to get involved like most people did. But you didn't, you were you. And you, Joseph Bogart, were just what we needed."

My face shone.

So, this is what self-worth feels like.

Julia returned with Aaron, like a nephew with his favourite aunt; she definitely had the trick – but then Aaron was a little bit special too.

Matt and Julia both hugged me when we left and then waved from their doorstep as we walked to the train station at the end of their road.

"They seemed so happy together, didn't they?" I said with pride.

Aaron didn't reply, so I glanced down and saw his head bowed and his hands tucked tightly into his little red jacket.

"What's wrong?"

He didn't look up at me straight away. "Why did they say I was your nephew?"

"Oh, that's just what I told Matt when he invited me. Did that bother you?"

"But why did you say that I was your nephew?"

"I wasn't sure how to describe the situation, so I thought it was just easier to say that you're my nephew."

"Couldn't you have told them about me and mum and how things are? Is it that bad?"

"No, not at all, it's just different is all. People sometimes find it hard to accept or understand things that aren't normal, that are different to what they know and expect."

"I'm not normal?"

"Not you, the situation. It's not that it's not normal, well, I suppose there's no such thing as normal, it's just different and some people find different difficult. Like when I was in school there was only one Indian boy in my whole class. He was normal but different, and some of the other kids found it difficult to be around him because he looked different and spoke different and sometimes acted different to them, and so sometimes they would pick on him and bully him because of it, but it wasn't because he ever did anything wrong, it was because he was just different and they didn't understand it and so they didn't like him and treated him bad, and that's wrong of course. It's wrong to ever treat anybody badly just because they're different."

"So if you're different what should you do?"

I stopped Aaron and crouched down to meet his eyes.

"You just be yourself. And if other people don't like the fact that you're different then who cares about them, they're not people worth knowing if that's how they want to think and act. All that matters is that *you* know who you are, that you know there's nothing wrong with you and that, in fact, you being different, you being you makes the world a better place. Don't let other people's twisted way of thinking affect you or what you do."

Aaron looked down at the cracked pavement; he seemed to be taking in my words. When his head rose, I was prepared to carry on explaining what I meant as I saw a puzzled expression on his face. Then he spoke.

"Then why did you lie?"

My lips moved in anticipation of a quick reply, but my mind was silent. I wasn't lost for words but I was lost for a reasonable explanation.

A few moments passed.

I stood up straight.

"You're right, Aaron. You're absolutely right."

I took him by the hand and with brisk strides we headed back towards Matt's house. Aaron remained quiet.

Matt answered the door holding a kitchen towel.

"Has the last train left already?"

Julia came from behind him wearing rubber gloves. "Oh, it's freezing, come in," she said.

"No, it's okay." I felt nervous and unsure. My forehead and neck became small furnaces; I didn't know what to say. They both looked at me, their smiles waning.

"Aaron's not my nephew. I lied."

They both immediately looked worried.

"He's my neighbour's child. I look after him most days after school. His mum isn't in often, she works in the evenings, and so Aaron ends up staying over most nights. He's a good kid, a really good kid. His dad isn't around so I... I help out. I try to look after him."

There was a short silence.

"Okay," Matt said with a shrug of his shoulders.

"That's so nice of you, Joseph," Julia said with a genuine smile.

"Why did you feel the need to come back and tell us?" Matt asked.

"Well, because I lied and there was no need to. For some reason I thought you guys might've found it a bit weird because you know, it's not... it's different."

"Why?" Julia asked.

Matt spoke before I could. "Where I used to live, about half of the kids in my block of flats weren't living with both of their parents. And most of them didn't even know who their dad was."

Matt looked towards Aaron. "I first met my dad when I was fifteen. You'd be surprised, you're not as different as you think."

Aaron nodded with a wide grin. "I know."

Aaron did know. At ten he knew what I was just realising.

We said our goodbyes again and they promised to invite us both back for a games night with a few other friends.

When we returned home, I gave Aaron a hug before bedtime. As he left, I sat on the sofa and whispered, "Thank you."

I wasn't sure if I was just saying that to Aaron or if I believed or hoped that someone somewhere was listening, but I felt the need to express how grateful I was.

<u>**Monday After Lunch**</u> -- (Specsavers)

Back at work, sat at my desk, my back to my computer, I looked out at everyone in the office.

At dinner, Matt had given me a brief breakdown on most of the people on our floor. I'm terrible with names and because I don't speak to them very often, I remember who they are by their distinguishing features.

The guy who looked like Mario Van Peebles (for years I thought it was Van Peoples) from when he was in Jaws: The Revenge, who sat next to the meeting rooms, lived at home with his dad. His mother was diagnosed with multiple sclerosis when he was eight and he and his dad became her carers until she died three years ago. After her death, his dad's health deteriorated and he was left on a dialysis machine and Van Peeps was left alone to care for him. He's been living in the same room on the same council estate his entire life. Since pre-adolescence death has been a constant reality. He's a good-looking guy. I always thought he sneaked out of work early to meet women.

The tall lady who covered reception during the receptionist's lunch break looked like the lady in that Humphrey Bogart movie where her sister goes missing (it used to come on Channel 4 all the time when I was a kid), the really tall and very pretty woman, I think they got married. Anyway, the Bogart lady lookalike was born in France. Her mother brought her over here when she was a baby. On her twenty-first birthday her mother revealed to her that she's actually her aunt. Her aunt, being a staunch Catholic, talked her mum out of having an abortion hoping that she would want her daughter once she was born. But feeding, crying and changing nappies didn't convince either parent. Supposedly she still calls her aunt "mother" and has never tried to contact her biological parents. She got engaged two months ago to a guy 15 years her senior, a painter from Combray according to Matt.

And my manager, who looked nothing like Chevy Chase and isn't funny in the slightest, but whenever I see him, for some reason, that's whose face pops into my head, he went to prison in his early twenties for assault. His whole life he's suffered with bouts of depression, but that has never affected how he dotes on his four daughters. During their fifteen-year marriage he cheated on his wife twice. Four years after the last act of adultery, they decided that what they had when they first met was no longer there. They divorced, quite amicably, he gave her the house and she gave him free access to the children. She remarried a few years later but my boss never did. Neither looked back with regret.

"There's no such thing as normal."

These were the highlights from Matt that, as surprising as they were, didn't stun me more than when Matt told me how unhappy most of my colleagues were. He asked why I thought they were always out every evening and why they always came back on Monday bragging about how much they drank and who they'd slept with and how much of an amazing time they'd had. He told me they put up the biggest front because they had the most to hide.

"'False face must hide what the false heart doth know,'" Julia said.

"*Macbeth?*" Matt replied.

"Well done," she said with pride.

"I tell you, Joseph, so many people in that place are completely fake. But if you look close enough, you can see right through them."

Throughout the whole conversation I sat there scared, terrified. I was waiting for Matt to say what he really thought about me, that he could see through my front and was going to say what he saw. Or even worse, that he would ask me what I thought about myself.

I missed certain comments and jokes because I begged louder and louder in my head for him not to start the sentence "So what about you, Joseph..." Thinking about it now, that's why I've always avoided group conversations and kept the topic about the other person in one-to-ones. That's why I don't speak as much or make any effort to get invited out. Or why I seem to just blend into the scenery.

Maybe it's not so much that people ignore me, but that I seek to be ignored. It's not so much that people don't hear me but that

I don't actually want to be heard. If people took more notice of me, I'd be forced at some point to talk about myself, and I can't think of a single thing in the entire universe that would scare me more than that.

My mobile rang; it was a call from a private number. (I always get apprehensive when I see 'Private Number' flash up on my phone. The hospital called from a private number the first time my aunty had a stroke and they couldn't get hold of my dad. I thought she was going to die. And it was a private number my dad called from when my mum left.)

It was Aaron, he was calling me from a phone-box near his school. I checked my watch, it was 3:30.

"I'm on my way."

I know I shouldn't have, but I lied to my boss and told him that I had to pick up my son from primary school. He looked surprised and a little embarrassed that he didn't know I had a child, and so without any questions, he told me that it was fine and I left.

Aaron met me around the corner from the front gate after sneaking out of his class. He was standing, hands in his bright red jacket pockets, watching the other parents go by; his chubby cheeks pinched pink by the cold. He ran over to me as soon as he saw me coming, playfully barging into my side. We went and treated ourselves to ice cream, even though it was freezing outside.

"What was your favourite subject in school?" Aaron asked as he munched away at his ice-cream-covered Flake.

"Mine was English. I used to love reading. I would go through a book a week, easily. Now I get a headache after reading for an hour. I think I need glasses. But I'm not that pretty as it is."

"You should go to Specsavers," he chuckled.

"I probably should."

"English is all right, I guess, but it's all about ICT."

"What's that again?"

"Computers. I *love* computers. I'm making up my own game, with different levels and tasks and baddies you gotta beat. It's an RPG, like Zelda, where you have to buy different weapons and armour and meet people on your journey and stuff."

"Wow. That sounds amazing. But what about English? Don't you like books?"

"I like books, I get loads of ideas for my game from books, I just hate reading. I love it when Miss Parsons reads to us on Friday afternoons. We're halfway through *George's Marvellous Medicine.*"

"Why do you hate reading?"

"Because it's boring."

"But you like being read to?"

"Yeah, it's like someone's telling you a story and you can sit back and close your eyes and think about the people and what they look like and what they're wearing and stuff. She does all the voices as well, it's soooo good."

"You know you can still use your imagination while you read, right?"

"I can't." Some of his ice-cream dropped on his jacket. "Crap!"

"Hey, crap's a bad word. You shouldn't use it," I reprimanded.

"I thought the 's' word was bad but crap was okay."

"No, crap's bad."

"But Mr Donner says it all the time."

"That doesn't mean it's okay... wait a sec, you've got a male teacher called *Mr Donner*?"

"That's his last name. We pretend that his wife's name is kebab."

I laughed before I realised it was wrong to. "That's bad, you shouldn't say that," I said in between chuckles.

"We've been saying it for ages. Then the other day he got upset and shouted that he didn't have a wife. Then he looked really sad. So now we say when he gets a wife, his kids are going to be called Pita Bread & Salad or Meat & Chips."

I cracked up with laughter and Aaron joined in.

We continued with our ice creams.

"Aaron, are you a good reader?"

He lost his smile and bit into the wafer cone. "I'm all right."

"I wasn't always a good reader when I was your age. I could help you practise reading at home."

"Maybe." His attention fell to the stones on the pavement, kicking them aimlessly.

I remembered hating it when my parents forced me to do things that were "for my own good."

"So, tell me about this computer game you're making. You said it's an RPG, what does that mean again?"

"Role Play Game."

Aaron brightened up straight away and talked all the way home.

When we arrived at my place, I had a plan in mind.

We made spaghetti Bolognese from scratch, including the sauce. We talked about our favourite computer games, and I realised that Aaron liked the 1990s not because of some new wave of retro appreciation, but rather because everything his mum bought him or that he "discovered" was at least fifteen years old; a Sega Mega-drive was the first computer console we both owned.

After dinner, I got up and turned off the TV. Aaron looked at me bemused and ever so slightly indignant.

"I've got a surprise for you."

His face lit up.

"We've just got to look for it first, though," I said. I think the prospect of a treasure hunt excited him more.

We went into the bedroom and started digging through the boxes of all my old things.

Aaron was kneeling over an old Walkers Crisps box going through each item as if he expected to find something extraordinary. "Why is all of this stuff still in boxes?"

"I've just never got round to going through it all; I can't actually remember what's in most of them, to be honest."

"So why don't you unpack them?"

"I will." I made no effort to hide my lack of sincerity.

I felt Aaron looking at me while I continued looking through the boxes.

"Who's this?" He held up an old photograph.

"That's my mum." I hadn't seen that picture in years; it took me a little by surprise.

His mouth opened and he looked back to the picture, bringing his face within an inch of it. "She's so pretty," he said softly.

"Yeah." I paused, trying to think about when that picture was taken but my mind was too preoccupied with the picture itself. "She always had soft hands."

Aaron sat on the floor, crossing his legs and kept his eyes on my mum as he spoke.

"The nurse at school has soft hands. She's always giving everyone warm hugs when we come in from playtime. She's never cold. We think it's because she's fat. But sometimes I think it's because she's nice."

I barely heard what Aaron had said. I didn't pay much attention until he asked me a question.

"Are your mum's hands still soft?"

I scooched over and looked at the picture again. I took it and I looked at her face. I couldn't reply.

I placed the picture in another box, and just as I felt Aaron gearing up to ask his question again, I saw what we had been looking for.

"Aha, I've found it."

I retrieved from under a stack of my GCSE certificates an A4-size bright yellow hardback book, and dusted it off. Aaron read the title as I handed it to him.

"*Bible Stories?*"

"This was my favourite book when I was a kid. When you talked about being read to, I tried to remember that feeling and I remembered our babysitter reading this book to us before we went to bed. My present is... that I'm going to read this to you."

He didn't speak, he just grinned. He took a deep breath and with pride opened the book and saw printed on the first page the words: 'This book belongs to' Both mine and my brother's names were pencilled in.

"Find a rubber and a pen and put your name in there."

He looked up at me, as if surprised that I would give him this privilege. Still, he didn't speak. He flicked through the pages and as he saw the colourful illustrations, his smile grew and he turned and hugged me.

His appreciation made me wonder how often he received gifts, or at least ones with any thought behind them.

His words were muffled but I heard them loud and clear.

"Thank you, Joseph. I mean, Mr Joseph sir."

As he ran into the living room to get a pen and a rubber, I hoped that, despite my slim stature, I was as warm as his school nurse.

He loved the book more than I did. He had so many questions but I could see that his excitement and eagerness to hear the next story were too strong to be halted by his present inquisitiveness. I never knew such joy could be found in giving.

<u>The Next Day</u>

I woke up with a slight headache, so I went to Specsavers. I got a pretty good deal.

<u>A Week After Getting My Glasses</u> - (Fifteen & in love)

We read the Bible stories book every night. When we got to the part about Samson and Delilah, Aaron wanted to see how strong he was and went around trying to lift up every moveable object in the flat. When he realised that he couldn't, he was convinced that if he grew his hair he would be able to. I explained that he needed to exercise to be stronger and attempted to show him how to do push-ups. After five it felt like my arms were on fire. Aaron mocked me. He stood over my exhausted, weak, meagre body and pointed and mocked me. So now we have a competition going that by the end of next week we have to be able to do twenty push-ups – straight out. Every evening Aaron's been going to the toilet to "make room for dinner." As I pass, I can hear him practising his push-ups, or at least I hope that's what he's doing. I've been doing the honourable thing by training in the front-room, after he's gone to sleep. I've got a pretty good routine going now.

When we got to the section about King David and Bathsheba, he asked me why she was having a bath naked on her roof where people could see. I didn't know the answer but thought that it was a good point. We talked about how attractive she must have been for the king to go through such lengths to get her and keep her. That turned into a discussion about which features he likes about girls, then to the girl at school that he likes; it turns out, it's not just blondes.

"She's got these amazing patterns on her hands, she said it's called Henna and her hands it's like... like she's never fallen over and scraped them or cut them or anything; they're so smooth. There's no marks on them!" He said this looking up at me as if I were about to call him a liar because such a thing couldn't possibly be true. "I think they're perfect."

Before I had a chance to ask him what else he liked about her, Aaron piped up again, his eyes bright with excitement, "But you know what, even more perfect than her hands... like the best-est thing about her... is her eyes."

The recognition of his words spread my smile wide and even.

"I sound stupid, don't I?" Aaron asked, looking disheartened.

"No, no, no. I smiled because… you sound like me."

"What do you mean?"

"Those small things that you like, like her hands and especially her eyes, are the type of things I'm attracted to in women."

Aaron's demeanour jumped from discouraged to enthusiastic. "What women?"

"Women in my past."

"What did they look like?"

"There's been a few that I've liked."

I could hear a tinge of irritation at my evasiveness in his tone. "The one that you liked most."

"Oh, that's a long story. I'll tell you about that another time."

"Why not now?"

"Another time, Aaron."

"But why, though?"

"I said another time."

"But you always say that." Disappointment flooded Aaron's face. With his hands balled into petulant fists, he stormed off. I sat kind of stunned as he pushed the bedroom door shut, but the thick carpet underneath prevented it from slamming.

My immediate thought was *how childish* and then I reminded myself, *he is a child.* This was the first time, however, that I had seen him act like one; and there was something inherently wrong with that fact.

He's ten years old. It's not natural. It's not natural and it's not right. He's too mature. What pressure must he be putting on himself daily not to mess up, not to upset me or his mum or his schoolteachers? It's not right.

I glanced over at the bedroom door; only silence came from behind it. Whether or not it was my place didn't matter, what kind of person would I be if I saw this and did nothing?

I made two cups of hot chocolate and grabbed the half-empty packet of chocolate biscuits in the cupboard on my way into the bedroom, with the intent of seeing how he was coping with everything.

"Aaron... WHAT ARE YOU DOING?"

Aaron was on his hands and knees trawling through my unpacked boxes. He froze in surprise but had a slight look of resentment in his eyes. He didn't reply.

"Aaron, what are you doing going through my private stuff?"

He remained silent, his face twitching to speak. I took a few angry steps towards him.

"It's not fair! IT'S NOT FAIR! You *NEVER* tell me *ANYTHING* about you. You say that you'll tell me later and then you don't, that's lying and that makes you a liar so I don't have to listen to you so I can look in the boxes if I want to!" He breathed in rapid bursts following his protest and held his position amongst my personal belongings with defiance.

"I'm not a liar, Aaron, don't call me that and..."

"Yes you are! You say you're going to do something and you don't, that's lying."

"I said I would tell you later, when I'm ready. Just because I don't tell you when *you* want me to doesn't mean that I'm lying or a liar."

"But when are you going to tell me, you could keep saying that forever and then I'll never know!"

"Never know what, why is it so important that you know these things?"

"Because I want to!"

"Why? Why is it so important?"

"Because it is." He went silent but held a look as if he had more to say. "I don't know anything about my mum, about my dad, about my sister, about Mum's friends, I don't know *anything* about *anyone*. Why don't people tell me about them, why don't they want to talk to me? What did I do? W..." He started crying and his head dropped. "I always tell people about me..."

I put the cups on the floor and put my arm around him.

"Why don't people like me?"

"People do."

Aaron shook his head with harsh twists in protest.

"I do."

He cried for a little longer before his tears abated.

Before he looked at me again, he reached behind himself and picked up a small pile of photographs he had gathered.

"Tell me..."

I felt apprehensive as he handed me the pile. The photograph on top sent a surge of emotion through my body.

"Her name's Sapphire. I think she's about twelve in that picture."

I didn't read to Aaron that night. Instead, I spoke to him, something I realised I hadn't spent much time doing with him, or with anyone.

About Fifteen Years Ago

She went to an all-girls' Catholic school. I went to a mixed comprehensive a fifteen-minute jog away; I always got to the gate just as she was finishing her last class. I'd never kissed a girl before.

She had got into an argument with Sister Finnegan about the mystery of the Trinity.

"I told her that the only mystery was that she still believes in it."

Sapphire's mum was a Protestant, but St Barnabas Catholic School for Girls had the highest achievement record in the county. They had achieved this by "the 'grades' of God," her mum had explained.

In the spring term, while we walked towards home, I would put my arm around her in that pally sort of way buddies do when they're "havin' a laugh". In the winter, she'd let me hold her closer; I looked forward to the days when it rained and snowed.

Since she had turned twelve, she struggled terribly whenever it was her time of the month. But in a funny sort of way, I looked forward to it; it felt like she needed me, she played me closer when she felt weak. It was on a day like this – a cold, grey, rainy day – that I realised I wanted to be more than her best friend; in fact, I realised then that we always had been more.

She came out of school later than the other girls, but I had a warm winter jacket on so I didn't mind waiting. We had missed the first bus, but when the next one came it was empty and we didn't have to stand. She had been silent and I didn't push her to speak. She sat with a small distance between us. I observed her from the corner of my eye – she was completely detached, as if she didn't belong to her own body. With all the discretion a young teen male could muster, I wiped my runny nose on the cuff of my jacket, and then looked back to Sapphie, her hands were in her lap, her thumbs rubbing the tips of her fingers and her face was covered in tears. I raised her chin in the crook of my finger and asked, "What's wrong?"

Her wide eyes glistened and she replied, "I don't know."

She crumbled into my arms. I opened my jacket and she fell into my chest, sobbing, crying through the cotton/polyester of my school shirt. I felt the warmth of her face in the dampness and, as she continued to weep, the softness of her cheek against my breast. Together, we felt alone on the bus. In that moment, I loved her completely.

The next day my mum was hosting a kid's party round our house for my little brother; Sapphie promised she'd keep me company.

I knew she loved me. I knew she loved me like I knew my heart was beating, it was something I didn't need to question. Armed with that truth my actions didn't take much courage.

I picked her up from her house and we walked towards mine. I held her hand and she didn't let go.

"I've got a secret," I started.

"Ooooh, tell me."

"When we were young, because the doctor said that you needed to be in the sun a lot and because the movie had just come out, for a long time... I secretly believed you were Supergirl."

"Are you serious?"

"Yeah! I used to sit at the bathroom window looking down at your house, waiting for you to fly off and fight crime."

"But I was weak as a kitten..."

"But you were honest, smart, always did good things and you were the prettiest girl I knew."

She blushed and her hand melted into mine.

"You know, Joseph, you're amazing sometimes."

Her words made me feel ten feet tall.

"And thank you for yesterday. I was all over the place and you were... you were just what I needed."

There couldn't have been a better moment. With a soft grasp, I pulled her towards me, placed my other hand behind her back and leaned in, and kissed her. I kissed her like a Hollywood leading male kissed beautiful starlets in those black and white movies my mum loved, I kissed her as I had practised on the back of my hand for months. I kissed her and felt her; I felt her soft mouth, the warm breath from her nostrils, then the uncomfortable tightness of her pursed lips, then I felt her hand let go of mine, I felt her head glide back and when I opened my eyes, I felt the horror of a terrible, terrible mistake.

The Morning After the Mistake the Day Before

Sapphie's dad was an avid rugby fan, but he gave religion "a fair go" for the sake of his wife and children. He was, however, a firm believer that Sundays were for rugby and not for God. When Sapphie's mum threatened to leave if he didn't support the family in Sunday mass, his eyes alone rose from the screen TV, his deadpan expression giving her pause,

"Rugby was here before you, and it will be here long after you leave." And back his eyes returned.

So that morning I knew Sapphie would be out and her dad still in. I woke up stupid early, in fact, I couldn't remember falling asleep. I got dressed before everyone else and sneaked out, while my brother was having his usual pre-church tantrum, and ran to Sapphie's house.

I couldn't keep still while trying to explain that I needed to leave a homework assignment for Sapphie. I held my arms, then my hands, then held my hands behind my back.

"Because we're in different schools, I need to check with her homework book to see which type of homework she needed to have, because it might be different to the homework in my homework book..."

At that point, Sapphie's dad walked back to the sofa and spoke as if throwing his words over his shoulder, "You know where her room is."

I kind of walked/jogged up the stairs as I was in a rush but didn't want to arouse suspicion. Sapphie and her siblings all had their own rooms. First was the youngest, her little sister, then her younger brother and then I reached Sapphie's bedroom. I nudged the door ajar. The scent of her was so strong that I stopped in my stride. "She's here!" my instincts cried and my heart pumped like a pneumatic drill wholly unprepared for this possible scenario. To my disappointment though, she wasn't.

My eyes darted left to right scanning her entire room, looking for her collection of books. There were tons stacked on two shelves and her windowsill. But there was one in particular I wanted, the one she'd been reading for the last few days. I couldn't see it anywhere amongst her collection or on her desk, so I bravely ventured into her school bag. Apart from her schoolbooks, lipgloss and a bottle of body spray, I found what I thought was a box of enormous padded plasters but nothing else. Then I spotted the tattered paperback I was looking for on her little bedside nightstand.

"Jane Eyre."

She had an old-fashioned leather bookmark three-quarters of the way in. I took the neatly folded A4 sheet of paper I had stored in my inside jacket pocket and placed it behind the leather strip with meticulous care. I closed the book, holding it with both hands, partly in accomplishment and partly hoping the depth of my intention would somehow transfuse through my pores, into the book, onto my note and translate to her just how I felt.

I descended the stairs like a terrorist, feeling like I'd done something wrong.

"Come on!" Sapphie's dad shouted.

I jumped, thinking he was talking to me. But his eyes were glued to the TV.

I shot out a quick and polite goodbye, and then ran home, stopping several times, wondering if I could go back and get the note before my parents realised I wasn't in bed. But I didn't go back, I assured myself of what I believed and squashed my remaining doubt with the weight of hope. Throughout the day that weight grew and its power intensified. It held me down when we returned home and I expected to find her waiting at the door. It kept me strong while I struggled through dinner and listened out for the doorbell. And it proved its worth when I heard the tiny rattle of small stones against my bedroom window. I looked outside and saw Sapphie in her nightclothes and coat waving me down.

It was dark but I was undeterred.

I snuck out without anyone noticing.

"I feel like walking." Her words were soft.

The air was cool but I felt a warm current beneath the breeze. There were no cars, no other people – no nocturnal activity at all. Instead, there was a stillness that hung around us, which only a gentle wind broke, reminding me that time hadn't stopped. Her smile made the silence cosy. I was filled with the sense that fate had conjured these ingredients in just the right amounts to create this perfect moment just for us. I felt we were strolling into love.

"I got your note." Now her smile made her words sweet.

"I know," I replied with soft omniscience.

She paused before continuing.

"You know, Joseph," she began, as she had done every day since I could remember, "you know I don't love you, don't you?"

It came like a painless stab to the chest. I knew I had been stabbed, but I just couldn't feel it. The knife stood protruding out of my chest as I continued to stroll on, looking down at it inquisitive, curious as to what it was doing there.

"I don't understand."

"You are the dearest person to me and I love you as much as I love my parents, but I'm not *in* love with you, and I don't think you are with me. I mean, I know you love me, but you don't *love* me love me."

I kind of poked at the knife now, with the dumbfounded naivety that a child has poking at jelly in his bowl for the first time, unsure of what to do with this confusing new substance presented before him.

"I don't know what you mean, 'I'm in love with you but I'm not and you love me but you're not in love with me'?"

"That's right."

"So you do love me?"

"Of course I do."

Now I looked at the knife indignant, wondering why it was there at all.

"Then why did you say that you don't love me?" I replied with a confused laugh.

I pulled the knife out and threw it behind me as if it were a crisp packet that had blown onto my chest and stuck there unwarranted.

"Because when you kissed me... I didn't feel anything. Well, the only thing I felt was that it was a bit weird – like kissing my brother."

Blood flowed from the open wound the knife had left. I went weak, numb; my energy fled me like a steady leak.

"Not weird, I don't mean weird," she started, "just not right. Friends aren't supposed to kiss like that, and that's what we are, Joseph, we're friends; best friends." I know I slowed almost to a halt because she was standing in front of me. "I think you're just confusing the love we have."

"But how? I mean, I want to be with you and live with you and spend all my time with you and... I wanted to kiss you; I've wanted to kiss you for ages. It felt right and normal... it... it felt natural to want to kiss you... I want to kiss you now, Sapphie."

"But I don't want you to, Joseph."

Finally, the pain arrived. Now it made sense. It was almost overwhelming. It kind of scooped everything out of me, including my breath. And then that vacancy was filled with hurt, upset and anger. The latter must've flashed across my face as Sapphire apologised, saying that she needed to get back. She walked the rest of the way by herself.

I was two minutes away from my house, but somehow, I didn't reach my front door until the moon was high in the sky and over an hour had passed.

Some Days Just *Have* to be Mondays

With two nights of no sleep, it was no surprise that I got detention for not concentrating in class. Being forced to stay late took the decision of whether or not to meet Sapphire after school out of my hands. But then at home, that relief was short-lived. I started to feel bad, wondering if she had stood there waiting for me, in the cold, alone, hoping that I would arrive, armed with one of my "quirky observations" to defuse the tension and allow us to carry on as usual, as if that weekend had never happened. Then the sting of rejection returned.

"I hope she did wait." I said to myself, walking home under a bronze sky. "I hope she waited for a whole hour and caught a cold waiting and went home and got into trouble and went to bed and felt bad, felt really bad about what she said and she's sitting there now, right now, thinking about how she can take it all back, just go back and not say anything..." my emotions impeded my speech so I continued in thought.

...not say a word, just kiss me and let me hug her and hold her. Then she could speak, then she would say that she loves me more than anyone, even more than her family. That she loves me the most and she doesn't need anyone else, she doesn't want anyone

else. That she loves me so bad, so bad that it hurts, it hurts her deep inside, it aches when she isn't with me 'cause she just wants to be with me all the time. She would want me that bad, she would want me and she would love me more than anyone else does, I would be the number one person in her life, I would be first to have her attention, to have all of her attention, and I would give her anything that she wanted. I would make sure that she had everything, I would make sure that she was happy, I would make her happy and she would love me... she was supposed to love me... she was supposed to make it all make sense.

A small void opened up inside me. It felt as though it had swallowed part of my soul.

On Wednesday she came round to my house. When I heard her voice my heart beat so fast I almost vomited. I heard my mum walking up the stairs. My skin started to burn. She called my name. I couldn't breathe. She approached my door and I flung myself onto my bed and threw the covers over me.

"Joseph. Joseph."

I froze.

"Joseph, Sapphire is here to see you."

I don't know why but my eyes began to water. I wasn't sad so it didn't make sense.

"Joseph!"

Then the feet walked away with the sweeping sound of a huff. I heard my mum explain that I was asleep and must be coming down with something as I had been coming *straight* home from school and going *straight* to bed. My little brother interjected, I imagined he was dancing around as he sang, "Joe's got AIDS, Joe's got AIDS, he can't see his girlfriend 'cause Joe's got AIDS."

Sapphire thanked my mum and left.

The following night I ignored the pitter-patter of pebbles against my window. As they rang against the glass, I ran through my mind how the conversation would go, but each time I failed to get past her saying "You know, Joseph..."

As the end of the week arrived, I missed Sapphire more than I was angry with her, more than I was sad about her rejection of me and I also felt a bit guilty for ignoring her. But still, I couldn't face talking about what had happened. So, after school that Friday, I ran to the gates of St Barnabas Catholic School for Girls and greeted Sapphie with, "Have you ever noticed that 'saint' and 'street' have the same abbreviation? If you saw it written down you might get confused, but then it would read 'Street Barnabas' which is a little weird... plus I don't think there would be many 'Barnabas Catholic School for Girls Streets' even if it were the other way round."

In an instant she understood, she told me this with her smile – that all-knowing, all appreciating, all understanding smile of hers.

"I almost missed meeting you today, I was supposed to have detention for pointing out that Christmas used to be outlawed in this country because it's pagan," she explained.

"My English teacher told us that Ronald Reagan was a racist," I replied.

"Reagan – Pagan?"

"You got it in one!"

And just like that, it was like the weekend had never happened.

<u>The Week After Getting My Glasses</u> - (Stephanie Zinone)

Every so often I would catch the HR Rep looking over at me, and every so often she would catch me doing the same; each time ended with a smile and a brief blush from us both. She was tall, had ridiculously straight teeth, and such a winning smile I wondered if Colgate might kidnap her; she wore it all day with ease, and you never got bored of seeing it. I'd been meaning to ask her if she wanted to get lunch one weekend – I didn't want it to be during the week because then everyone at work would know and make jokes and I thought of Joanie and Chachi on the set of *Happy Days* pretending that no one knew they were dating off-screen but knowing that everyone knew and having to keep up the pretence anyway. But because I'd been with Aaron on the weekends, I hadn't had a chance to ask.

That Tuesday, however, I was in the stationery cupboard trying to find white envelopes with no window and overheard her arranging a date for the coming weekend. There was no real reason for this to bother me, but it really did.

Strolling out to the shops to pick up some biscuits for the office kitchen, I was wondering why I hadn't asked her out earlier and if she was just humouring me with her looks and if she'd been with this guy all along.

On my way back with a packet of Jammy Dodgers, I saw a woman who, despite the weather, made me think I was 'California Dreaming'. She must've been mid-twenties, with cheek-length blonde hair that fell like leaves on a palm tree. She was dressed in that kind of trendy way that you wanted to stop and applaud. And she had these eyes, these cat's eyes that were both dangerous and sensual. I instantly thought:

Michelle Pfeiffer – Grease 2 (a great film; I don't care what anybody says).

We shared the same side of the pavement, me going up towards Liverpool Street, she going down towards St Paul's. As Stephanie Zinone approached, she sized me up with one glance – she took in my ungroomed hair, the luggage under my eyes, my scuffed faux-leather shoes, my trousers that hung a little too baggy, the self-made extra hole punched in my belt, my 85 percent polyester shirt, my nails bitten to the nub and hands too small for a grown man. She weighed me up and found me wanting. Yet, I smiled. She smiled back and even said "Hi" as I passed her by.

In an instant, I stopped worrying about the HR Rep. That smile just then, it validated me. Not the one she gave, but the one I gave her. I wasn't overcome with nerves, a sweat attack or crazy eyes that would look everywhere other than at her. I didn't need her smile. My smile was for me. I thought back to the girl on the train with the shaved head and piercings, and I remembered her smile. As much as it touched me, it was for her; that was her light shining.

Despite the frosted car roofs, dark clouds and even darker skies, my light shone that day and I couldn't wait to tell Aaron all about it.

That Weekend - (1 for every 5)

Aaron had brightened up a fair bit since his dad's visit. I'd been thinking of what more I could do to cheer him up and was thinking about buying him a few classic Gameboy games or a console made in this century. Then one evening, without any obvious prompt, he stated, "We spend a lot of time indoors."

The next day I picked up a half-price football. Neither of us really followed the Premiership, but if there were something big like a Cup Final or the World Cup on TV, we would give it a watch. That Saturday afternoon, we dressed warm, took the football, a pre-diluted bottle of orange squash and a portable radio down to the park. I got Aaron to tune the radio into one of the sports stations and we had the early afternoon game between Liverpool and Manchester United playing in the background for atmosphere. We used our coats as goalposts (well, my coat and Aaron's jumper; he didn't want to put his favourite jacket on the floor) and had a good old-fashioned kickaround. Aaron pretended he was Man U, as that's where his Grandma Doreen lived, and I was Liverpool because my mum had had a thing for John Barnes.

We were worn out after fifteen minutes.

As we sat on our coats, drinking juice, and catching our breath, two Saturday league teams turned up and prepared for a game just a stone's throw from where we were. As we approached them, the smell of damp grass mixed with Deep Heat and unwashed football kits collided with creative swear words, hoarse laughter, and pre-match cigarettes, making for something that felt so absolutely British.

We chose to support the team in blue, cheering every time they made a good play and booing every time the ref gave a decision against them (booing is so much fun). Aaron was on his feet jumping up and down every time a shot was taken or a free-kick given. A burst of energy took him rushing up and down the side-lines chasing the flow of the game. He screamed "Come on you Blues!" at every opportunity and suddenly adopted a cockney accent when he chose to reprimand the referee.

"Oi ref, ya 'avin' a laugh ain't ya...Flip me, someone needs to go to Specsavers!"

He had the substitutes cracking up and even the managers were having a chuckle. It was like seeing a new side to him, bounding with energy and confidence, happy to be the centre of attention.

One of our players fell to the ground injured from a bad tackle. I jumped to my feet and joined Aaron in leery protest. We were lovin' it!

There's no way I would've been able to afford tickets to a Premiership game, but then I'm sure there's no way Aaron would've had this much fun.

We got back home, sweaty, muddy and hungry. I put some chips and chicken burgers in the oven. Aaron drank a pint of milk.

"I feel like listening to music," he said.

"You know what, that's not a bad idea. What should we play?"

"I don't know. What do you like?"

"Ah, now this may surprise you, but in my younger days I was quite the Drum & Bass fan."

"What's Drum & Bass?"

"Oh, now you've got me started." I went over to my unpacked boxes and started rifling through them for my old cassette tapes.

There was a knock on the door. It was Aaron's mum. We hadn't seen much of her that week. Some mornings we would knock on her door and receive no reply and I would take Aaron to school, but last week this happened more than usual.

Aaron led her into the flat by the hand telling her about our front row seat to the game of the year.

"It was 3–3, the ref had given two minutes extra time, and we had a free-kick. It was about thirty yards out, wasn't it Joseph?" he called to me.

"Maybe even thirty-five," I called back from my room.

"Thirty-five yards out, Mum. And I tell ya what, he bent it like Beckham, right into that top corner."

"Really?"

I could hear her smile in her reply.

She explained that his grandmother was on the phone and wanted to talk to him.

Aaron yelled out, "I'll be back in a minute," and closed the door behind him.

I found my old Notorious B.I.G. double album. I put that to one side for when Aaron was out, laughed at the cover of the Fatboy Slim album with the obese American kid wearing a T-Shirt saying "I'm #1 so why try harder", and under that found my collection of Jungle Drum & Bass mix-tapes. I grabbed them all and amidst the pile, a photograph fell out. It was a picture of my brother and me. On the back, all that was written were numbers '6' and '8'.

He was a cute kid. He would've loved the kickaround we'd just had, and knowing him, he would've talked his way into coming on as a substitute for the Blues and scoring the winner. For the first time in a long time, I really missed him.

When Aaron returned with his mum in tow, they found my front door vibrating with the bass delivered by UK Apache's big hit "Original Nuttah." I opened up with both hands in the air, head down, bouncing on my tiptoes as the chorus' bass-line kicked in, and I went mad!

Aaron, caught up in the spirit, joined in jumping around waving his hands and repeating the chorus in his newfound East End accent: "mi ah di nuttah, original madmah madmah mad nuttah!"

Aaron's mum stood at the door, chuckling at her son and nodding to the beat. When I realised she was still there I stepped closer to the door.

"I just wanted to say sorry for not being around as much," she shouted over the music. "Things have been a bit up and down."

"That's fine. I'm happy to have him here."

Looking down at her son throwing himself around the room she replied, "He's happy here too." A flash of sadness fell over her features.

"Why don't you come in and join us? We've got chips, chicken burgers, this party could go on all night."

"No, you're all right. I've got to head off anyway."

"You sure?"

She smiled and nodded, but lingered as she left, watching her son and then glancing back at me.

When we had danced until I pulled my hamstring and Aaron dropped to the floor with cramp in both legs, we crashed on the sofa with our meal, a bottle of ketchup and whatever was on the TV.

"How was your grandmother?" I asked.

He spoke of her with fondness, and mentioned that she wanted to come and visit next weekend, but that his mum didn't want her to.

"And Joseph, I didn't want to lie, but my mum said that I can't tell Grandma Doreen about you, or me staying here."

"If that's what your mum told you then it's okay."

We slept right through to the afternoon that Sunday. Following a Beef Biryani and Chicken Korma takeaway for dinner that evening, Aaron's attention went from the television to pulling faces, to flicking his lips, to blowing bubbles with his saliva, before he asked if we could read instead.

I got him to read one paragraph for every five that I read. He lacked confidence and needed a lot of help, but he wasn't that bad at reading. I had researched on Google and found that one in five children have a language-based learning difficulty, but that with the right support that difficulty wouldn't hold them back.

We were on the chapter about Abraham and had just read the part that said God would bless Abraham to have more children than the stars of the heavens. Aaron looked up at me as if to say "big deal".

"It's saying how big Abraham's family would be. God told him to look up to the sky at night, at all the stars that he could see, and that his family would be even more than all of those stars."

Aaron's expression looked even less impressed.

"Okay, when you look up at the sky how many stars do you see?"

"One or two. Sometimes more but they keep moving or you get the ones that flash."

"Aaron, those aren't stars."

"Yeah they are, look."

He jumped up and ran over to the window, drawing back the curtains.

"There's one moving now," he pointed out. "That's the only one I can see, the others must've gone."

I reached the window and placed a hand on his shoulder.

"Aaron, that's the light from a plane flying really high."

"Planes fly that high?"

"Yeah. And the lights that stay still and flash are satellites out in space that beam down TV shows for us to watch."

"Aaahh." He looked up in awe. "So which ones are the stars then?"

"Well…" I looked up and scanned the sky. "I can't seem to see any at the moment."

"See, I told you, they're gone."

"Stars don't move, Master Aaron, it's just that the sky isn't very clear tonight so that we can't see them."

He pressed his face against the window, trying to see through the clouds.

"It looks the same as always to me."

I turned to him. "Apart from the lights that flash and the ones that move, have you ever seen a light that just stayed still and shone or kind of twinkled, you know, like 'a diamond in the sky'?"

He shook his head, unmoved by his admission.

We returned to the book but he fell asleep before we finished the chapter. I struggled to get to sleep – which hadn't been much of an issue for weeks – I felt troubled, a little disturbed. To me, being a kid and not seeing a star was like saying that you've never had any friends or never tasted chocolate. There was a gift out there that we have all been given, but through no fault of his own, he had been denied.

The Next Day – (The best-est)

His jaw dropped, and his little arms went waving behind him when he found me waiting outside his school the next day. He didn't ask why I was there, he was just happy.

He started telling me about how Mr Donner almost swore when he spilled coffee on his crotch, but when all the kids couldn't stop laughing, he called them little... then Aaron stopped, noticing that he was walking alone. He looked back to see me standing by a car. His look of confusion turned to one of surprise when he saw the lights flash and locks pop open as I pressed the key.

"You bought a car?" he said rushing over.

"Nah, just rented it for the day."

"Oh."

"But I've got a surprise for you, though?"

"What is it, what is it?" His face beamed as we jumped inside.

"We're going on a road trip, and tonight you are going to see your first star."

He didn't ask where we were going or how many stars we would see. Instead, he sat and examined every inch of the car his eyes could take in. We drove off past all of the school kids and their parents.

"This is the new Astra, isn't it?" he asked while setting the climate control.

"Yeah. How did you know that?"

"I like cars."

"You never mentioned this before."

"We've never been in a car before," he said locating all of the hidden compartments. "My dad's good with cars. My mum says that's the only thing he's good with."

"Okay."

"I guess that's where I get it from. Mum lets me look at the car magazines when we're at the dentist. He's always saying that I eat too many sweets but always has loads of lollipops that you can take for free."

"Have you ever worked with your dad on cars before?"

"Nah." Aaron moved on to adjusting the seat recliner. "I've only ever seen him three times." He spoke as if he were talking about the neighbour who lived between us.

"Three times?"

"Maybe more... when I was a baby, but I don't remember."

"What's your favourite car?"

He stopped fiddling and fell back in his seat, his open-mouthed grin revealing several fillings. "The BMW number 4 co... cop-e? C-o-u-p-e."

"Coupe."

"Ah, that's how you say it." He started tuning in the radio.

"I don't know much about cars but... we could learn about them together. If you like?"

On finding a radio station, *Spandau Ballet's – Gold* was playing, he turned to me for the first time all journey. "Do you like cars too?"

"Not really, but with your help I'm sure I will."

"Sounds like a plan, Batman."

"That's what's poppin', Robin."

"Hey..."

"I've been waiting ages to drop that one."

"I'm going to use that tomorrow on Nicky Peters."

"Hey, reach in the back seat there. I've got us some packed lunch."

He pulled the seat adjuster and flew backwards. "Wooooo!"

Mid-chew of the ham, cheese, pickled onion and crisp sandwiches I'd made while he was asleep that morning (I was very proud to announce that they were handmade and had my signature ingredient – prawn cocktail crisps), Aaron asked, "So how many stars will we see when we get there? And where are we going again?"

"We're going to Cambridge, the sky's quite clear up that way. We should see at least one or two stars." He was content with that and I smiled with mischievous glee. "The last time I came here, my mum was taking us out for the day. We went shopping and stuff, ate ice cream and then she saw that the university was performing the play *The Importance of Being Earnest*. She bought us popcorn and a few tickets and I remember being surprised that the play was done outdoors, in the college gardens."

"Did it rain?"

"No, the weather was perfect." I think he was disappointed; and thinking about it, the idea of the play being called off and my brother and I running around the garden in the rain did sound like a lot of fun. "My brother and I didn't really get the jokes so we just ate our popcorn and watched the bees hopping from flower to flower. But I can't ever remember my mum laughing so much."

I felt Aaron's gaze on me, his attention now caught, yearning to hear more.

"She was never the type to really laugh out loud that much, she didn't like drawing attention to herself in that way, but during the play she laughed until she cried. She was louder than anyone else but didn't care. We stopped watching the bees and just watched her as she covered her mouth trying in vain to hold in the laughter. When the play was over, because my brother and I were so well behaved, she took us to a sweet shop, but this was one of those proper old-fashioned ones where they weighed the sweets you were buying on a scale. I would get strawberry bonbons and my brother would get the lemon ones; he was always a bit crazy like that, he loved the sour sweets that made his tongue tingle and face screw up. Then she let us run around in the park by the canal chasing ducks. She just sat on a bench watching us, still smiling from the play. It was a good day; a really good day."

"Was it your best day, though?"

"How do you mean?"

"Was it your best-est day... ever, like... like you were soooo happy but like I mean the most happiest you've ever been?"

"I don't know. I suppose I've never..."

"I know mine." He smiled with that bound excitement of someone who asked a specific question with the sole intention of you returning the query, so they could tell you their answer. At uni, it irritated the daylights out of me when people did this, but with Aaron, it was a special kind of cute and I was almost as excited to hear his answer as he was to tell it.

"Well, it was when I was like six and it was the summer holidays. We all stayed round my mum's cousin's house, and I mean all of us, me, my mum, Grandma Doreen, my great aunt and uncle from America and my two cousins from my other great aunt but she didn't come and their dad just dropped them off. They lived with their dad and spent the holidays with their mum. Nobody likes their mum, though," he whispered. "I thought she was okay but Gran would leave the room if someone talked about her. I never talked about her and neither did my cousins, we just used to talk about computer games all night. They would bring their PlayStation with them and we would play it all day and talk about what games we would play tomorrow at night. Three of us shared the blow-up bed. It was fun. I didn't wet the bed anymore so I didn't have to sleep by myself. We would play tug of war with the duvet because everyone wanted more covers. That was a lot of fun too."

"So, the whole of the summer was your happiest time?"

"No," he said, critical of my impatience. "We only stayed there for a week 'cause my mum's cousins were moving to America. But on the Sunday, we were all together in the living room eating chicken and roast potatoes and my gran made the best Yorkshire puddings ever and we were watching *Home Alone.* The living room was packed and us kids had to sit on the floor and everybody was laughing and my mum was laughing and I was sitting at her feet and I was allowed a big cup of fizzy drink and I didn't spill it and then when they came home from the holiday in the film and found him safe and everyone was happy that he was okay, my mum held my shoulders and I held her legs and then she picked me up and hugged me and just kept kissing the top of my head and nobody else was getting hugs and kisses, my cousins didn't have their mum there but I did. I went to get my cup of fizzy drink but my mum wouldn't let me go and I wasn't that thirsty so I stayed and watched the rest of the film through her arms. And then when it was bedtime my cousins had to go to bed even though they were older than me, but I got to stay up with my mum and all the grown-ups and watch films through her arms until I fell asleep."

I glanced down at Aaron; he seemed transfixed, lost in that memory and filled with its joy.

"That was the bestest day ever."

It was early evening by the time we arrived. The sky had a cosy glow and almost everyone we passed had a smile on their face. We walked through the town centre for a bit and stopped in a few bookshops and toyshops, but just to look, as I was broke till payday. We found the same old-fashioned sweet shop still there – the owner had retired but his daughter and her children had taken over; Aaron preferred the lemon bonbons – he had me cracking up as he exaggerated their taste by twisting his face, squeezing in his cheeks and making his eyes roll around.

We bought a couple of Cornish pasties and some hot drinks and sat inside and ate them as it was a bit chilly outdoors. When we finished, I wanted to take him over to the canal to see if there were any ducks to chase... then I stopped, noticing that *I* was walking alone. I looked back to see Aaron staring up at the night sky – I joined him. It looked like tiny diamonds had been sprinkled across a sheet of black velvet.

"You said one or two." Aaron didn't break his awe-struck stare to address me. I could see his eyes trying to take it all in, his face twitching with delight as the diamonds in the sky seemed to wink for him.

When we got home, we finished the chapter on Abraham with a new appreciation. I closed the book and Aaron sat there looking up at me, eyes wide with anticipation.

"Aaron..."

"Yeah...?"

"You look like you're waiting for me to say something."

"Yeah..."

"What?"

"I want to hear more about Sapphie." His grin was infectious. "Can I call her Sapphie, is that okay?'

I checked my watch, it was late but not too late, so I put the book down, tucked him in and began where I left off.

Fifteen Years Before - (What wasn't to be will be)

I stayed on at my school's sixth form, Sapphie went to college further away to do her A-Levels, but we stayed in contact. There was a pub around the corner from her campus that made it no secret they were happy to receive business from under-eighteens, so we would meet there often for lunch/dinner/a few too many pints. With each winter the pain in her joints increased and her arms would bruise easier and easier, yet her eyes grew brighter, her lips fuller and her femininity blossomed, producing that perfect mix of pretty, yet humble. I hated the first year of college and almost failed. My teachers made an exception with me and for the second year, I just put my head down and got on with it.

I tried not to be disappointed when she didn't seem to feel anything but humour when I went out on my first date with a girl from my English class. In the end, I guess Sapphie was right to laugh. The girl was nice, in that "plain Jane" sort of way (is that phrase a reference to Jane Eyre?), and was... frontally well endowed... so to speak, but suffered with that nervous readiness to outdo you in conversation – always attempting to finish my sentences and repeat my comments as if they were her own. I would say, "There's such a difference between African and Western culture," and she would reply, "The dichotomy between the two cultures is incredible."

Or I would say, "That's nice," and she would respond with, "That's beautiful."

"Isn't that sad?"

"It's such a catastrophe."

If I complimented her on how good she looked she would contrive bashfulness and proceed to detail the process of her wardrobe and make-up choices.

Towards the end of the date, I commented on her competitiveness and she responded as if I'd called her that horrid four-letter word that women hate more than herpes.

Apart from her "aesthetical features" swaying my decision, I later realised that I'd only asked this girl out to see how Sapphie would respond; it was a while after we broke up that I realised they both had the same dark shade of hair, were the same height and had similar chiselled features; only their eyes were different. And as luck would have it, Sapphie knew the girl and laughed heartily at my choice. There was no spite or bitterness in her mocking; I took their absence as notification that it didn't bother her at all.

It was coming up to the Easter break in our second year of A-Level studies when the faeces truly hit the fan – for Sapphire that is.

She was upstairs studying when she heard the front door slam shut and her father scream her mum's name. Sapphie heard the steady footsteps make their way down and a violent argument erupt. All three siblings gathered in Sapphie's room, too scared to be alone and too scared to watch. Sapphie said that she held the house phone in her hand ready to dial 999, but all the physical violence seemed to be coming from her mum – her father only armed himself with bad language.

As soon as they heard glass smashing Sapphie dialled. Then they heard their father leave the house followed by another glass object smashing against the front door. Then silence.

"What's your emergency, please?"

"Um... I'm not sure. I'll call you back," Sapphire had told the operator.

She crept out of her room, her siblings in her shadow. They all looked downstairs and saw their mum, physically unhurt, cleaning up the mess it seemed that she had made.

"Don't come downstairs without your shoes on," she ordered. Her mum continued the evening as though the two glass vases had annoyingly smashed themselves.

Two days went by without any mention of their father. On the third day, Sapphire approached her mum,

"When's dad coming home?"

She replied that he had a drinking problem, one he'd had for some time, and that as soon as it was resolved he would be back. Sapphie's mum made no real attempt to mask her lies when questioned; her father at least tried. It ended up being my aunty who became the source of truth. I overheard her talking to a friend on the cordless house phone while in the bath.

Since her father left, Sapphie had been spending more and more time with me – confused, perturbed, sad and vulnerable. Because of her state, I didn't want to be the one to tell her what had happened.

She came round that night with a bottle of white wine and red eyes. I'd finally got my own room as my dad and my aunty gave in to my protest that we never had guests.

We sat side by side on the edge of my bed, the bottle resting in between her legs. "I need to know, Joseph. Their lies are killing me. I want my father to come home, but I need to know why he left. The thing is... it's the not knowing that's driving me crazy. I stay up all night thinking the worst things and then get angry with him and then have to tell myself that I can't do that because I don't know what he's done... if he's even done anything at all."

Exasperated, her head fell into my lap. The open wine bottle toppled over, but only a little of its half-empty contents escaped. She looked up at me, her eyes wide and bloodshot like finely decorated marble orbs. She stared through me without blinking. Then those orbs glistened as a thin film of water rose over them.

"I know what happened," I said.

Her eyes refocused, she rose and with a blink, the tears receded.

"Tell me."

"I overheard my aunty talking..." I started. Sapphie held my face with a soft firmness and cut me short with a whisper.

"Tell me!"

"Mrs Welton, who goes to your church..."

"Dad no..."

"She found out that your mum and her husband were having an affair and... she told your dad."

A surprised look of relief loosened the tension in her face.

"Okay..." She sounded lost in her comprehension.

She stared off, that big brain of hers contemplating not just something, but everything. I waited in silence, trying to guess how she would react so that I would know what to say and how to say it.

"Thank you." As the words still hung on her breath, she kissed me. It was a kiss on the lips like a mother would give a child – or a friend to a friend. She inhaled on seeing me smile, and then seemed to just shake off her sadness with immediate effect.

"I'll call you tomorrow." And with that, she left.

I sat on my bed feeling that that kiss confirmed that we were friends and nothing else. But as her scent lingered and filled my senses, I yearned towards a hope of us being so much more.

There was a light tapping on my window that night, the former guestroom was downstairs. Sapphie was outside in just her nightclothes. I opened the window, and before I could speak, she was making her way inside.

"I can't believe it's so chilly in April," she commented.

I didn't know what to say or expect. She closed the window and turned towards me.

"I felt cold at home," she continued. "Can I sleep here?"

"Yeah, of course." I kind of stumbled over my words, still half asleep and trying to make sense of what was happening. "I'll just grab one of the pillows and sleep on the floor."

I already had a pillow in my hand when she stopped me.

"Can we not lie side by side? I... I don't want to sleep alone."

"Oh," I started, "yeah, erm... okay," I said with a surprised smile.

She's just a friend, she's just a friend, I kept telling myself as we both got under the duvet.

"Thanks again, Joseph." This time her words were followed with a kiss on the forehead, before she rolled over and had her back facing me.

I lay there still thinking: *She's just a friend, she's just a friend,* but feeling something completely different.

For some unknown reason, I felt a duty to wait until she had fallen asleep before I could consider doing the same. I was dozing off, with my back to her, when I felt Sapphie roll over and her nose nestle between my shoulder blades. I could feel her small hands, balled up, against the curve of my ribs and her knees brush the tail of my spine, as though she were lying in the foetal position, snug in the arch of my back.

My alarm woke me; she was dead to the world. Strands of her hair fallen across her freckles, her cheeks puffy, her lips ajar with a droplet of dribble at their corner; it felt criminal to disturb her.

"Sapphie, Sapphie..." I whispered.

She stirred, her eyes opening.

Her dream must've been sweet.

"What's the time?" she asked.

"Seven."

"Okay." Her eyes closed, her smile remained.

"Sapphie, my dad will be up soon, and so will your mum."

She drew in a deep breath, trying to savour her last moments of slumber. She opened one eye.

"Can I borrow a jumper to wear home?"

"Sure." I got up and went into my wardrobe taking out my favourite hoody. She thanked me again, but with no kiss this time. Watching her climb through the window, I stood, my arms feeling empty, my mind feeling that there was something symbolic in her sneaking in and out and something significant about the passive role I played. Once outside, she flung the hood over her head and walked off, causing the same uncertainty she'd instigated on arrival.

That night she returned, wearing my jumper, but took it off once she got under the covers; she had her nightclothes on underneath.

Every evening she came, every morning she left, and throughout every night she drew closer and closer. On the eighth night she got into my bed and hugged me straight away, saying, "Goodnight" before I had a chance to respond. I rested my cheek on the top of her head and I believe we gave in to slumber at the same time. That felt nice.

Two nights later, we were lying on our sides facing each other, still dressed in our college clothes and close enough that I could feel her breath. She was telling me how the separation had been affecting her little sister more than her little brother. I spoke, interrupting her, without a single thought of what I was about to say.

"I never stopped loving you."

Her face froze.

"And I know you'll say I'm wrong and that you don't love me. But I'm right, and you do love me and you always will, and one day I'm going to marry you and I'll make you feel safe and loved every single day of your life."

She stared back at me, her mind teetering on the thin rope of indecision.

"Tell me I'm wrong," I softly demanded.

Her lips moved.

"Tell me you don't need me."

Her lower lip quivered.

"Tell me you don't love me."

In reply, her lips pressed together as she answered with her silence.

We both allowed that silence to linger. I waited for her to see sense and reprimand me. She waited for me to do something – so I did.

I unbuttoned my shirt.

I took it off and returned her voiceless stare.

She unbuttoned her shirt.

She took it off and stared back with anxious eyes.

Next my jeans, and her skirt.

I pulled the duvet over the both of us.

A silent moment passed.

She drew near to me; I felt her nervousness.

I held her close to me.

My eyes swallowing her whole, without effort.

She raised her cheek to mine.

Lightly, she brushed my face with slow rhythmic strokes.

She relaxed in my arms.

She felt gentle and fragile; her lips parted.

Her brown skin glowed with heat.

I felt her heart pulse softly against my chest.

She pressed closer, closer.

Her breath blew warm caresses against my cheek.

She continued closer.

Her heart beat faster as every breath quickened.

Closer still she pressed.

She kissed me; kissed with such soft intense passion.

I knew straight away, without the need of a second thought, that this was a mistake, but my conviction, though sure, was impotent.

Realising afterwards that I didn't love her was the shock of my life.

Telling her, afterwards, that I didn't love her was the worst thing that I have ever done.

There's wrong, and there's wrong, and then there's this.

<u>Fifteen Plus Years on & Two Weeks with My Glasses</u> - (Come dine with me)

I was walking home from the shops after popping in to get some Sunday evening Ben & Jerry's for Aaron and I, and grabbing up as many reduced food items as possible (shops knock the price off of food reaching its sale-by-date, this is how I survived uni). As I was on my Jack Jones, I strolled along bopping my head and mumbling the words to *Blur's - Country House*, it was playing in the chippie next door to the corner-shop and I couldn't get it out of my head. Aaron's mum had picked him up in the morning so he could help tidy their flat.

Since our road trip, I'd been thinking about what I could do to cut back on costs so that I could buy a car; just a little run-around so that we could take more drives outside of London; I sometimes forget I grew up outside the city and take for granted what a blessing that was.

We could do a different road trip every other weekend, because Aaron was right, we do spend too much time indoors. And then when the car gets a problem, we could work on it together; that would save us on maintenance costs too. But insurance won't be cheap because I haven't got a no-claims-bonus and if it's old then the road tax payments will be through the roof. I'll actually need more money. I could speak to my manager about a promotion; no one's filled Mac's old role yet.

I was stopped in my thoughts by a surprising sight.

Aaron and his mum were walking towards our block of flats hand in hand carrying a few shopping bags. She was smiling, and even broke out into laughter as they strolled. The joy she expressed brightened her face in an incredible way, making her prettier, almost beautiful, and that glow was reflected in Aaron as he bounced along looking happier than I'd ever seen him before. The joy I found in his happiness drowned the touch of jealousy I felt. She let go of his hand and in a playful burst of energy dragged him into her side, burying his head in the soft fabric of her overcoat. He giggled as they continued towards the building. Then she noticed me.

"Joe." She beckoned me over.

With clumsy steps, I dodged the traffic dividing us and approached them. Her face looked fresh, and for the first time I noticed that her left cheek dimpled when she smiled.

She glanced down to Aaron who was bouncing with excitement.

"Can I tell him? Can I tell him?" he asked.

"Go on," she replied.

"You are cordurally, cor…"

"Cor-dially," she enunciated.

"Cor-di-ally invited to our home for dinner tonight. Mr Joseph sir."

She gave him an approving nod. He stood taller on receiving it.

"I'm cooking steak," she said, her eyes rising to meet mine.

"I happily accept your invitation, Master Aaron," I replied.

"I told you he would. I told you. I'm doing the salad and the peas," he responded.

"Well, I've got dessert right here," I said.

"Perfect. Is about an hour okay?" she asked.

"Perfect."

"Okay, let's go, Mum, let's go, let's go." Aaron tugged at his mum's arm.

"We'll see you in about an hour then."

"Yep."

They entered the building and I followed behind with that awkwardness you get after saying goodbye to someone, and then realising that you're both going the same way.

With youthful ignorance of the awkwardness, Aaron bounded up the stairs towards their flat. My mind scoured its crevasses for conversation resurrectors. I was about to start complimenting Aaron's politeness when I noticed that she seemed perfectly comfortable walking up the stairs at a slow pace, while silence stood between us. I took a quiet deep breath and attempted to contrive "comfortability".

Sharing silence shouldn't be a scary experience.

But sometimes it was. I looked over at her and wondered what made her so confident. I noticed that she'd had her hair done; her roots now matched the rest, which seemed to have been trimmed.

But her confidence couldn't have just come from a trip to the hairdressers.

I didn't realise at the time, but the silence became less apparent as I contemplated the person behind the gentle stride.

<u>**That Evening**</u> – (It's funny how things turn out)

I knocked on their door an hour and fifteen minutes later; I assumed she would need the extra time. Aaron opened up and their small table was decorated with an appealing assortment of food. His mum gave me a mock reprimand, tapping her watch and raising her eyebrow. Aaron followed up on her gesture just to make sure it wasn't missed.

"You're late," he said.

"I'm really sorry."

"Come on, let's get started," she replied with a lightness I hadn't heard in her but which came across more natural than her usual brash tone.

She put my ice cream in the fridge and we sat down together around the table, and not the TV.

"So, Joe, Joseph, have you always lived in the city?"

"No," I started while chewing. I didn't want to break away from the meal – the steak was delicious. "I grew up in the country, my dad's still there, I moved down this way when I started university and never left."

"Oh, what did you study?"

"English for two years," I said with another mouthful. "Then I realised that it would only really qualify me to be an English teacher and I didn't want to spend more time at uni doing teacher training so I changed over and did business studies."

"Why business studies?"

I hadn't realised that inquisitiveness was hereditary.

"Well, that was the course everybody did when they didn't know what they wanted to do."

She smiled as if I had made an insightful quip about the pressure on youth due to the supposed necessity of a university degree. I played along and smiled as if I had.

"Did you study?" I asked.

"I took a law degree. I completed it but got side-tracked before starting my training with a firm." She sipped from her glass. "You look surprised."

I was. "No... I was just curious. You wanted to be a lawyer, then?"

"That was the plan. I wanted to work my way up to being a criminal defence Barrister. I loved the challenge. I wanted to see if I could free a guilty man with just my words."

"Wow. It sounds like you were pretty confident."

"A little." She glanced away bashful, her lips pursing together. Her lower lip was full-bodied while the top one was sharply curved. When she wasn't speaking, she wore a slight pout like she was about to blow a kiss.

As we moved on to dessert, I asked her about her school days but her answers were short and concealed. She told me that Aaron had been finding it difficult to make friends at school.

"I'm not good at sports. I like running around but I'm crap at football."

It felt inappropriate for me to reprimand him in front of his mum. "You were pretty good when we had our kick-around the other day."

"Yeah, but at school, I always get picked last. I can't dribble and I'm rubbish in goal – I'm scared of getting blasted in the face."

"Yeah, but it's not all about being good at sports, is it?" I stated.

"If you can't fight or play football then nobody cares. And I'm not smart enough to hang out with the nerdy kids."

I wanted to disagree but would've been lying if I did.

"I keep telling you, Aaron, loyalty goes a long way. Never grass up one of your schoolmates and cheer on your school team at football matches. They'll respect you, then they'll like you. To make friends you have to be friendly."

"But the school team are rubbish. I hate watching them play."

"More than you hate not having friends?" his mum retorted.

Aaron sulked into his ice cream.

"I'm going to have a glass of wine. Do you want a beer?" she asked.

"Yeah, that sounds good." I replied a little too greedily.

While alone at the table I told Aaron we'd practise over at the park. That didn't move him, so I told him about my plan to buy a car we could work on.

He was so surprised he whispered, "Really?"

"Yeah."

Something slight changed then, between us. It was in the kind of joy he received from what I was happy to give – I hadn't experienced anything like this since fighting sleep to stay up and hug my mum. Aaron was no longer just the kid next door.

When his mum returned, she let him drink the foam on the top of my beer, which he did with a little too much enthusiasm, and burped with the skill of a sailor.

He was soon sent to bed, both tired and reluctant. He kissed his mum on the lips and hugged me before leaving.

"I loved the last few years of school," she started, once Aaron had closed the door to their bedroom. "But a little too much, though."

I couldn't discern whether or not she was wearing make-up. Her skin and complexion looked clear and smooth but naturally so. The red wine disguised the fact that she wore no lipstick.

"How do you mean?" I replied.

"I was always getting into trouble." She took a long sip and continued. "My dad died when I was eleven. I loved him more than life. He was where I got my confidence from." Her head tilted to the side, her lips curling into a sad smile, hiding her dimple. "When I started secondary school my mind was all over the place. My dad didn't have any brothers, just younger sisters. I guess that's why he was so kind. Mum had a brother and a sister but they lived in America. I didn't have a male figure in my life anymore and I was struggling to cope. I used to get teased a lot by the other girls and the boys."

"Why?" I asked, too eager to let her pause.

"I was really skinny and flat-chested, until I turned fifteen." She smiled, looking embarrassed. I instinctively glanced down at her chest. She noticed but just continued as if she hadn't.

"To begin with, I hated going to school and I hated feeling so insecure. But I felt like I would be dishonouring my dad if I spoke to my mother about these things like I used to speak to him. So I didn't." I only realised that my glass of beer was empty when I reached for it.

She got up without a word and went over to the fridge.

Her skirt wasn't short. It stopped just above her knee. She walked with a light step, her legs were long and shapely.

"I'm out of beer." She already had the bottle of red in her hand.

"I'll join you with the wine then."

She brought the bottle over, poured two glasses and leaned back, crossing her legs.

"I went through a growth spurt when I was thirteen. I was the tallest in my form. I ran 100, 200 and 400 metres for my year and the year above. My bum got tighter, my legs got longer but my boobs went nowhere." She chuckled and then drank from her glass. I had almost finished mine. "The boys still didn't like me. Boobs are everything to a thirteen-year-old boy."

I smiled in agreement, like a thirteen-year-old boy.

"But my teachers weren't boys." She let her words linger for a moment, before placing her glass to her lips and emptying it.

She poured us both another round, her motions gliding through the silence. I didn't want to ask her what happened, I wanted her to dictate how the story progressed, just in case my prompting caused her to miss anything out.

"When I was fourteen, I slept with my history teacher. He played hard to get for months, but I finally wore him down."

The wine in my throat stopped moving as all my muscles paused. I wanted to avoid asking her to repeat herself so I played her words back in my mind to make sure I'd heard her correctly.

"*He* played hard to get for months, but *I* wore him down." I finally swallowed.

"He was a young widower. He doted on me with constant attention. He wanted to see me before school, after school and even on the weekends. He would hold me and talk to me for hours.

I loved it." Her lips pressed together into a full pout and her body moved as if invisible hands ran down her sides.

"One night, after a few months, we were lying on the rug in his front-room when he kissed the freckles on my nose and told me he loved me."

I leaned forward, my chin resting on my palm. "Did you love him?"

"I only realised when he said it, but a part of me always knew I didn't." She held her glass with just the tips of her fingers. The freckles on her nose were barely discernible; I had to stare for a moment to make them out.

"Two weeks later I was sleeping with my French teacher." For some reason, to me, him being French gave the scenario complete plausibility.

"He found every possible way under the sun to call me beautiful. He told me in different languages, using illustrations about flowers, fruits and all sorts. He introduced me to red wine and cigarettes." Her smile broke off into a chuckle as if saying, "how crazy were we?" "Every night I would sneak the cordless phone into my room and he would call me. He would tell me how much he wanted me, then I would ask him if he thought I was beautiful. His words would send me to sleep."

I assumed it was the wine that made my body temperature rise.

"But after a while, it wasn't enough. Our PE teacher was a notorious womaniser, but never showed any of the girls a shred of attention, including me. I remember it was a Thursday night, I was fifteen now. I turned up at his house; it was 9:30. I was supposed to be at a study night sleepover with Lucy Scott-Davis. He opened the door and was shocked to see me standing there. We stood in silence for a moment and then he stepped back and I walked in. He took a little longer than the others, but even the toughest men go weak when they're satisfied. He fought it for months, he wanted me to be first but it was easy for me to stick to my guns; he would say he only *wanted me*. I didn't respond. He said he'd never felt for someone like this before. I acted like he was boring me. 'I'm telling you I love you,' he finally admitted. I made sure that night was the best night of his life."

I was compelled to ask her how she accomplished that. But my smile made my thoughts transparent, and hers did the same.

"When I started college I... fully bloomed." She glanced down at her chest as she filled our glasses.

"What happened in college?" I asked, taking a mouthful of wine.

"I went wild! I targeted older students who were in relationships and teachers who were married. The boys proposed and the men wanted to leave their wives. Because the boys were not as discreet as the men, I got slapped by one angry girlfriend in the toilets during lunch. Then a few months later, just before we broke up for the summer holidays, I got beaten up by a gang of girls at the train station," she chuckled at the memory, "I'd only been with one of their boyfriends, the rest just hated me." Her eyes examined my body. "There's something different about you, your frame, your shoulders..."

"Oh... really?"

"Yeah," she replied leaning forward, concentrating on my chest.

"Well... Aaron and I have been doing push-ups for a while..."

"You look bigger."

I couldn't help my pride from swelling.

"So, err... what was it that you did to have all of these guys eating out of your hand like that?"

She sat silent, her slow deep smile acknowledging my question.

"Nothing makes a man feel like more of a man than when he's making a woman happy. Men are better fathers than they are husbands, because it's easier to make a child happy than it is a wife. What a man wants more than anything else is a woman who is easily pleased. I let a man feel like a man." The rim of her glass rested on the thickness of her lower lip, slowly parting her lips and opening her mouth with a moistened glow.

I lunged towards her. She let her glass fall to the carpet and drew in my embrace. I grasped the back of her neck, pressing my lips hard against hers. Her chair began to topple as my weight pressed her forward.

With strength I was unaware of, I scooped her out of her seat and cushioned our fall onto the thick carpeted below, and rolled on top of the wine-soaked material. She received every touch and kiss, regardless of how soft or rough, with increased ecstasy. I'd never known anything like it; I felt like Hercules amongst men.

In the Early Hours of Monday Morning

Partially covered by my shirt, she lay on her back, relaxed; one hand on her stomach, the other on her thigh; enveloped in a memory. My head in my palm, I rested on my side, tracing the outline of her face with my eyes, following the rise and fall of her brow, her nose, her lips. As if speaking to the ceiling, she explained how her mother found out about her behaviour when the wife of the college's media studies tutor turned up on their doorstep with her two young children and told both mother and daughter, in no uncertain terms, what she would do if her husband left her and their kids.

She shivered whenever I kissed her behind her ear. It distracted her so that she forgot what she was saying. I was filled with delight, amused by the power I possessed with her.

"You were talking about how your mother reacted."

"Oh yeah. She was disgusted. But that didn't stop me."

Like a seal swimming to the surface only to find it covered with ice, it seemed like a smile was about to rise on her face, but before it could form, the corners of her mouth fell into a quiet frown.

Her tone and flow of words sounded a lot more sober than they did when we had been sitting at the table. She told me that once her mother knew of her exploits, she just became more flagrant. It all came to a head when one night, during one of their frequent rows, her mother called her a whore.

"I called her a poor excuse for a wife." She produced a hollow smile. "Then she said the most unforgivable words she could've spoken. She said that, *for years*, I'd put my father up on a pedestal, making him out to be something he wasn't 'when the *truth* was he was a worthless, miserable, selfish...'" a flash of pain darkened her features and contorted her lips, leaving her unable to say the word, "...she said 'he only cared about himself and barely deserved a decent funeral'. I slapped her across the mouth, she slapped me back harder and I left the house that night. I knew what my father was and I knew what she was, so I never went back, until I had Aaron."

We lay silent for a moment. I read her need for a cigarette before she pointed to her handbag on the coffee table. I handed it to her and she took one out and a box of matches. Taking her first, long, deep pull, her chest swelled, her back arched, her eyes closed and with an exhale her whole body sank back into the carpet, looking more relieved than satisfied.

I smiled, thinking *"Who still uses matches?"* There was something in this small detail that infatuated me.

She stared up at the ceiling, her chest rising and falling slower and slower. The rhythm was calming. I felt sweet.

She rolled over to face me, her eyes taking in mine.

"You feel good, don't you?"

I leaned forward for my lips to answer her question. But she held me back, awaiting a verbal answer, her expression sombre, almost severe.

"I feel great," I reassured her.

I was about to ask how she felt, when she smiled. It was that peculiar kind of smile that made the recipient stop and think. Then I saw it, my own naivety reflected in her expression.

She kissed me on the tip of my nose and said,

"I'm glad I finally got to thank you."

She stood up, turned her back to me, and walked with brisk strides into her bedroom, switching off the front-room light and closing the door behind her.

I sat in the dark and went cold with realisation, remembering the last time she tried to "thank" me. A weightlessness filled my body; I felt empty.

How foolish. How foolish. My goodness. How foolish was I?

With skin still damp with sweat, I pulled my clothes on. My eyes struggled to find the front doorknob as I left. That sweetness I felt only moments before had become as bitter as wormwood.

It's funny how things turn out.

Tuesday Evening – (To be loyal)

I found Aaron sitting in the hallway in between the doors of our flats. I asked him why he hadn't called me to pick him up. He shrugged and I didn't chase a reply.

He was quiet all evening. A cloud of uncomfortable tension formed above us as the guilt I felt combined with the increased detachment he displayed. The cloud descended, darkened and developed into a small electric storm between us. I suffered a sharp shock every time I got too close.

Standing, looking over at him from the kitchen, a cup of tea in my hand, a Gameboy on silent in his, an ache began to grow in my stomach.

What on earth was I thinking? That's his mum. Joseph, you idiot!

I shook my head.

There are no excuses – it wasn't exactly a grey area. I just failed. All I had to do was not sleep with his mum. It seemed like a fool-proof plan, but my foolishness seems to be on some sort of non-stoppable superhero level. Or maybe I am just like his dad, and every other man who has passed through his life.

As I finished my cup and went to start on the growing pile of dishes in the sink, I told myself I was too old to be making such horrible mistakes with such ease, but more than that, I knew that Aaron deserved better, he deserved a better me.

As the evening and the silence wore on, Aaron's expression began to change. The storm cloud grew and pulsated, I felt I was about to be hit by a bolt, and I wondered if he had heard us – how could he have not – and if I should apologise and try to explain, or just apologise.

"I had a fight today," Aaron's words fell from him with a sullen thud. "It wasn't really a fight… I just got beat up."

The cloud shrunk and evaporated as I strode over and sat close to him, subtly checking him for cuts and bruises.

"What happened?"

"Nicky Peters, a boy in my class, he's into the same RPGs as me."

"Yeah..."

"We chat about games and stuff sometimes, he ain't good at football either." Aaron's foot kicked at an invisible object. His eyes refused to meet mine. "He asked me if I want to come round his to play the new Zelda game next week, his dad's getting it for him for his birthday on Saturday."

"Did you two get into an argument?"

Aaron screwed up his face and shook his head. "Nah... there's some guys in the older year that are in the same class as Nicky's brother Ricky."

I ignored the obvious joke to be made and kept listening.

"Ricky grassed up the boys in his class for having cigarettes because the whole class was going to get in trouble for it. The boys were looking for Ricky today to beat him up but Ricky bunked off today and me and Nicky were playing penny up by the fire exit...'"

"Penny up?"

He looked at me. "Yeah, you know… where you flick a coin up against the wall and whoever's coin is the closest wins all the money?"

"Oh, okay."

Aaron continued with more pace. "So, we were playing penny up and about five of them tried to rush him. I pushed the biggest one off him and pulled Nicky up and we ran to the headmistress's office and just stood outside her door until lunch was over and the boys had to go back to class."

"That was brave… and loyal. And like your mum said, that's how you make real friends."

Aaron continued as if I hadn't spoken, gesturing more and more as he went on. "At second break, I snuck out to the water fountain to get a quick drink. I kept looking out and then I saw two of them coming. I ran back to the door to run to my class but two more of them were coming through that door. Then Nicky came around the corner to warn me that the boys were coming. But when he saw them already there, he just ran away, and left me. They didn't bother to chase him, they just did me in. When I got back to class… Nicky didn't even talk to me." Aaron's eyes rose, searching my face for an answer.

I felt like I'd paused for too long. How could *I* talk about what a real friend should've done? How could *I* explain what loyalty was?

In the silence, he got up and went to bed. I was sure he was crying. But when I went into the room he was just lying there.

"Can you read to me?"

I didn't dare speak any words other than those written in his big yellow book. The story comforted him, it was about the young boy Samuel whom God had chosen to speak to and protect. He fell asleep as soon as the chapter ended.

<u>**Wednesday**</u> – (Slippery ground)

I almost slipped over three times on the way to work today; that black ice is serious stuff. The local authorities make no attempt to hide the fact that the less affluent parts of the city are always last to get their roads gritted, even though they're the most overpopulated. I had told Aaron to get his mum to buy him some winter boots; she'd said she'd look into it – I didn't feel ready to confront her, so I left it to them.

Aaron was hoping it would snow and settle. In his excitement at seeing a few icy showers he reminded me that "every single snowflake all over the world is absolutely different from every other one ever made ever before". That type of complexity is beyond me; much like women. I don't know whether it's because they're too complex for me to understand or whether in my fascination with them I choose to *believe* that they are.

Did she just want to get one over on me? Did she just want to display her power and expose my weakness, or did she just want to be touched by someone who cared, but no more than that? Maybe she just wanted attention or maybe she was testing herself and not me at all?

That time I wouldn't let her kiss me, she could've seen that as a rejection. It would've cut my confidence. Maybe she's more self-conscious than she lets on. But that doesn't explain why I consented; in fact, I made the first move! I wasn't feeling in need of attention from her. And when I think about it, it wasn't even her words that caught me, it was how she said them. It was the way she moved, the way she looked at me, it flattered my ego in a way mere compliments never could.

But what now?

Something bad, something wrong had taken place and my mind was so preoccupied with assigning blame to the act that I hadn't thought about what this meant moving forward. Do I confront her and tell her this can never happen again, do we speak to Aaron to find out if he heard what happened, 'cause goodness knows she wasn't quiet, but then neither was I?

You selfish, selfish... stay focussed Joseph. If he does know, how do we explain what happened? Wait, what if he's happy about it and wants this to happen – if he wants us to be together? Could I really see myself with Aaron's mum?

<u>Wednesday Afternoon</u> – (The dangers of black ice)

"Mum said that she would be here at 3:30 on the dot 'cause I've got to go to the dentists, but she didn't come."

"Okay, I'll leave work now. Wait inside the block, it's pretty cold out."

"Okay."

His money ran out in the pay phone before I could say goodbye. He didn't sound himself. A flash of his mum biting my lip shot through my mind like a round of friendly fire.

On my way to his school, I resolved to use the guilt I felt in a positive way; to let it heighten my resolve to do what I knew was right and be the kind of person Aaron could be proud of, the type of man in his life he deserved.

We were back in the flat for five minutes before there was a knock at the door. I was in the kitchen making a cup of tea, so Aaron answered.

"You better be ready to go or we're going to be late," she said.

I stayed in the kitchen and kept my back turned. I knew I wasn't ready to see her.

"I've just gotta use the toilet, Mum."

Use the toilet at the dentist.

I heard the toilet door close. Then I heard her footsteps near the kitchen.

I turned around, and as soon as I saw her, I felt ashamed. She, however, moved with an impenetrable air of authority that made me nervous. She stood at one end of the kitchen while I looked on from the other.

She didn't speak. The toilet door locked.

She approached me with a slow rhythmic swing in her stride.

"Why do you look so uncomfortable?"

"I'm not." Small balls of sweat speckled my nose.

"I think we should talk about what happened the other day."

I nodded, refusing to trust my lips and tongue to work in tandem. She picked up an empty *Stars Wars* mug from the side table - probably assuming it was her son's. She started her sentence still looking at it.

"So, how did it make you feel?" She waited a few seconds and then looked up at me from under her eyelashes.

Do what you know is right Joseph.

I looked over to the toilet with caution before answering in a low tone.

"Guilty. It was wrong or at very least inappropriate. And I feel bad."

Her eyes widened, her cheeks paled, and she seemed to swallow her confidence.

"Is that how you felt at the time?"

"No, no, of course not." I wasn't trying to offend her.

She took an inquisitive step towards me, her head tilted down to the left.

"So how *did* you feel?" There was a tone of genuine insecurity in her voice. Her eyes searched for reassurance. Although I wanted to be flippant, I didn't want this to end with me feeling a new load of guilty towards her.

"It felt good…"

The toilet door was still closed.

"Where?" She almost hummed the word.

I was confused at first, then her eyes slowly fell to my abdomen. I instinctively placed my hand on the top of my stomach, just below my diaphragm.

"Here," I replied.

She mimicked my movement and asked with all seriousness, "Did it feel warm?" My heart beat slower as her words entered me. I began to recall the feeling, and nodded.

I didn't see her take a step forward, but somehow, she began to dominate my vision. Her hand swayed downwards over her flat stomach.

"How did that warm feeling move?"

I was no longer reminiscing but felt that warm feeling again in my stomach. She stretched out her free palm and touched my lower abdomen.

Arousal combusted within me as her other hand rested on the top of her low-cut jeans. Our lips were locked before I could work out who was kissing who.

The toilet door opened with a bang.

She fell to her knees. Aaron looked over to me straight away I was sure he could hear the shame and embarrassment screaming from my pores.

"Sorry about the spill, I'm so clumsy sometimes." She rose behind me. "Come on, Aaron, we've got to get there in ten minutes, or they won't see you."

Aaron grabbed his red jacket and tried to smile. I couldn't muster the gall to utter a word. The door closed.

"So much for my resolve."

I turned and put the kettle on for the second time in 5 minutes, but as I lifted my hand to reach for the box of PG Tips, I failed again for the second time in 5 minutes.

"I hate her," I said in response to the accusing voices in my head.

It's one thing to discover your own weaknesses, but it's beyond humbling for someone else to expose them as if for sport.

"I hate her."

As soon as the words left my lips there was a banging at the door. I paced over and opened up, she was standing right outside, Aaron was only a few feet away.

"I forgot to say, I got a call from a 'friend' this morning. You should get checked for, erm..." she looked over at Aaron and back at me, and then clapped and nodded with a conspiratorial wink.

"What?"

She clapped again and nodded with impatience.

"Are you giving me a round of applause?"

"The clap you idiot," she blurted out in a harsh whisper.

"The clap?" I was still confused, but then her annoyed glare moved from my eyes to my nether-regions. "Chlamydia?" I exclaimed, loud enough that Aaron turned to face us. "I mean, er… Midichlorians yeah, I just may be a secret Jedi Knight, I'll get that checked."

She smiled at me, as if to say 'well saved'.

My eyes scolded her, as if to say 'what the hell?'

And with that she was off. Aaron turned back to me before they disappeared down the stairs but he didn't say goodbye, or wave or even smile.

My guilt deepened, but so strong was the fear her words had impressed upon me that I didn't stop to consider Aaron's feelings. I fled into the flat, jumped onto my laptop and Googled 'STD same day tests near me'.

<u>Half an Hour Later</u>

Sometimes in life, you sit down and you find yourself asking the question 'how did I get here?'

Sat in the waiting room of a private doctor's clinic off of Liverpool Street that specialises in testing for STIs & STDs late on a Wednesday afternoon, dressed in my work clothes and the first pair of trainers I could find, I whispered under my breath while my eyes perused the equally uncomfortable looking customers of this establishment,

"How did I get here?"

No deep deliberation was needed, the voice in my head replied without hesitation,

'Duh, you had unprotected sex with Aaron's mum you idiot!'

As I took in the fact that there were a lot more men there than woman and tried to make sense of that, I then noticed the number of wedding rings, and then my name was called.

"Mr Ryan Reynolds."

I made my way to the reception desk. It's not that I want Ryan Reynolds to get an STD - it's true, I don't like him and consider him to be a terrible actor and generally a turd but I don't wish some penile degenerative disease to strike him - I just couldn't give my real name and his was the first to enter my mind.

I was led into one of the testing rooms, the door was closed and I was asked to take off my trousers and underwear. There was no verbal back and forth, no internal jokes. I thought of my anal examination and the feeling I had surrounding that, but this was very different. Cancer would've been something that happened to me, an STD was something I had done to myself.

That sense of failed responsibility, that sense of failure, only compounded the awkwardness, discomfort and shame I felt while this strange woman swabbed my urethra for diseases and infections I may have contracted whilst doing something I never should've been doing. And yet, the question still persisted 'how did I get here?'

She placed the swab in a medical vile and checked the chart with my written details on it again.

"You specified a Chlamydia test only?"

"Yes."

"It's procedure to ask and suggest, would you like a HIV test?"

And that's when it hit me. It was while I sat there in silence. While the nurse stood, looking at me, waiting for a response. It was during those moments where I could not speak that it hit me, and the question 'how did I get here?' was crushed by the weight of 'what have I done?'

"Sir?"

I thought of her stories, of Aaron's Dad's 'visit' and of what I heard behind that closed door beyond the music, of every time Aaron was left with me while she needed to 'work' and of the lack of hesitation, the absence of caution, the ease with which we both proceeded without a second thought.

"Yes. Yes please."

"Would you like to read the information about the rapid HIV test, it…'

I shook my head and pursed my lips until she stopped talking.

She swabbed again but this time the sample was taken from my gums, and this time I had to fight to keep a tear from escaping my eye.

I didn't ask, and I don't know if it was due to them having a slow day or if this was normal procedure, but the nurse allowed me to stay in the examining room while I waited for my results.

I counted the medical books on the shelves and then read their names, and then mentally put them in alphabetical order. I was deciding if *The Scars of Venus* should be placed in the T's or S's as so many books started with 'The', when she returned.

She handed me the printed results.

'Chlamydia: Positive.'

My eyes flew down and moved to the next page.

'HIV: Negative.'

"Oh my goodness, thank you." I released the biggest sigh followed by the biggest smile.

"The doctor has written you a prescription for a course of antibiotics. You can..."

"Thank you, nurse." I wanted to shake her hand but then remembered where we were and what she does. "I'm so relieved. It's amazing how positive the word negative can be, I'll never look at that word the same again."

She smiled and I sighed again.

"It's amazing how something stupid you did on Monday could turn your life upside down by Wednesday."

"Sir?"

"Yes,"

"On your form you didn't state when your last sexual encounter was you just wrote, 'Chlamydia test'."

"Yeah, I hadn't even considered HIV before you mentioned it."

"When was your last sexual encounter?"

"Monday night." She stopped smiling, and so did I. "Why?"

"HIV tests are only accurate 4 weeks after possible exposure. The test you've just taken won't..."

Her voice faded out as the words 'four weeks' sank in.

I leave the clinic £200 lighter but feeling an indiscernible amount heavier. Sat on the bus on the way home, the phrase that had been on my mind since Monday morning returned again but this time, I wanted to read it in full. So, I searched 'Wormwood bible scriptures' and Proverbs Chapter 5 Verses 3 & 4 came up and spoke, what were at that time for me, the truest words I'd ever read.

That Night

I did not sleep at all.

The Following Day - (His favourite red jacket)

At 3:30pm I checked my phone; it didn't ring. Every time I looked down and saw a blank screen I thought of how mad Aaron must be with me.

He must've heard us Monday night, and he could've caught us kissing yesterday. He must be wondering if I'm either using his mum, like all the other men or if I'm truly the man I have made myself out to be and am pursuing a serious relationship with her.

Then it hit me again:

'4 weeks.'

I was lost in a daze of 'what ifs' 'buts' and 'maybes.'

Then the sound of my mobile phone ringing snapped me back into the here and now.

It was a private number, but it was 3:33pm so I answered it with a smile.

"Joe... Joe, I don't know what to do they won't let me see him! They won't let me see my baby they..." Aaron's mum cried down the phone.

"What do you mean, what's happened?" I stood out of my seat, the HR rep walking past took a step back.

"They say he's lost a lot of blood, Joe, I don't know what to do..."

"WHAT? WHAT HAPPENED?" I dashed out of the office and started running down the street, while still on the phone.

"He looked blue, and couldn't open his eyes..."

"What hospital are you in?"

She tried to talk through her tears. I was trying to listen and decide what was quicker, for me to take the tube or a cab.

"...Queen Elizabeth..."

I looked out at the rush hour traffic. "I'M ON MY WAY NOW," I yelled, heading for the underground.

I stuffed my phone in my pocket as my network reception cut out, and rushed through the barriers and fled down the escalator. The doors to my train were just closing as I reached the platform. I dashed forward and stuck my hand in between the sliding doors ignoring the pain. I squeezed my other hand into the little gap I'd made and tore those doors apart.

We moved off agonisingly slow. I gripped the metal bar by the door wanting to drag the train down the line; I swear, with the anger and frustration that was combusting inside me, I could've dragged that train all the way to the hospital.

Every pore in my body began to sweat, I felt itchy all over and started fidgeting, bouncing my right leg up and down on my tiptoes then turning to the left, then to the right. In my frustration, I began pushing on the door while the train was moving. A woman glared at me.

"Don't look at me like that."

She took my advice a step further and didn't look at me at all.

I tried to focus my mind and plan the rest of the journey in my head and what I was going to do at each point.

"Ah!" I exclaimed.

Her phone number, I don't have her phone number and she called me from a private number.

My hands started to shake and my breathing became rapid and shallow.

I fastened my fingers around the metal bar again and looked through the glass into the darkness of the tunnel. My eyes refocused and I saw my own reflection, I saw my eyes. A flash of Aaron in the state that his mum described filled my thoughts and ignited those volatile fuels within me and I couldn't control the explosion. I kicked the door with all my might and swore viciously at an invisible foe. I wanted to smash my fist through the door.

The urgency to hit something and distract my thoughts swelled, and I punched myself in the thigh, the pain calming me. As if it were a knock-on effect, the train began to slow. It was my stop.

As I bundled and barged through the crowds of commuters I fumbled in my pocket for my phone. I ran up the stairs ignoring the packed escalator, hoping that she was trying to call me and that the quicker I made it above ground and got reception, the quicker she could update me.

While rushing through the barriers and up the stairs towards daylight I kept trying to push "what ifs" out of my mind; but they were too heavy and I was too weak.

"Please don't die," I whispered.

I ran up the side of the stairwell where people were coming down. I had never been so happy to see the sun than when I neared the street exit.

I gathered my bearings in microseconds and began sprinting down the bustling high street. My heart beat quicker as I spotted the hospital. I felt a sharp queasiness but I kept running. My legs went weak but I kept running. Tears blurred my vision and streaked across my face as I refused to stop.

I almost jumped out of my skin when my phone vibrated in my pocket and began to ring. I was nearing the hospital entrance as I fought to free it from my trousers. I bolted towards the main reception desk and looked down at the phone. It was a private number. A wave of fear flowed through my body as I stopped just short of the receptionist and saw the entrance to Accident and Emergency.

"Where are you?" She was crying through her words.

I barged through the doors, shoulder first, into A&E and was about to reply when I heard her crying without my phone. I turned and looked in the far-left corner of the ward and saw Aaron's mum running alongside a hospital gurney where a lifeless figure lay strapped with a neck brace and medical apparatus attached. It didn't feel like I moved, it felt more like I was carried across the ward. The bed disappeared behind a pair of double doors before I could see Aaron's face, but I caught sight of his favourite red jacket, cut and torn to shreds, hanging off him; then I looked closer and realised that it was his shirt I saw and not his jacket; the red was his blood.

"This is your fault!" A woman I didn't know with a strong Irish accent came shouting towards Aaron's mum. "Your neglect did this and if he survives, God help me, you'll never see him again!" Her short heavy strides drove her straight to Aaron's mum.

"That's my son! You can't do that. I'm his mother!" Aaron's mum screamed, pounding her chest.

Without breaking stride, the woman struck her across the face with a slap that shook the room. Stunned into silence she just held her cheek.

"How dare you? You've never been a mother to that child. I'm going to call the police and the child services and have you arrested!"

Aaron's mum stood frozen to the spot while the other woman stormed out of the ward.

I approached Aaron's mum and placed my hand on her shoulder. She didn't move, the shock of the slap giving way to a look of fear.

"Who was that?" I asked.

Her cheek reddened and her lips quivered, but she didn't reply. She stared off into space as if her attention had been captivated by a screen that only she could see and on it played a film only she could understand. Once the film had finished and its message passed on, she turned towards me, but didn't look directly at me as she spoke.

"Please stay with him."

"What do you mean?"

Before I had finished my question, she had already begun walking away. A sense within fought my instinct to reach out and grab her arm. I knew my effort would be futile.

She glanced back at me, and walked out of the hospital.

I sat down, put my head in my hands and had no idea what to do.

Twenty Minutes Later

I spotted one of the doctors who had taken Aaron through the double doors.

"Doctor, how is he, how's Aaron?"

"Excuse me, who are you?

"I'm his... his father, Joseph. Please tell me, is he okay?"

The doctor paused, expressionless.

"He's stable, at the moment. But the injuries that he has suffered are severe."

"Where was he? Why was he by himself?"

"We don't know. The ambulance report said that the road was icy and that the car couldn't stop. The best thing to do is to ask his grandmother about the other details. She was on his GP's emergency contacts and came here first."

"Was he far from his school?"

"We really don't know." The doctor moved to leave. "The only thing the ambulance staff added was that they found a Gameboy, some loose change and a phone number on a piece of scrap paper. I'm sorry but we don't know anything more than that."

I wanted to thank him but I couldn't breathe.

"Here's his grandmother now. I'm sure she can help you more."

Drained and worn, Doreen approached.

"Doctor..." she began.

"He's stable for now but we will keep you updated."

Her whole body sagged as she sighed.

"But as I explained to Aaron's father, he has suffered very serious injuries."

"His father?" They both looked at me.

"I can explain..."

"I'm sorry," the doctor said, "I have to go."

Doreen looked like she wanted to stab me.

"I'm not sure how to explain..."

"You're one of her men, aren't you? She asked you to stay here for her, didn't she?"

"No, no, it's not like that... she did ask me to stay but..."

"Just as I thought."

"Look, you've got me all wrong..."

"Tell me you haven't slept with her." With that one statement she stripped me of all my freedom of speech.

She smiled and was about to turn away.

"You've still got no right to tell her she can't see her son!"

Doreen turned back towards me with the coiled anger and cruel intent of an insulted street brawler.

"What did you say?"

I didn't answer quick enough. But if I had, Aaron's mum would've always been a mystery to me.

"Let me tell you something." Within two menacing strides she was in my face, staring me down with bloodshot eyes. "She never wanted Aaron; from the day he was conceived he was just a means to an end. His father was the only man who didn't fall for her. No matter what she tried, no matter what she put up with from him, he just didn't want her and she couldn't deal with it. Her father spoiled her and so did every other man after that, except for him. The only thing she hadn't tried was getting pregnant."

"How do you know it wasn't just unplanned?"

"Because all the other 'unplanned' ones saw the abortion clinic before they did the light of day. She thought that carrying his son would stop the fights and make him love her. So she waited until she knew it was a boy, then told him. The foolish girl thought the beatings would stop there; but you know what he did? He tried to beat the child out of her. But she kept going back. I tried talking to her and she wouldn't listen. I told the police and she said that I was making it all up."

I tried to look away but her eyes, surrounded by heavy bags and engraved lines, wouldn't let me.

"He almost killed the both of them. But by that time, she was five months pregnant and couldn't get an abortion." With indignation she drew a deep breath through her nostrils and pressed her finger deep into her chest. "*I* raised that boy while she got drugged up and whored herself around the city. She did the same after her father passed. I didn't want to take a child away from his mum, but now she's left me with no choice." Her tone dropped and her contempt now narrowed in my direction. "I don't care who you are or what you want, but you'd better leave now and stay well away from my grandson."

"But..."

"If you don't leave right now, I will call the police and have you arrested."

"But I haven't done anything wrong."

"Fine!"

She turned and marched off back down the corridor she'd come from.

I sat down, put my head in my palms and thanked God that Aaron was still alive.

Time Passed

I didn't feel hungry or tired. I wasn't happy or sad. I was lost in the same trance that Aaron's mum was in. On my invisible screen played, not the things I had seen and experienced with Aaron but, all those that I had hoped to.

"Excuse me…" It was a female voice that sounded friendly. I raised my head. She was one of the nurses from the A&E reception desk. I didn't speak. "I'm not supposed to tell you but I've been watching you sit here for the last few hours and felt I should say something." I didn't move and my expression didn't change as I looked up at the nurse, leaning forward with her hands on her knees. "Aaron's gone…" The words echoed in my mind and I could only see her lips moving and not hear her words. "…they left about an hour and a half ago."

"Who left?"

"Aaron and his grandmother. They were moved to another hospital."

"He's alive?"

"Yes, they…"

"Oh God…"

I fell to my knees in breathless relief. She knelt next to me and placed a hand on my back.

"Where did they take him?" I asked.

"I don't know."

"Can you find out?"

"No. I wasn't even supposed to tell you that they had left. But it felt wrong not to."

"Is there any way I can find out?"

When she shook her head, I knew that she wasn't lying. As she stood, I followed.

"Thank you." And with that, I left.

It was 1am when I got home. I felt hungry but I didn't want to eat, tired but sleep was the last thing on my mind. My thoughts were completely blank for the whole journey home; I couldn't recall a second of it. I didn't know what to do. So I just stood there for a while, a long while. Then I walked back out and over to Aaron's mum's place. I knocked hard a few times and put my ear to the door but heard nothing. As I walked back to my door I thought,

Just call every hospital in London. Call them all.

I got in, threw down my jacket, put the kettle to boil and clicked onto the Yellow Pages online. When I saw the long list of hospitals I wasn't deterred in the slightest.

"Good evening, my son was moved to your hospital a few hours ago from Queen Elizabeth's A&E..."

"Sorry, sir, we have no one here of that name."

"Sorry, they must have given you the wrong details."

"I've double-checked and no one has been moved here this evening." "This is a hospice."

"We have a girl named Aaron from St Bartholomew's who arrived this afternoon..."

"Are you sure it's a girl?"

"She had a gynaecological emergency."

I had my third cup of coffee and began dialling hospitals on the outskirts of the city. Some of the receptionists could hear my lack of conviction and knew the distance between the hospitals made my claims unlikely. They began to ring Queen Elizabeth's to check out my statement so I hung up before they got through.

They'll tell the reception Queen Elizabeth that someone is calling around for Aaron, and then the reception desk there will call the reception at this 'secret' hospital where he is and so even if I find it, they won't tell me.

I went to the toilet and then came back and tried a few more hospitals anyway.

As night turned to day, I sat on my sofa staring out of the window, trying to retrieve the joy I'd felt in finding out that Aaron was alive.

I emailed my boss and told him I wouldn't be in that day because of a family emergency. I tried to Google Aaron's name and then "hospital" in a desperate attempt to find him, but Google was not yet that powerful.

I struggled to get to my feet. I walked over to their flat again and banged on the door as loud as I could. I knew she wasn't in; I'd been listening for any sounds out in the hallway and hadn't heard anything, but felt I needed to be trying something.

I walked back into my flat, picked up my jacket and wallet and made my way back to the hospital.

Nobody would talk to me.

On the way home I went to Aaron's school. The parents were dropping their kids off; I was alone but seemed to blend in. His teachers knew nothing about the accident, nothing about his grandmother and very little about his mum. His form tutor's initial expression of caution when she first saw me approaching now simmered into one of concern.

"Are you going to be all right?"

I was so drained at that point that I wasn't sure if it was tiredness or contemplation that led me to pause for so long before answering.

"I'll have to be."

I thanked her, not really sure what for, I suppose for her concern, and then turned to go, almost tripping over a boy who stood staring at me.

"Sorry," I didn't have enough energy to look down at him. But he didn't move. "Are you okay?"

"You're Joseph, ennit?"

"Yeah... how do you know me?"

He looked up at me with an expression that I didn't understand.

"Aaron talks about you *all* the time."

I crouched down, leaned towards him and replied, "What does he say?"

"Philip!"

A woman who more resembled a witch than a teacher scolded us with her eyes and then, with a bony-fingered beckoning, called the boy over to her classroom. He scurried away in fearful obedience. I was too tired to be scared but equally too tired to argue with her about why she should allow her ten-year-old student to talk to a dishevelled, red-eyed stranger who didn't even have a child in the school.

I left frustrated but somehow with more energy than when I arrived.

On the way home I made every effort not to think about anything at all. The harder I tried the more impossible it became.

I was trying to convince myself that it was okay for me to go to sleep, that I had done everything I could, that...

"Oi!"

The man trying to break into Aaron's mum's flat heard me, saw me and then ran. I started to run after him but a pain in my stomach stopped me in my tracks and I found myself holding the spot where I'd been stabbed.

But he might know where Aaron's mum is or how to contact her.

So, I continued a half-hearted chase but he disappeared out of the fire exit and was gone.

Back in my flat it felt cold.

I dozed off sitting up in the sofa with my jacket on.

BANG! BANG! BANG! BANG!

I jumped up out of my sleep and dashed to the door. I flung it open and shoved my head into the hallway. Two police officers stood outside Aaron's mum's door and jerked their attention towards me.

"She's not in."

"Do you know where she might be?"

"No."

The officers looked at each other with satisfied resignation.

"Has it got anything to do with her son, Aaron?"

Their expressions changed. "What do you know about her son?"

Caution made me think on my feet.

"One of the neighbours told me that he was involved in a car accident today... yesterday." They gave nothing away through their expressions.

"If you see or hear from her, advise the lady that we have a warrant for her arrest."

I stood in shock, then realised that I hadn't replied.

"Err, okay, yes, officer... officers, I will if I see her, I'll... I'll let her know, I'll tell her what you said."

They didn't bother to reply. They put a notice through her letterbox and left.

I stood in my flat leaning on the closed door. My stomach moaned, as did my mind and heart. I slid down the back of the door until I was slumped on the ground.

"I'll never see him again,"

With every breath, I felt my body sink and wilt.

I should've forced his mum to buy him those winter boots. Maybe he would have been able to run out of the way of the car if he'd had decent boots on, or just gone out and bought them myself. Or just gone and met him at school, why was I waiting for her to pick him, we all knew that wasn't gonna happen. But I didn't. I didn't do anything because I was too busy feeling guilty about having slept with his mum.

"Please God, please let him be okay."

Ten Days Later

I still hadn't heard anything about Aaron; not where he was, how he was or even if he'd survived – nothing.

My beard had returned, my skin had paled and my weight decreased, but not in a good way; I didn't look slim and healthy, I looked weak and malnourished.

I hadn't left the house, bathed or slept in my bed. I only left the sofa to go and grab another mini can of baked beans and to use the toilet. The house stank. The battery in my wall clock had stopped and I had drawn all the curtains in the flat. Night and day was a thing of the past.

I had to wash out my mug; the clumps of leftover cookies in the bottom were forming an unsightly mountain too large for me to ignore. I'd had no more than ten hours' sleep in the last fourteen days, yet all I wanted to do was drink coffee.

The weather outside had worsened. A cold chill passed through the living-room, feeling its way through the emptiness. I walked into the bedroom and over to the sock drawer. On top of that chest of drawers was the photo of Sapphire and I that I'd showed Aaron.

The sight of this memory provoked within me the desire to see more, to reminisce and have thoughts of the past drown out those of the present.

In my weakened state, it took me a moment to get to the floor. I sat beside my box of memories and for the first time since moving here and living alone, I wanted to unpack. One box half peeked out from under the bed. I placed my palm atop of it, feeling so nervous that I took a deep breath. I was so anxious that I wanted to pray.

I reached in the box, half not knowing what I would find, half knowing what I was looking for. It was still lying there, neatly tucked away at the bottom of the box, the picture that Aaron had found of my mum.

A stew of emotion stirred within me as I looked. I felt an overwhelming compulsion to tear it to shreds and return to my sofa and single duvet. But I imagined Aaron was sitting next to me, looking up at me, his eyes asking me to tell him about her.

"Well, for years I thought that I had nothing to be upset about, and in comparison to some, maybe even most, I didn't. But knowing that someone else was in more pain didn't stop mine from hurting. In fact, the more I ignored it, the more it found new ways to hurt me. And the more damage it did."

Then he would ask, "Then why did you ignore it?"

"Because I knew that dealing with it was going to cause me more pain than I wanted to feel."

"But weren't you in pain already?"

I would look away from him for a moment and take a deep breath. "You're right. I was, and I still am."

He would look up at me, wondering why I hadn't put the obvious solution into action. And I would respond, "I guess it doesn't make sense for me to carry on like this."

I picked up the picture and kissed it.

<u>Five Minutes Later</u> - (When home isn't home)

I walked up to the window and opened the curtains. It was night, well, evening at least. I leaned on the ledge and looked out at the cars and people below steadily going about their business: going home, going to work, paying bills, buying stuff, selling stuff; doing this and that. A quote from a poet I'd heard on a radio talk show at work last summer came to my mind.

"In three words I can sum up everything I've learned about life: it goes on."

"Maybe for everyone else."

In the evening air I caught the scent of fish and chips from my local chippie, and my stomach groaned. I had eaten every morsel of food in the place – including two out-of-date packets of ready mixed macaroni cheese; a bad idea on so many levels.

As I left the flat, I noticed that bailiffs were removing everything of value out of Aaron's flat. My landlord stood outside shaking his head and muttering "Damn dirty, liberty-taking tenants!"

On my way back from the chip shop I thought about having to make an appointment to see the doctor and get a sick note for my time off. That reminded me of having to go back to work. Then I remembered that Matt had called me a few times and left messages but I hadn't replied.

I'll feel really bad if I go back to work and I haven't returned his calls. I'll text him... nah, that's a bit weak. I'll call him and explain what happened. He trusted me and I think I can trust him. I hate talking on the phone for ages, though. What time is it?

"Excuse me, what's the time, please?"

"Seven twenty-five," the passer-by replied.

You know what, I'll just go there, I'll go there now. Who knows, they may even be able to help.

So, without further thought, I jumped on the over-ground train and was at Matt's house in twenty minutes. I kept my empty chip bag in hand so as to have a good excuse for why I didn't want any dinner.

They were both glad to see me, so glad that they couldn't let me sit at the dinner table with them without a plate of food in front of me. Julia told me that my beard made me look distinguished. (I'm sure that's polite code for "haggard".)

They knew I had something to tell them because after they poured me a glass of wine, they both sat back in silent anticipation with concerned smiles. I told them everything about what happened on that day.

It was weird, the events were obviously not new to me but when I spoke them out loud, that was when I felt them; and it was still raw. I think at that moment the reality of it all just hit me. When I explained how I felt on the train I began to choke up.

When I told them about seeing Aaron on the stretcher I had to pause and take a breath. But when I got to the point where the nurse told me Aaron was gone, I couldn't finish my sentence. The wave of emotion took me by complete surprise. All the way on the journey there I knew what I was going to say and felt my anxiety. But as soon as I opened my mouth, my emotions receded, like the tide does just before a tsunami, and as I spoke those emotions built up, rising and rising until I couldn't speak. Then this gigantic wave of feelings just came crashing down. Julia leaned across the table and held my hand. The room was silent for a long while.

Once the sea had settled within me, I went on to explain what I had done to try and find Aaron and then about my conversation with the police.

"On the way here I thought that maybe there was some way you could help, some idea that I hadn't thought of. But after explaining it all... I know he's gone, and that there's no way that I'll find him."

"If that is true, Joseph," Julia began, "then you have to start thinking about how you're going to cope with that reality." Leaning towards me, her eyes brightened. "To begin with, I'll take you out shopping. How about that?" She looked at Matt and me for a response. Matt's nod was enough for her to continue. "On your next payday we'll all go out together and buy you a new wardrobe, give you a new look and you'll be surprised how much of a difference that can make."

"Okay." I wasn't convinced.

"And we can redecorate your flat, maybe change the arrangement of your furniture. I've read up all about Feng Shui and I tell you what, that stuff works." She glanced over to Matt for his vote of confidence and he nodded, with dutiful enthusiasm. "When you walked in here today didn't you get a warm open feeling that induced comfortability?"

"I think so." *No, I didn't.*

"I used to do a bit of painting and decorating when I was a teenager. We could make a weekend of it, and if not for anything else, it will take your mind off things," Matt added with his touch of pragmatism.

"That's true. Thanks for wanting to help."

"That's what friends are for."

Out of everything, hearing Matt say that felt good. He glanced at my untouched glass of wine.

"Do you fancy a beer instead?"

"Please." We all smiled. Matt walked over to the kitchen, giving his wife's shoulder a gentle squeeze as he left.

"I miss Aaron as well." Her comment caught me by surprise.

"Really?"

"I had a great little chat with him last time you both came round. It's amazing how innocent he is, isn't it? But how at the same time he's like a small grown-up, mature beyond his years."

It was strange hearing someone talk about Aaron in the same way that I saw him. It felt good knowing how his little light touched others.

"He was worried about you, you know?"

"What do you mean?"

"He said that you never slept a night all the way through. That no matter how early he woke up, you were always already awake."

I was speechless.

She looked at me with eyes kinder than those Sapphie watched over me with; they reminded me of my aunt, but in her expression – for the briefest of moments – she looked like my mum.

"How long has it been since you had a proper night's sleep?"

"About five or so years."

She leaned back, tilting her head, her eyes still on me. "What happened five years ago, Joseph?"

My mum was beautiful, and she never looked her age.

"I really don't know."

Looking through it, I brushed the base of my glass with my finger, noticing how it distorted the room. Julia could tell my mind was split between the past and the present.

"Did something traumatic happen, did you lose someone or break up with someone you loved?"

That question snapped me back to our conversation. "No. Nothing much was going on at that time." I bit the inside of my cheek in thought. "Well, we lost... I mean, my dad sold our old house, but that's the only thing that happened or changed in my life around then. I'd been in my flat for about a year by then, so I know it wasn't the move..."

"How did losing the house affect you?"

"It didn't."

"What do you mean?"

"It didn't really bother me."

She had a look of intent in her eyes, but I had no idea why.

"Why not?"

I looked at her confused. "It was just a house."

Her reply was quick. "Did you ever live anywhere else?"

"Yeah. I moved away for university and then got the place I live in now after my degree."

"No, no, I mean as a child, did you move a lot when you were young and live in different places?"

"Oh, no, I grew up in that house, I was born in the hospital just up the road from it."

She leaned forward, her brow rising and her index finger falling on me.

"So that house holds... held rather, all of your childhood memories then?"

"No, my *memory* does that, I hold all that stuff up here. The house was just bricks and mortar. Don't get me wrong, I was a bit upset when I heard Dad was selling it, but I put that down to the fact that I had never thought of it not being in the family; you know, not being able to just pop in or stay overnight if I'm in the area... or if everything in my life went to pot knowing that there's always a bed in the old house with my name on it." I smiled at the thought of my old room. "I do literally have my name on the bed. I carved it in as soon as my dad allowed me to have a Swiss army knife. But I did it under the bed borders so that no one could see."

Julia laughed. "What was the point of that?"

"Well, if they saw it, they would've taken away the knife and that was the coolest thing I owned at eleven. Besides the inscription is there for me..."

"*Was.*"

"'Was' what?"

"*Was* there for you. The inscription, the bed, the house *was* there for you. It isn't anymore, Joseph."

I understood what she was trying to get at, but she didn't understand me.

"I'm serious, it wasn't a big deal." My words came out louder than I wanted. She paused for a moment and I hoped I hadn't offended her.

"I believe you, I do." She placed her hands on the table and interlocked her fingers. "You know years ago, before I met Matt, I used to work in Birmingham. It was a nice private nursery on the edge of the city. One of the teachers I was close with there was from Ethiopia, she was born and grew up there but had spent most of her life in England; lovely girl, really maternal, she had four children of her own and another two who were her husband's nephews. But anyway, over there, in Ethiopia, about twenty years ago now, the government decided it was taking control of the land and was going to relocate millions of people from their homes and move them elsewhere; she was just a child when this was happening. But she told me that whenever her parents talked about it, she could see the pain in their faces as if it had happened only yesterday. So one night, when she was in her teens, she asked them why it bothered them so much, why being forced to move all those years ago still hurt." Julia's fingers slid away from each other and she brushed her hands, palm against palm, as she spoke. "Her father said that they'd eat first and then answer her. So, after dinner, they sat down, and it was her mother who spoke first. She explained that it wasn't just the fact that they lost their livelihood off the land, but what cut deep was that their home had been theirs for generations; it's where they'd grown up, where they got married, where they had mourned and buried their parents and where they had their children and where their children had grown up to be men and women. Her father told her that there were many family heads who couldn't deal with the loss. Grown men, well respected in the community, couldn't deal with losing all of that history, all of what was so much a part of them. It cut them so deeply... that many took their own lives."

Her eyes glided away from mine and her hands were still. Her empathy was clear, and infectious.

"Apparently, one of her father's friends was in tears the night they destroyed his house. He explained that demolishing his home was like them digging up his parents' bones. That they weren't only disrespecting his memories of his parents, which were tied to the house, but that they were tearing them away from him; it felt like he was grieving all over again. The next day her father found his friend hanging from the ruins of that house."

I shrank into my seat.

"It is a big deal, Joseph. Don't just ignore it."

As I took in her words, Matt joined us again holding two beers.

To lighten the sombre mood he had returned to, he updated me on work stuff. The Bogart lady had got married and posted in her resignation while still on her honeymoon. The office busybody got the manager to make up the role of assistant manager for her, and the HR Rep has been really worried about me. Julia then went on to kill us with a host of naughty jokes her dad had told them at Christmas. When they mentioned it, I realised that the end of the year had come and gone and a new one started and I hadn't even noticed.

I had such a good time with them both that it was hard to believe how bad I had felt just hours before. I now felt more equipped to deal with returning to an empty home, revived by an evening of warm company.

In the hours where I couldn't sleep that night, I thought of our old home. The memories brought more pain than smiles. I couldn't think about the house without thinking about *her*, and I couldn't bear to do that; but without sleep, I was at the mercy of my thoughts.

<u>The Following Monday</u>

I returned to work. The HR Rep did seem pretty happy to see me, although my beard caught her by surprise.

I was apprehensive about speaking to my manager; the company's really hard on sick leave, plus because I'd lied about Aaron being my child and I didn't want to dig a deeper hole, I couldn't play the sympathy card. But he was away on annual leave so that was a big relief.

I'd been feeling better for the last few days. When I'd told Matt and Julia that I would never find Aaron again, it gave me hope that I would. I realised I hadn't said those words before but I'd believed them, but then as soon as I said them, I didn't believe that they were true. Then I remembered the conversation that I'd had with Aaron about hope and belief. I believed that I would see him again and that belief softened the soil of my heart and allowed the seed of hope to take root. Every day I watered it and every day that passed brought me a day closer to seeing him again. I decided that I would do everything in my power to help Aaron grow up to be a good person – a strong person – and to do that I must be one myself. I arranged to go shopping with Matt and his wife over the weekend and I already had ideas for redecorating the flat. I had a plan and purpose, and it felt good.

<u>Wednesday Night</u> - (Falling)

I was cooking Chicken Cordon Bleu and at that stage it tasted better than the one Aaron and I had made what seemed liked years ago. My mobile rang and I strolled over to the sofa to answer it. It was a private number. I felt sick. I silenced the call and sat and watched the screen flash. It stopped flashing and I felt my heart thumping.

Ring Ring, Ring Ring!

I jumped as the phone started to vibrate and ring in my hand with 'Private Number' splashed across the screen again.

It might be Aaron. "Hello..."

"Joe, it's me, I need your help." Aaron's mum sounded frantic, making me even more nervous.

"Is it Aaron? Is he okay? Where is he?"

"Forget about him, he's with my mother. He's not coming back. Listen, I need bail money as soon as possible. I swear I'll get it back to you straight away, within a week..."

"I don't have any money, at all, I'm sorry. But are you sure Aaron's okay, have you spoken to hi..."

The line went dead.

"Hello... Hello..."

"The person you are calling has hung up. Please redial the number and try again. The person you are calling has hung up..."

I sat down.

The silence hurt.

She was right. Aaron was never coming back.

I wrote a text message to Matt saying I couldn't make shopping at the weekend and one to my boss saying I was ill again. The last message wouldn't send. I gave up trying.

I turned off the cooker and the TV and went to bed.

The splinter-sharp thought that every foundation I build on crumbles, wove in and out of my mind that whole night, piercing through memories and stabbing dreams.

I couldn't find a reason to leave my bed. So I didn't. I couldn't sleep, so against my will I gave in to my thoughts. When the same thoughts kept circling my mind with no answers in sight, I wrote.

That Thursday

Matt had called and sent a text in the morning asking if I was okay. After that I put my phone on silent and left it on the bedside table.

I lay there, hours passing, feeling the love I had for Aaron decay into loneliness. Then that loneliness frustrated itself into anger. And that anger become bound by the bonds of bitterness. I wanted to jump out of the window. I wanted to fly away from these feelings, to be somewhere else, to feel something else, to let rip, to let anger have its day. But the chains of bitterness chilled my pain while holding my anger to burn within. And that anger hurt so much that I wanted to hurt myself; to remedy pain with pain. I was angry with Aaron's school teachers for letting him sneak out, I was angry with his mum for not being there to pick him up, I was angry with her mother for taking him away, I was angry with the hospital staff for not telling me where he was, and most of all I was angry with myself. I should've been there, I should've just arranged to pick him up every day or told him never to sneak out, just to call me from the school, I should've done something. I should've done more!

This hot rage carved jagged lines into my chest and hurt me with a pain I'd never felt before. I wanted it to stop; I had to stop these thoughts. I crawled out of bed and on my hands and knees dragged my boxes of forgotten burdens towards me, reached in and grabbed the glass-framed picture of my family at one of my father's many award ceremonies, he dressed in full British Army regalia. I stared long and hard at his unnerving expression. It was one I knew all too well.

"You should've done more for me, for us... for *her*." My jaw clenched as my eyes narrowed in on his face. "Was it that hard to love me?"

I stared at the picture and thrust my mind back to his disappointment, his embarrassment, his regret. I relived the beatings, the tears, the fear, the anger, the hatred. I tore open the scar tissue on my heart and squeezed out the pus festering inside, and with every thought I squeezed harder and harder.

Closing my eyes, my mind dashed back to when I was ten years old; I would call my dad every Wednesday evening and Sunday night while he was away with the army. At the end of every conversation I would say, "I love you, Dad."

He would reply, "Okay, goodbye."

He would never say it. Its absence stayed with me and I craved to hear the words. So, one Sunday I said, "I love you, Dad." I pressed the phone receiver close to my ear

"Okay..." he said.

Grasping the receiver with a tight grip, I waited, and then said again, "Dad, I love you."

He hung up. He actually put the phone down. It broke my heart. I couldn't understand why it was so hard for him even to say it. And that day, when I needed him the most, when I was at my lowest...why couldn't he love me then.

And that's when the realisation hit,

"I never told Aaron I loved him."

That makes me as bad as my dad.

I shook my head, my mouth wide open, my eyes closed.

I can't believe I never told him, and now I'm never gonna get the chance.

I opened my eyes and my knuckles were covered in glass and blood. I didn't feel any physical pain. I was too empty to be shocked. I walked over to the bathroom and ran cold water over my right fist. I felt numb.

Going back to my bed I sat down. My hand kept bleeding. I could see bits of glass in my flesh. Wrapping my hand in a tablecloth, I walked to A&E.

I looked around the Accident & Emergency section and recognised where I had stood, watching Aaron being wheeled away, and where I had sat afterwards for hours. I felt nothing. I saw a teenager with what looked like a stab wound being pushed through the double doors followed by his tearful mother and scared siblings; nothing. I saw a young woman with a bruised and swollen face, and a man with red knuckles sitting beside her. I didn't want to comfort her.

I didn't look at the nurse as she took my details and I used only monosyllabic replies when I was forced to speak. After two hours of waiting, they cleaned and stitched up my wounds; I didn't know that pain could lose its potency when you ceased to care.

As I was leaving, I averted my eyes from the ailing in waiting and glanced out of the window. The deep crimson skyline took me by surprise. But no more so than the little boy who, with his face to the glass, was looking up at the sky. I couldn't help myself from hoping that the child knew that he was loved.

<u>Monday Morning</u>

On my way into work, I kept telling myself,

"It could be worse, it could be worse. Be grateful for that at least."

A smile from the HR Rep gave me what my morning coffee couldn't. I reached my desk feeling more confident about the day.

"Joe..." My manager appeared behind me and continued before I could greet him "...can we have a quick word?"

It was quick. I was fired.

My "unauthorised absence" on Friday was considered an act of "gross misconduct" – I'd forgotten to resend the text message. He said it would've made little difference if I had sent it, due to my string of absences and practically being absent even when was I was in. I threatened to take the decision to a tribunal. He saw straight through my bluff, but without condescension humoured me.

"Do you really want to stay here, Joe?"

"What do you mean?"

"I've watched you come in this place every morning and leave every night like you're taking a long toilet break away from home. I don't know you well enough to say that you could be doing a lot better, but I can't understand why you would want to keep doing this." His point wasn't rhetorical, but I had no worthy reply.

He ended with explaining that I'd get paid till the end of the month, then he shook my torn hand.

The End of the Month

The end of the month was the end of that week. My payslip showed numerous deductions for "sick absence", leaving me with half my normal wage. My landlord called to ask why he hadn't received my rent's direct debit. I explained the situation. He said that I needed to pay my rent by the end of next week. I told him I needed to find another job first. He asked how long that would take, I said I didn't know. He went quiet. I waited, and he finally said, "Okay."

The Next Day

A note was slipped under my door informing me that I was in breach of my tenant's agreement and had two weeks to pay my rent or move out before the bailiffs moved in. With the letter still in my hand I walked over to the sofa.

My phone vibrated in my pocket. I was half inclined not to check it but the buzzing sensation annoyed me. It was a series of text messages from the Liverpool Street clinic reminding me of the appointment I had made and asking me to confirm my attendance.

I didn't care. I genuinely didn't care at all.

I sat down. Then I lay down. I closed my eyes and my body folded in like a child's pop-up book being closed.

In the dark silence, her name called out to me from some deep place within. But not the usual location of my heart; this was from somewhere darker and its tone without that familiar sweetness. "*Sapphire.*"

She's the only one who ever understood me, who ever made me happy; she's the only one who can help me now. She has to. She must.

I found her letter, and true to her character she had written a return address on the back of the envelope just in case it wasn't delivered. I read it again, but this time saw indications of tenderness and the possibility of unspoken love. The words were just words. But now, in my current state of mind, I was able to perceive the *true* meaning behind them.

I rummaged around the flat collecting loose change until I had enough to top up my oyster card with. I hadn't bathed and was wearing house clothes that were ready for the bin, but as I ignored the odd looks when entering the bus, I rationalised that my appearance would add visual honesty to the plea I was about to make to her heart.

I was on her street. I stood outside number 73. She lived at number 127.

"This is the right thing to do," I told myself. "But..." I sighed and my head began to drop. "No. No, this *is* right. No one has the history that we have together, no one has that depth. No one can love me like she can. Like she *does*. She's probably been waiting for me to make this trip ever since she sent that letter." I started walking. "I was stupid." 81, 83, 85. "I was a coward too. She's what I've wanted, what I've needed this whole time." I moved with a swifter stride. 97, 99, 101. "I won't be scared anymore. It's crazy, I see it now, it's so clear, this is it, this is what everything has been building up to. All those other women, they could never be

Sapphire, they could never really give me what I wanted." 111, 113, 115. "And I knew they couldn't, deep down I knew I was wasting my time. Looking back now, those relationships didn't end because of the women, I ended them, I ruined them." 121, 123, 125. "I didn't realise what I was doing then but I see it as clear as day now. Everything's been leading to this moment!"

I knocked.

The automatic porch light came on. I hadn't noticed how dark it was.

The concerned-looking face of a man at least seven years my senior answered the door.

"Hello?"

I was thrown for a second.

Don't be a coward!

"I'm here to speak with Sapphire... please."

The man looked at my clothes and frowned. He was about to speak when her voice rang out from behind him.

"Who's at the door?"

He turned as she approached him and in the gap, he created she saw me.

"*Joseph?*" She was holding their child. I was silent.

"Is everything okay?" he asked her. She broke from her gaze to respond.

"Yeah, err... take him inside for me, will you?"

He took the child, smiled at her and nodded a cool goodbye to me. As soon as he left, she closed the door behind her. We were alone. An impulse inside of me screamed "Kiss her", and then she spoke.

"What the hell are you doing here?"

"I needed to see you."

"I thought I was clear in my letter. And how did you even find me—"

"Sapphire, I know how you feel about me and I finally know how I feel about you" – *be brave Joseph, this is it!* – "I love you."

She paused, staring at me. "So, what!"

"No, you don't understand, Sapphire, I've been through so much and I—"

"You selfish, selfish so…" She turned back and glanced at the door then took a step towards me.

"I know it's hard to believe but we were always meant to"

"You narcissistic fool. You self-absorbed, conceited, childish"

"I need you, Sapphire."

"And it's all about you, isn't it, Joseph? It's all about what you want and about what you need. You want someone to make *you* happy. You assume that their happiness will be a by-product of your own. You think that your happiness is some sort of right, something that the world owes you and if you don't receive it, it's everybody else's fault – even mine."

"Sapphie, I—"

"I haven't finished. You turn up here, in the middle of the night, looking like a mad person and you tell me that *I* need to realise that I'm still in love with *you*, and *I* need to leave my wonderful husband and beautiful child and, presumably, run away with you tonight. And why should I do this? Because *you're* unhappy, because *you're* at your lowest point, because you're *needy* – but what you don't realise is that you always have been! You want someone to fill that gap in your life. But what gap would you be filling in mine?" The question was rhetorical but she allowed it to linger. "I bet you never gave my needs a second thought when you decided to come here." She gave me the opportunity to lie but I let it pass. "The best thing I can do for you right now, as a friend, is to tell you to leave my doorstep and never come back here like this again." Her expression was unwavering, her conviction true. She wouldn't hear another word from me, even if I had one to utter.

My internal desolation must have been clear on my face as, when I turned to leave, she spoke, not in a regretful tone but one of exasperation, tailed by care.

"Why did you come here, Joseph?"

I couldn't even turn to face her as I spoke.

"I'm at the lowest... the... I'm desperate, Sapphie, and I couldn't need your love more."

Silence.

"I can't be what you want. In truth, nobody can. I know you never speak about it and I know I swore I never would either, but Joseph, you need your mother."

I could barely speak.

"I need you."

"You never needed me. You convinced yourself that you did because what you needed was gone. You were so desperate for love that you convinced us both that we needed to be together. But you soon realised that even when you had me – and you had me Joseph – that I wasn't enough, that something was still missing. Joseph, I couldn't then, I can't now and I can never replace your mother; nobody can. You've never moved on from her death and you never will until you accept that she can't be replaced." She looked at me without anger, and must've seen what a complete mess I was, because she came down from the doorstep and kissed me gently on the lips and told me.

"I can't help you, Joseph. I'm sorry."

As she went inside, she looked back, sincere pity attempting to mitigate her priorities as a mother and a wife. Then she closed the door.

That Night

I tried to hold it in. It took everything I had just to hold it at bay. I allowed the pain to turn to anger just so I could control it long enough to get home. But anger wasn't strong enough to contain my pain and as I stumbled through the door of my home, I dropped my keys, fell to my knees and cried. I cried as if I had just got the call from Dad to come home from college straight away because my mother was dead. As if I was standing at the foot of her coffin at her funeral knowing it was empty because, as my dad put it, 'there was nothing to recover from the plane crash'. As if I were sixteen, alone in my room at night filled with guilt for every bad thought and word I'd ever had against her.

I cried for all the nights of all the years I never did. I gave into the pain that I had feared heart and soul, and grieved without shame or restraint. I thought – I truly believed that it wouldn't stop, that I would cry myself to death. God Almighty, the pain was unbearable.

It didn't end; it only abated, from a sea to a river.

My phone flashed. I'd received a text. "It must be Sapphire. Dear God, make it be her." I grabbed the phone and opened the message.

Joseph we hope ur okay If theres anything u need just let us kno. Try 2 remember that ur happiness isn't dependant on somebody elses. Ur a good guy Joseph, b happy being u. because what r we here for if not 2b happy?

"What?" I scrolled back to the top of the message. It was from Matt. I sank into myself. My head was pounding, my eyes sore. My breathing stuttered and my nose ran. I wiped my face and looked at the text again.

"If I'm not happy, what am I here for?"

I thought of my aunty and the peace she must be in.

"If I'm not happy, what am I here for?"

I opened my bedroom window, taking it off the latch to allow it to open to its full extent. The rush of cold air cooled my face and brought relief to my throbbing head. I lifted myself onto the windowsill and I hung one leg over the ledge. I looked out and not down. I was on the third floor. I remembered lunging at Aaron's mum, full of lust. I lifted my other leg over and was now sitting on the ledge of my window facing the street outside. I remembered how Aaron wouldn't look at me when he came out of the toilet while his mum and I were kissing. I moved closer to the edge. There weren't many people out and the trees obscured my view of the apartment block across the road. I had nothing left. There was a strong wind that evening, so, I waited.

I hoped for a sign. I thought maybe my life might flash before my eyes or that I'd have some type of spiritual experience, or just simply that the strength of the wind would carry me one way or the other; allowing nature to decide.

Then, for the very first time in my life, I wondered, I dared to think,

Is this how my mum felt before she died?

Because of never seeing her body, my mind could never accept her death. I knew she was gone but refused to believe it.

When we were kids, my brother and I had found the code to my dad's safe amongst mum's papers one evening. We found his army medals, his will, and his gun. I closed the safe, tore up the paper with the code and told my brother to immediately forget it; I didn't though.

As the months following the funeral went on, my need for proof continued to grow. A part of me understood she was dead, another part of me was convinced that she had run away and no one wanted to tell me the truth. The one thing that was certain was that something wasn't right, something was missing – I could feel it.

It happened the same week I broke Sapphire's heart. Everything just felt too much, nothing felt certain and I wanted nothing more than to have my mother back, and in that state of mind, I allowed myself to believe that she was still alive. That she was unhappy was clear, that my dad would cover it up I could believe and that my aunty didn't know... that was a jump, but one I was willing to make.

So, a year after the funeral, driven by this new conviction I jumped on the internet and looked up the details of the flight all over again. A plane had crashed from Lyon to Strasbourg at the time my mum was away, but when I had searched there were no details of the passengers available. But a Memorial site had been created by the families of those who had died. Everyone's name was listed; but my mum's wasn't there! My first thought wasn't to confront my father or aunt, I wanted to have the upper hand, I didn't want them to know that I knew she was still alive. So, I went to the one and only place I thought I could find evidence of this dark secret – my father's safe.

Somehow, I remembered the code. My heart thumped wildly as I consumed the idea that my mother was still alive, that maybe she had tried to make contact via letter and that dad had hidden them in the safe, that maybe her address was on those letters, that within 24 hours I could be with her again, that the world would make sense once more...

Beyond the medals and the gun, and his will I found my mother's name, on the front of her death certificate.

It felt like she had died all over again.

The disappointment was gut deep and felt like it squeezed my intestines, in the way you wring dirty water from soiled clothing.

But unsatisfied with the pain I had already created, I read on:

'Cause of death:
Suicide.'

I became faint and fell to my knees.

This, it was too much.

Something within, something very powerful swallowed that shock, that pain and all the anger and confusion. And I found myself moving again. Putting everything back into the safe the way I found it. I got up and walked to my room, in a daze, like I was watching myself sleepwalking. I began to pack my clothes. I wasn't due to leave for Uni for another month, but I had to go.

I told my aunty that I was leaving and before she could protest, I just said that being here is too much for me. She nodded and hugged me and let me go without fighting me. I informed my dad via text message, his reply: "Okay."

It was the greatest shock I've ever suffered, but somehow it made more sense.

I wanted to blame my dad but I didn't want to confront him about the truth. I wanted answers from my aunty, but felt I couldn't handle hearing them. I never spoke a word of what I knew to anyone. I didn't want to spread the pain and confusion I felt to my brother, I didn't want Sapphire to think differently of my mum, and I was happy to blame my dad.

It wasn't a conscious decision to bury it all, that dark force which had devoured the shock and anger and pain, in time took my questions too. I had always thought that this force this power was grief, but now I know that it was something greater, something darker - desperation.

Now I know just how my mother must've felt.

For 15 years I've kept this secret, locked in me as it's been locked away in my dad's safe. Many answers passed with my aunt's passing, and today, tonight I hope the remaining questions die with me.

After an hour on the window ledge, it didn't even feel like I was breathing anymore. As the cold air ran through me, the clouds, almost directly above, parted and a full moon shone down like a spotlight.

This is it.

I stared up at the glory of the night's sun, mesmerised in its gaze.

This is my moment.

I closed my eyes... and a pigeon crapped all over my face.

"What the... You little b...."

I jerked back, unsteadying my position on the ledge and feeling my bottom slide closer off of the edge.

I swung my legs inside and fell back into my bedroom. As I rushed into the bathroom, the mess had started to drip down my face and passed my lips – I could taste it.

I ran hot water into my mouth and then spat it out with force. I cupped hands under the tap and then bathed my face, feeling the water's warmth against my cold, filth covered cheeks.

Some of the bird poo had mixed with the hot water and ran down my neck and chest, so I took my jumper off and the cold flooding in from my open window hit my naked torso. I closed the door. Shivering, I turned on the shower.

Hot water crashed down on me like Victoria Falls. I hung my head, allowing it to flow down my back. Feeling weak, I held onto the shower curtain rail, gripping the aluminium bar with might.

Tears ran unnoticed, and sobs escaped my lips unheard while heat brought life back to my limbs.

I stayed in there until all the hot water in the boiler ran out. Condensation hung heavy in the room. Afraid of the cold, I wrapped myself in the thickest, largest towel I owned. I wiped my mirror and, on sight of it, ran my fingers through my beard. I missed my old face. My hands moved while my mind was elsewhere, nowhere. I took out the shaving cream, my razor and felt heavy clumps of me fall into the sink.

When I'd finished, I looked like a little boy, smiling without knowing why.

On stepping out, I slammed my bedroom door and turned up the heating. I put on the kettle and strolled to the fridge. There was some jam and old breadsticks inside which I had 'borrowed' from work. I headed to the sofa with my snack and a hot chocolate. I sat down on the remote control and the TV switched on, playing the news. A reporter was talking to a Palestinian about his people's recent conflict with the Israelis. He spoke clear English, despite his accent, but they put subtitles beneath the image anyway.

"I don't understand, I don't understand why there needs to be war. We are brothers, we are brothers, Jews and Arabs, we both come from the same father, Abraham. Why must I kill my brother?"

"I didn't know Jews and Arabs both came from Abraham," I said aloud to the television. I grabbed my laptop, opened up a new page on Google and did a little research. with the remaining shekels in my account, I ordered Chinese halfway through and ended up watching loads of short documentaries on YouTube about Abraham's sons Isaac and Ishmael, then on Judaism and Islam and somehow, by the time I finished my special fried rice with pork balls, I was hooked on watching conspiracy theory videos.

I opened my bedroom door on the way to put on my house clothes and was surprised to see the window wide open. Then I remembered why. I closed it and sat on my cold bed wrapped in my warm towel. Goosebumps ran up my skinny calves and I got up to find a robe. Then a quote my English teacher used to say all the time ran through my mind and began filling me with understanding. But I couldn't for the life of me remember the exact words. I knew it was David Hume and I was sure I'd written it down somewhere.

So, I rummaged through my boxes flicking through my old anthologies, assignment books and homework notepads. Then, written in my stolen (long-term borrowed) copy of *The Great Gatsby*, right next to the line-up and formation for my dream England football team, was the quote - written how I remembered it:

> We can never achieve absolute knowledge. But nature mitigates our scepticism compelling us to believe. – David Hume

I went over to my window and looked outside. I read Matt's text message once more. "What are we here for, if not to be happy?"

My aunty used to say, "As apples of gold in silver carvings, is a word spoken at the right time."

"I don't want to die; I just want the pain to stop."

And with that, I closed the window.

A Day Later - (Deeper underground)

The door knocked and knocked and knocked and knocked and knocked. I first thought it was the postman, then maybe the new neighbours, then I thought it might be something important and then it just got annoying so I rolled out of bed ready to swear at someone.

I flung the door open and standing there with a six-pack of beer was Matt.

"Aren't you supposed to be at work?" I asked.

"It's Sunday." He walked inside and took two bottles out of the box.

"Isn't it a bit early for alcohol?"

"It's four in the afternoon." He turned my TV on. "You got Sky Sports? The second half of the rugby should be starting any minute."

"No. I've only got the 'I'm broke' channels."

He found Sky Sports News and was content with that. I put jam and breadsticks on a saucer.

We spent the next forty-five minutes drinking beer and listening to the match commentators get excited over a game we couldn't see.

"So, they sacked you."

"Yep."

"Are you appealing?"

"Nope."

"Have you been looking for another job?"

"Nope."

"Do you have any money?"

"Nope."

"None at all?"

"I've got an interest savings account with a few grand... but I can't touch it for another three years."

"So, you've got no money?"

"Nope. I mean... yeah, I've got no money. I'm dead broke."

"How are you going to pay your rent?"

"Ah, I won't have to."

"How come?"

"Because my landlord is kicking me out in two weeks."

"So where are you going to stay?"

"I was thinking of making a treehouse." I downed the last of my third beer. "Or moving to live under the sea 'where there's no accusations just friendly crustaceans.'"

"That's maybe Julia's favourite episode of *The Simpsons*."

I smiled; Julia was cool.

"Pack up your stuff and come and stay at ours. You can keep most of your stuff in our storage unit round the corner and the adoption process takes months, so the spare room will be spare for a while."

"I can't do that."

"Oh, I've got selfish reasons too. All that talk of redecorating got Julia excited and full of bright ideas for our place. So, it's going to be trips to Ikea every weekend for the next month, and as you're to blame you can help bear the load."

My smile grew with the gratitude that the beer in my system stopped me from articulating.

"Just take things a day at a time for now."

"What does that actually mean? I hear people say it all the time, but I don't see how that's possible."

"Don't start stressing or even thinking about the 'ifs, buts and maybes' of next month, next week or even tomorrow. Just do today. And today, you pack!"

Matt drove us to the supermarket where he bought me some food and we asked for any spare cardboard boxes, and they gave us loads that they were recycling. He said he'd come back at the end of the week to pick up what I'd packed so far – as long as I promised to stop ignoring his calls and messages. I felt blessed and cursed at the same time.

Why couldn't Matt and I have been friends before all of this?

The answer was obvious, it started with an "m" and ended with an "e".

I opened the car door to leave, then just began speaking.

"Matt... has someone that you've loved ever died?" I was still facing the street outside so couldn't read his expression in the silence.

"Years ago, a friend from school..."

"Were they someone you loved?" My hand gripped the handle that still held the door open.

"No."

This is going to hurt.

"I lost my mum... my mum died when I was sixteen. It was four months into my first year at college. It was a Tuesday afternoon... the 21st."

I closed the car door.

"The College receptionist didn't say anything, she just transferred the call to the phone in the corner of the office. The caller display showed 'Private Number'.

'Joseph,' my dad said, 'you need to come home from college now. Your mother has died. Your aunt is here.' I couldn't speak, it was the weirdest thing, I couldn't form words, the function failed me and I couldn't focus. I... I just stood there. Then he hung up. The change to the dialling tone kind of shook me. I dropped the phone and walked out of the reception office. I could hear the receptionist say something but it was like she was shouting from miles away. I couldn't really hear anything; it was just all noise. By the time I got downstairs I was running and I remember I burst through the main doors and I just couldn't hear anything, and then my vision started to blur, I was crying and didn't know that I was. I was running and wiping away tears and then I couldn't feel my legs, they were like... like numb stumps and I had to consciously move them and consciously make them stop when I got to a road. Then the sound of my breathing got louder and louder in my head and I was deaf to everything else. I... I got hit by a car – wow, I don't think I ever told anybody about that, I don't think I remembered it happening – it just knocked me over, not badly or anything, I just got knocked to the floor and then got up, my eyes were full of water and I couldn't make out the car so I just kind of waved and then carried on running. I remember the sound of my heart pumping louder and louder, until it hurt. And then I was home.

I couldn't get the keys out of my pocket; my fingers were numb. So, I banged on the door. My aunty opened up and stood there already in tears, and then it started to hit. She held me while I bawled but then I tore back away from her. I wanted to know everything that had happened, I needed to understand exactly what had happened before I could accept this, I wanted to see her, to see my mum. I ran past my aunty to my dad who was in the living room alone. I remember him standing when he heard me coming. He just put out his right hand, that was his way of telling me to calm down, so I stopped a couple of feet from him. He told me that her plane from Lyon to Strasbourg hadn't made it. I stood there. What he said made no sense to me. The only words I could get out were 'Where is she?' And he looked at me like... like he was angry with me for asking such a stupid question, for making him explain, and he just said 'She's dead.' And walked into the dining room and closed the door behind him."

I wiped a few loose tears from my face. It felt like Matt hadn't moved a muscle.

"After that day, in fact that evening, I stopped crying and told myself that until I saw my mum with my own eyes and saw her not moving, then it wasn't real and I didn't care what anybody said, this hadn't happened and I wouldn't accept it. And I didn't. Even at her funeral, I refused to cry because I refused to accept she was gone. And then I started to get angry with her because she wasn't there and almost made myself hate her in her absence, believing she had left me; not us but me. Then I convinced myself that I didn't need her, that my aunty was there and as far as I was concerned, she was twice the mother my mum was, so if she didn't want to come back then that was up to her, it was fine, I'd just put it behind me and carry on."

I paused, running out of steam.

"Did you carry on thinking that way?"

"I did, until…" I thought of telling him about how she died but it was too much too soon, "well, for a long time. I carried on… in complete denial and just grew closer to my aunty who became my mum's replacement; so much so I stopped referring to my mum altogether. I refused to even use the term mother when speaking of her, and I… I never spoke her name again."

I shook my head, filled with shame.

"I didn't know what I was doing," I started, as if I'd been accused of something. "I had no idea what I was supposed to do to cope." With a deep breath and a silent moment I accepted my own argument and continued.

"Where I had drawn close to my aunt, my brother had got closer to my dad, and the distance between him and me grew. I wanted love so badly, and couldn't even get a hug from my dad. My mum had left me. Then my aunty had left me..."

"And now Aaron's left you too."

My head swung round to Matt, shocked at his words. And slowly, ever so slowly, they began to sink in and make more sense than I could deny.

The immediate thought that everybody leaves me because I'm worthless, sped through my mind.

I don't deserve to be loved.

But the thought that slowed its pace and circled my mind before taking rest, was that Sapphie was right; I thought I'd been trying to replace her my whole life but there was a deeper loss that she was being used to cover over.

Then what of Aaron?

Matt hugged me before he left and made me promise again that I wouldn't lock myself away or ignore calls and texts. When I closed the door behind me, I stood there and physically felt lighter, realising what a burden I'd been carrying. I thought of how I could continue to lighten my load.

I got inside, stood in the middle of my small living room, and said my mother's name out loud; it was a whisper. It hurt, but less than I had imagined.

With a freedom I'd long forgotten, I spoke the word. There was a dull ache in my chest. I said it again, this time mustering the courage to speak louder, then louder, again and again until the tears started and stopped and started again and I stood calling out her name for the first time since her funeral.

"Rachel, my mother Rachel. My mother Rachel is dead."

That Night

I was mentally and emotionally exhausted. I lay in bed, trying to fall asleep. My eyes closed, and I begged for all of this to be a dream, everything: Aaron's accident, my decisions in life, everything following my mother's death. It felt too much to accept. It must be false. It must be make-believe. I don't want it to be true.

It would be so easy for this to have all been an elaborate nightmare, and for me to wake in the morning in my old home, my mother telling me I'm late for college, Sapphire waiting to see me at the pub for lunch. If God had mercy, he would make it so. I squeezed my eyelids shut and I prayed.

The Next Day – (The magic hour)

In the morning, I started my packing in the kitchen first. I found that I had bought appliances that I'd never used and had then bought shelves and storage units to keep them in while I wasn't using them and had to paint and varnish these additions so that they didn't look out of place in the flat. All of that money, space and time wasted on appliances and gadgets that I bought to save time, space and money. Seeing this made me realise that not everything I had there was worth keeping.

In that frame of mind, I went straight to the old boxes in my bedroom.

During the day I would pack only what I needed, and every night I went through my boxes seeing which memories deserved holding onto and which needed to be left behind.

I took out that picture of my mum again. She looked beautiful. I placed the picture on my bedside table. The thought swam into my mind on a wave of emotion.

"I want to go home."

My sleeping had improved but still wasn't right. Something was still missing.

I lowered my wall of stubbornness and allowed inside the thought of what Felicia had said and what Julia had told me. I called Matt and explained. He let me borrow his car.

By the time I reached my old home, it was early evening. I stood outside on the lawn looking up. The windows were dark; it was hollow and lifeless and empty behind those eyes; the house was abandoned. I stood there staring as day turned to night, feeling the grief of this lost loved one; it *was* more than just a house. That magic hour came and went, and I was present for every second of it.

My old home drew me in and repelled me all at once. I remembered a voice over the phone telling me that I was scared of life. What more did I have to fear? The very worst things have already happened to me, and here I am – still standing. The front door was locked but the downstairs toilet window was left ajar.

I'd never been in a completely empty, derelict house before; it was like a skeleton – not just bare but barren. The owners after us had painted the walls white, but nothing else had changed. The floorboards still creaked in the same places and that brown patch of damp above the dining room door had re-emerged. As I entered that room, I recalled the story I told Aaron about my brother. I could see our dining table, our chairs, my brother, who always sat to the right of my dad, my mother who sat to his left and me, I sat opposite her. I could see her so clearly now.

It took only a minute to wander around the dining room, to float without thinking. Then I was drawn upstairs, to the bedrooms. I almost broke into laughter at the sight of the room I used to share with my brother. Sword fights with coat hangers, bedtime burping competitions, tying all of the sheets together to make a tent for indoor camping; fighting over who got to use the mirror, fighting over who should get up and turn off the light at night, fighting over what colour to decorate the room, fighting just because fighting was what siblings did. The room looked so small now but I could still feel the life that once filled it.

I moved to the bathroom, the only safe haven in the house; when that door was locked nobody could bother you. I used to stand on the ceramic toilet lid and look out of the window, just watching – enjoying the view of life happening around me.

Then there was my parents' room. I walked in and curled up against the wall where the bed used to be and I closed my eyes. In that moment, I missed her more than I could bear. I loved her more than I ever knew, and I wanted to see her again more than anything else that life could offer me.

I opened my eyes and it was morning; afternoon to be exact – 12:43pm; I'd slept the whole way through. Squinting from the daylight, I glanced around the room, taking it all in again, then wiggled myself back into comfort, and went back into a deep sleep.

After waking again, I began driving back to my flat, planning to buy our old home, knowing all the while that it was impossible, but enjoying every thought of living there once more.

Then it tugged on my mind again, the dream, the vision. I had wanted to wait till I reached the flat to re-live it and let it sink in, but the memory of what I saw and heard while I slept wouldn't wait for me, it kept pulling at me, urging me to re-live it; so I pulled into a side road and followed it round to a quiet cul-de-sac which lead onto an empty park, and I closed my eyes.

<u>Earlier That Day</u> – (Innervisions)

I woke up in my old home but somehow it was night. I felt rested and awake and drew in a deep breath. Moonlight broke into the house like a slick invader, being everywhere but moving nothing. I got up and began walking as if I had purpose but not knowing where I was going. I trotted down the stairs but made no sound. I smiled at the sight of the front door, thinking of the thousands of times I went in and out of it, and now looked on at it as an old friend who's hand I hadn't shaken in years.

There was a smell, something so familiar, I thought at first it was food, maybe baking, perhaps a neighbour was making a midnight cake, but the scent was too strong, too familiar, it was sweet but light; somehow it smelt warm and I found my feet leading me with pace, not to the kitchen or dining room, but to the living room.

I entered and turned to my left. And there she was. Dressed in a white linen shirt and linen trousers, she stood barefoot with that smile of someone waiting to be found, waiting to be seen, then that smile broke out wide and tears began to trickle towards it. I ran and embraced my mum with all of the joy the world could muster. I grabbed her and held her close as she shed tears of joy while I cried rivers of relief.

"You're back, you're back... oh God." My words struggled to make their way out through my sobbing. Then I stopped and held her back from me, my eyes soaking her in.

"It's me, Joseph it's me."

I fell into her chest and my tears started again. Hers were replaced with deep inhalations and soft strokes bestowed upon my head. She pulled me in closer and then pulled us down to the floor where she sat up and I rested my head on her shoulder, with the side of her face on my hair.

"I've missed you, I missed you so much." I fought hard to articulate my feelings, and then the words came. "I've missed you so bad I've wanted to die."

She stroked my hair with her cheek. "I know, I know."

"Where have you been all this time?"

Her chest rose and expanded as she let out a heavy sigh.

"I had to go away."

I lifted my head so that my cheek was on her shoulder, I could just about see her lips.

"Why?"

"You know why."

"How could I know?"

"Do you remember what your friend told you, the one who worked for the Samaritans?"

I wanted to say no.

"Yes."

"I wanted the pain to stop, but it wouldn't."

Her mouth barely opened as she spoke, her lips moved as if knowing the words they uttered were full of sadness. I kept looking at the unhappiness in her lips, seeing that they would produce nothing more by way of an explanation. I watched them purse together and create small creases around her mouth and soft chin. The muscles in her throat moved up and down, she swallowed, then her jaw clenched, then those lips, drenched in sadness, opened again.

"Why are you here?" Her words were spoken with no weight, but left her with a tone of reluctance.

Looking up at her I didn't know what to say, but after a moment's thought, the answer was very clear.

"I came here to see you,"

Her lips came together and turned downwards. She swallowed again, and before the muscles in her throat had taken her saliva away, a tear dripped and flowed around the corner of her mouth, riding on the crease her downturned smile had made. It hung from the side of her chin, not heavy enough to fall. I watched it hang, dull and translucent. The droplet somehow escaped the grasp of the moonlight as it escaped the fall and sat there as we both did, hanging onto each other. Then with a swiftness made by the path already trodden, another tear rushed down and stole its predecessor from its position and the two fell, disappearing, leaving behind only the single streak of where they had both been.

"You know I can't carry on without you?" I tilted my head up higher and could now see her eyes. They were closed, not squeezed shut, just not open, as if the need for her sight was vacant. "I don't want to carry on without you". I continued. "It's not right. How can I live my life acting like the worst thing that could ever happen to me hasn't happened? I can't, I won't; it's not right, and it's not fair."

Under their lids, I saw her eyes look down in the silence. Then she replied, with a light nod:

"It's not fair and it's not right. But you can't mourn me forever."

I arched my chin upwards bringing my mouth closer to her face, closer to her eyes feeling like I was talking to them, pleading to them, waiting to see their reaction.

"But if I stopped mourning you then it's like I'm saying 'I've forgotten you', it's like I'm saying 'I'm okay with you not being here, I'm okay with this!' How can I enjoy life while the person I love most is dead? You gave me life!"

"Is it guilt you feel?"

I paused.

"All the time." My voice trembled at the last. "I should've been kinder to you, I should've talked to you more, I...I can't remember the last time we spoke - I don't know what my last words to you were." Tears now hung from my chin. "And every time I smile or laugh or have a partially good day, I feel like it's a sin against you, like I'm saying I can enjoy life without you."

"Why is it wrong to enjoy life without me?"

"Because I don't want to! There should be no life without you. I shouldn't be able to move, to talk, to walk, I shouldn't be able to breathe, the pain should kill me!"

Her eyelids tightened and a thin line of moisture was squeezed to the fore.

"But why Joseph?"

"Because you mean everything to me. And if everything goes then I should have nothing, but when I function without you it's like I'm saying you weren't everything."

Tears clouded my vision and I bowed my head back down onto her shoulder, sobbing as she drew me in closer.

"Joseph,"

I didn't move.

"Joseph," her tone was somehow kinder.

"Yes,"

"Look at me."

I didn't want to. I couldn't.

"Joseph, please,"

Her gentle tone lifted the weight of the unexplained fear I felt to look up at the face I had yearned to see for years.

I lifted my head, wiped my face and looked up. Her eyes, her beautiful soft dark eyes, looked down on me and her lips smiled and then parted to speak words I would never forget.

"Would you die for me?"

I took a solemn breath and spoke as if giving an oath.

"Everyday."

She held my stare and matched my solemnity.

"Then live for me."

Her words were so large they filled the room. Yet the silence that ensued was so strong it gripped my heart. With all my strength, I was only able to mutter:

"But..."

"Live for me, Joseph." There were no tears in her eyes or sadness on her lips. "Live for me and let me live through you. Let every person that meets you know just how much you love me and how much you were loved by me, through knowing how wonderful you are. Let them all see what I see in you."

"But I..."

"Live for me, Joseph. If you would die for me, if you love me, if you have ever loved me, live for me, and make me proud by making you happy."

"I don't think I can, I don't think I have it in me."

And that's when she smiled; I knew that smile, I've known that smile from the day I learned to breathe, and I trusted it like I trusted day to follow night.

"I know my son."

And she did, even more than Sapphie, even more than her son knew himself. Yet still, I didn't want to.

"But why can't I just stay here with you, like this?"

"Because this isn't real Joseph. I'm not really here. I only exist now in God's memory, and your heart. But if you stop trying, if you stop living, then what happens to me?"

She paused, and I allowed her words to sink in.

"You have no reason to carry guilt, but what you do have now is a responsibility. Love is more than just a feeling, to love someone means to take on a responsibility, a duty, an honour. You are responsible for keeping our love alive and for sharing it and making it grow. Let the world know just how much you were loved."

She knew her son.

"Will I see you again?"

Her smile was deep as she breathed the word. "No."

My eyes dropped. I knew every word she had spoken was true, including this one.

"But you will feel me; every time you smile, and every time you laugh, every time you have a 'partially' good day; every time you make someone happy and every time you feel happiness you will feel me and remember me and honour me with your joy."

I could feel a swirl of emotion rising, rushing past my chest, making it difficult to breathe.

"Look at me son,"

I looked up.

"I'm dead Joseph. I'm dead, and I'm so sorry, I'm sorry my son, but I am. I've gone."

Her lips trembled, and her words trailed off as tears streamed from her eyes and she cried. She tried to control herself but couldn't. Seeing her cry, seeing her pain, seeing her miss me, hit me harder than her words. Then her words continued, despite the tears.

"But know this Joseph, know that you can make me live." She put her hand on the side of my face, holding it firm with a gentle touch. "Will you?"

I tried to speak but I knew that if I released the hold on my face, I would lose all control, so I nodded, but she waited; wanting more.

I forced the words out.

"I will."

"Do you promise?"

"I promise."

"Please, for me... say it."

I clenched my jaw, my fist and my stomach and fought for control over myself, fought for the strength to grant my dead mother her final wish.

"I will…" I struggled so hard to get the words out, "I… I will make you live through me." I took the deepest breath my shaking body could hold, and continued. "I'll make you proud by making me happy."

"That's all I've ever wanted."

The smile she produced was like seeing heaven open up. I closed my eyes and wrapped my arms around her, and like that… she was gone.

She was gone and I was awake and it was early evening. I touched my face and it was dry. I touched my chest and my heart was thumping. I looked around the empty room, the empty house and felt the desire, the need, to go home, to my home. I looked out of the window and felt blessed at the sight before me – it was the magic hour.

<u>Later That Day,</u>

Sat in Matt's car, parked in a cul-de-sac facing an empty park I re-lived the moments with my mother with dry eyes.

"I'll see you next week. Don't forget the chocolates."
Those were the last words I spoke to my mother.

She had replied, "Don't forget to brush your teeth." as a quick rebuttal. Then she said, "I love you, bye Joseph."

I only said "Bye." It would've been nice if my last words were "I love you too." But they weren't, and that's fine. Instead, I can live those words, those words I didn't say will be seen, and everyone who will know me will know them to be true.

My eyes were dry, my heart was calm and my face was smiling, as I thought about my dead mother who I knew I would never see again.

I turned the car around and made my way home.

<u>The Next Evening</u>- (Self-raising)

I don't know what time I fell asleep but I didn't wake up until 3pm the next day. Despite the time it didn't feel right to eat anything besides cereal.

I found an out-of-date mini variety box of Coco-Pops under my bed.

As eating cold cereal, in my view, was reserved for POW camps and scenes from Dickens novels, I put my bowl of brown deliciousness in the microwave for 30 seconds, and stood, listening to the hum of the machine in its dull orange light whilst watching the numbers count themselves down.

Just as I anticipated the ping and then heard it, I realised, in the silence that followed, I realised that it had stopped, it had actually ended; I had stopped crying.

For so many years, the thing I had feared most was facing my pain, and, in the face of its enormity, being crushed by it. I feared that I would breakdown and cry and cry, until I cried myself into a madhouse or to death.

But I didn't go insane, nor did I die. I returned from that place I had feared for so many years, that black despair that I believed would consume me, and I'm here. Not just still living and breathing, but lighter, warmer...

Then her eyes struck me, not those of my mothers, or Sapphire's or Aaron's mum's, but the woman with the wide eyes full of fear. Her face, that look, filled my mind as it had before, but this time I felt different, I didn't feel connected to her as I once was. I thought back to that night, that scene, to her face, and realised it wasn't the fear in her eyes that had connected us, it was the desperation.

She saw no way out, perceived no saviour and so resigned to her fate. But for her, it was just in that moment. For me, I had lived the last 15 years of my life in that state. My situation was now worse, even more uncertain and the scope for failure was vast, but now I had seen the face of my fear, and I did not die, I did not break beyond repair, I was still here, living, breathing and now hoping. Not just wanting hope to be real, but really feeling hope.

I heard the noise of people in the hallway, and thought that my landlord might have sent the bailiffs early. I crept to the door and looked through the spyhole. It was a team of decorators going into Aaron's flat.

Instead of sadness, a warm joy filled me as I wondered:

What's Aaron up to – who's cooking for him now, who's reading to him, who's answering all of his questions, and are they doing a good job?

As I thought of him, I couldn't help but think of her, his mum. "The test!"

As I had done over 4 weeks before, I grabbed the nearest trainers I could find and made my way to Liverpool Street. So much about that journey felt similar, but so much, so much was different.

The test came back negative, but it was weird because I wasn't as relieved as I was with the first negative result. I recognised that it was good news, I recognised that not having HIV was something to be joyful about, even celebrate, but I also recognised that this was a reminder, not just of what I did but who I was.

As my mind pondered on the 'Joe' so many, including myself, had seen me as, to the Joseph my mother had always seen, I smiled, appreciative of one less scar to bear, thankful that this mistake could be left in the past, with the old Joe who made it.

When I returned home, I looked on the many boxes that I had marked for storage, and took them down to the bins.

"Letting go, means letting go."

By the end of the night, my flat was bare. It looked naked and a lot more attractive in that state. All that was left were a few boxes with my last essentials, some photos and my sofa, which we would need a van to move. I looked around at all of the empty space, and I felt good. As if all the unnecessary clutter in the flat and all of the hoarded relics in my boxes had been clogging my mind.

It was like living through an earthquake and surviving the destruction and upheaval it brought, then in the aftermath discovering that the quake had turned up many hidden treasures from within. Although these riches couldn't in any way compensate for what was lost, they did help rebuild what was crushed and fortify a stronger foundation to cope with the next disaster. Because without any doubt, sooner or later, there would be another one. But that was life, and I wasn't scared anymore.

I sat on my sofa drinking the last hot chocolate I'd ever have in my flat. Matt said he'd be round again in the evening so that we could move the rest of my stuff. I laid back on the sofa and sank into a comfortable nap.

About two months ago, my block was allocated the laziest postman alive: my post now arrived halfway through the day as a standard.

The sound of mail coming through the letterbox woke me up. I looked at my watch and it was 4:37pm.

"This postman takes laziness to a new level."

As I got up I thought it might be from my brother. He had emailed asking how I was getting on, and for the first time, I responded with the truth and told him how I was feeling. He hadn't replied, so I thought the letter must be from him, especially as I noted the airmail stamp on the front.

But as soon as I picked it up and saw how my address was written, I knew without a doubt that this wasn't from my brother.

Joseph,

I had to wait until I could get to a computer to write to you. I can't use the one here coz then people will see what I'm writing so I waited until I joined a school and then started to write this letter in my lunchtime every day. It took me ages. Plus, I needed to use spell check. I'm in America now I'm living with my great aunt my gran's smaller sister. My gran took me to her house for a couple of months until I was better and she was sorting stuff out with my aunt so that I could move to here. I tried calling you loads of times but I kept getting the number wrong I'm so stupid I didn't listen to you and memorandum it. My aunt wouldn't help me becoz my gran told her that you are a bad person and that I'm not allowed to speak to you but I remembered the name of our block of flats and Googled it to get the right address so I didn't need her help. My aunt is nice but the kids in my school are so cool they think my English accent is really cool to. People over here are different though everybody talks so loud and then becoz it's so noisy you have to talk even louder for people to hear you. My mum called she said she's coming over soon I hope she means it I don't think she does coz my mum and my aunt hate each other. We've got a cat and a dog here I thought that was a bit weird. I had to start my computer game again but that's ok becoz the softwares over here are better. The TV shows over here are so good and so funny but there's more commercials and no one likes to watch football they call it soccer and that's so stupid becoz they call American football football even though they use their hands. The house my aunt and uncle live in is nice my uncle is ok he is really quiet he just works and reads his newspaper he's alright though. Things are okay I love you Joseph and sometimes I feel sick becoz I want to come back home so bad.

You can write me back if you want to.

I put the address on the bottom and if you do write back put it in a big envelope so that they think it's the comic books I send off for.

Please write back.

Aaron.

I sat down on the sofa and placed the letter on the top of the box in front of me. As I stared at it, something bright and yellow distracted my gaze. I reached into the box and pulled out Aaron's book of Bible stories. I opened it to the page where he had written his name. Joy bubbled within me remembering how happy he was that day.

"Sapphire was right. She was absolutely right. I never gave. I always wanted and expected but never really gave until Aaron…"

It was different with him. I didn't want anything from Aaron, I wasn't using him to fill a gap in my life – I was needed to fill a gap in his. My joy was in the love I gave him more than in the love I received.

Then it came to me as the most obvious thing in the world.

I pulled my laptop out of the box and jumped on my neighbour's wireless – using "password" for a password.

I needed money and now. I had pretty much nothing left in the bank. Once again, the answer was simple. I closed my laptop, grabbed the power pack and ran out the door.

The cash converters down the road only gave £75 for it. I went back again with my TV – £50. All of my DVD box sets – £27.64. I offered them my watch.

"We don't do jewellery, mate. There's a pawn brokers down the road, but," gesturing at my wrist, "I don't think that counts." I was out of the shop before I had time to comment on his comedic skills. Unfortunately, he was right.

I sprinted home, sure that there must be something left there of value. I remembered the cufflinks my brother sent me two Christmases ago as I came through the door. I dug through the boxes looking for them and instead found a small, dark green velvet box. Inside were my aunt's engagement and wedding rings.

I didn't want to, but I had no choice.

As I walked back out, holding the rings in my jacket pocket, I saw a couple moving into Aaron's old flat. My slow pace offered them the opportunity to wave. I smiled back and turned to leave, then stopped.

"Do you have furniture already?"

"Yeah, we do, thanks," the man said, his sleeves rolled up his long thin arms.

"Oh..."

"Not all of it has arrived yet, though," the woman said, dressed more like they were going out for a picnic than moving home.

"The sofa we want isn't in stock so will take about a month or so to arrive," the man added, picking up another box.

"You can have mine... or at least rent it until you get yours. I'm moving out."

They stood looking a little confused – too confused to just say no.

"Come and have a look." They glanced at each other and before they could answer I ushered them over and they followed with a little reluctance.

"It's quite nice." She looked at her husband with a smile.

"Okay. How much to... rent your sofa?" he asked, too tired to argue.

"Two hundred."

"That's a bit—"

"One hundred, final offer." I was firm.

He didn't need the not-so-gentle nudge from his wife to take the offer – £100 was exactly what I needed. We went to the cashpoint, he took the money out and I paid in all the money I had. I sprinted home, grabbed my notepad and pen, Aaron's letter, ordered a cab, and wrote these words on the in the back seat:

It's the only way I feel I'll be able to express to you all the things I want to say to you now, but also all the things I would want to tell you in the future, in case this is the last time I see you – if I get to see you at all. I've just booked a one-way ticket to New Jersey over the phone, I'm in a cab on my way to the airport – the flight leaves in an hour and a half, there's traffic and because I sold my laptop I couldn't check-in online – but I know I'll make it. I have to.

45 Minutes Later

I couldn't do it. I just couldn't do it. I got to the check-in late and they were a bit suspicious at the fact that I didn't have any luggage, but they checked me in, let me through and led me to the departure gate.

I froze. Fear gripped and tightened all the muscles in my body. The stewardess called up the first-class travellers. I watched as they strolled out to the plane. The "premium" travellers were next. Then the queue for the economy seats started and trailed back to where I stood, bearing an empty expression while the bitter taste of defeat lined my lips.

"But I'm scared," a little boy a few feet from me told his mother as he refused to step forward with the queue.

"Where's your father?" his mother replied exasperated.

At first, I thought it was just a strong sense of déjà vu, but then the memory filled me like a breath of air, clean, crisp and complete.

We were all at the airport, me, my brother, my dad and my mother. We stood in line at Heathrow, ready to board. I was about the same age as the little boy in front of me now, and said those exact words to my mother.

She, however, replied in soft tones, "Of what, Joseph?"

"I don't know." My uncertainty was tinged with embarrassment. She took me over to the metal seats a few feet away and knelt down.

"Tell me."

I looked out of the window at all of the planes, and then held my rucksack close to my chest.

"Something bad might happen."

"Something bad might happen on the way home too, should we not go home anymore?" She spoke as if this was now a real concern.

"No."

She smiled and took my hand from my bag and placed it in hers.

"Darling, you're right, something bad might happen. But, so might something really, really good. Something amazing. So amazing that you'll be so upset you ever missed out on it."

My eyes glowed at the promise of new wonders, but I didn't move. I glanced once more out of the window. My mother stood, took a step towards the queue and turned with her hand outstretched to me. I ran towards her, grasped her arm and smiled with unspeakable joy while we talked about the impending trip.

We went. We *did* go. I was six and we flew to Jamaica during the school summer holiday. I couldn't believe it. I couldn't believe that all this time I had never remembered, never recalled the fact that I had flown before!

I can do this, I have to do everything I can to make sure that I see you again; it's my duty, my responsibility.

The final call for boarding rang loud and clear.

A Minute Later - (Epitaph)

The weight of my last words sank deep in me. The final call rang out again.

This, what I'm doing here, is not everything. This is impulsive, poorly planned, and likely to fail; just like that night at the bar, and when I turned up at Sapphie's house. I can't allow the most important thing I do to be another last-minute, slapdash effort. That's not responsible, that's not love.

I won't try to see you. I will see you; but not like this.

Three Months On

I wrote to your aunt and uncle. I realised that if I called and I didn't say the right thing in just the right way and straight away, that they could hang up on me and that would be the end of it. So I wrote to them. I took my time, drafted out word for word what I wanted to say, and I handwrote them a letter, explaining as much as I could.

I moved in with Matt and Julia; that turned out to be a great experience. I got a temporary job as a Teaching Assistant in Julia's primary school as a bit of a stop-gap, but after two weeks they offered me a six-month contract, and I jumped at it. I emailed my brother and asked when he'd next be in this part of the world, as I really wanted to see him in person. He messaged me back saying that he would let me know soon, and ended his email saying that he missed me.

Then, although I had to really push myself, I went to see the doctors; not about my stomach or about my toe but about my mental health, and they referred me for counselling. It's been tough but it has really helped. In fact, it led to something very, very unexpected.

Halfway through my twelfth session, my counsellor asked me the unaskable.

"Have you ever thought about going to see your dad, and asking him about your mother?"

"No way, no way. I want nothing to do with that man."

"Does anyone else have the answers you are looking for regarding your mother?"

I didn't have to think about it but still paused.

"No."

She let the silence sit.

"I know what you're trying to say but I can't; it's his fault that she's gone, I don't want to face him on this, I can't do it."

"What are you afraid of Joseph?"

"That I might hurt him." My tone was cold.

She paused again and made me think on my words. I would want to hurt him but I knew I never would.

"Are you afraid that he might hurt you?"

"What? What do you mean? How could he hurt me? What, physically?"

"Not physically."

"Then..."

And it hit me. She was right.

I don't know why my mother took her own life. What if he told me something I didn't want to hear?

"It's the uncertainty. I have no idea what he might say?"

"Joseph, do you know if your mother left a letter or a note?"

The suggestion took me by complete surprise. I had never considered the possibility.

"I have no idea."

"If one exists, would you want to read it?"

"Of course."

"There's only one way that can happen." She gave me that reassuring smile you see doctors give patients before surgery. "Don't see it as a confrontation, or a situation where you have to bring up every bad thing from the past. You could just start with a simple request."

"And if there isn't a note?"

"What is the main question you want an answer to?"

"Why, why did she do it?"

"Then start there and ask him that. It's not an argument, it's not blame, it's just a question. How do you feel about that?"

Shaking my head I looked down as I answered. "I'm not sure."

"Okay. Let me ask you a different question. Do you want to know 'why' more than you fear the answer?"

It sounded like a complicated question but I didn't have to think to answer it.

"Yes."

She sat there silent, trying to mask her smile. I looked up at the clock in her office. We had 20 minutes left of our session.

"Can I call him now?"

She raised her eyebrows in surprise.

"Of Course."

So, I did.

He picked up.

He knew my number but still answered the phone with his formal: "Good afternoon, Winston speaking."

"Dad, it's Joseph."

"Joseph, are you okay?" He sounded detached but still concerned.

"I am. Thank you. I have something I need to ask you."

"Okay."

I took in a deep breath and spoke the words.

"Did mum leave a note?"

He was silent.

"I know dad. I saw the death certificate in your safe. I've always known."

His silence continued and started to hurt. I went to speak again.

"Yes, she did."

His words took the breath from my lungs. Before anger could set in and I start shouting, demanding to know why he never told me, I allowed my first and most natural response to proceed.

"Can I... I want to see it."

"Okay. I'm next in London..."

"I want to see it now."

"I leave tonight for a Conference..."

"Are you at home, now?"

"Yes."

"Is it in your home with you now?"

"Yes."

"Then please can you take a picture of it and send it to me now. Then, maybe on another day, we can meet and talk."

He was silent again. I was taken back by my own confidence.

"Okay. I will send it to you now and will let you know my schedule over the next month."

The right thing to do was to thank him. But I didn't want to.

"Alright then."

There was an awkward silence this time, we hadn't ended a conversation in a pleasant way in over a decade.

"Okay. It was good to hear from you son."

I went to hang up.

"I... I also have your mother's ashes." He said.

I was speechless.

"I think it's right for you to have them."

I had to force the words out, no longer because I didn't want to say them but because it was so difficult to speak.

"Thank you."

He hung up.

I looked up at my counsellor, and was shaking.

"He has my mother's ashes." It was hard to breathe. "He wants to give them to me."

Her smile was warm. "And the letter."

I inhaled a sharp breath through my nose. "He's, he's going to send me a picture of it now."

She sat up straight, jubilant, looking like she wanted to shake my hand. Then we both looked down at my phone.

The next 10 minutes were excruciating.

My counsellor and I waited in complete silence, until my phone beeped, and then beeped again. Two messages. I opened them. There were two pages.

I read them to myself.

I couldn't speak.

I couldn't say goodbye to my counsellor or even greet Matt and Julie when I got home. I couldn't speak for two days. It scared me and rattled me to my core. I read the pages again; it was as if I had written the letter myself.

I spoke on the third day, when I received a call from your great aunt.

She was stern to begin with, but we eased into comfortable conversation after the initial awkwardness; she has a very dry wit. She told me that you had owned up to writing to me, but that you didn't know I had written to them. I asked if they could keep it a secret, because I wanted to fly over to meet you all and I wanted to surprise *you*.

Three Months On

I'm on the plane now Aaron, well rested from 6 months of *real* sleep and 6 months of real stability. I'm determined, beyond any obstacle, to place this, my diary, into your hands. And to achieve this I'm armed with the most necessary tool: hope – our unique ability to believe that we can make the dawn of our tomorrow shine that much brighter with the realities we hold true in our minds today. I see now, without hope we are less than mortal. Without hope we don't bear the burdens of life or feel the glow of joy on our backs, instead, we carry our coffins.

You see, it wasn't fear or even desperation that had been destroying me, it was hopelessness.

And then you came along.

From my heart, Aaron, I swear, I cannot thank you enough.

P.S.

Stuck on the back of this page is the letter my mother wrote before she left. I have shared this with no one, but I think it will give you what it should've given me many years ago:

Of all the dreams that we can dream, how many do we see fulfilled? And if not in fulfilment, joy must be found in the venture of attempting to traverse the line between those aspirations of our imagination and the realities that we behold. But what joy can there be found in ventures never made?

Which of us has never dreamt of greatness, has never felt that burning desire in their heart to accomplish a single act or all-encompassing goal that could be replayed and reminisced with increased joy on each occasion, whether that goal be to raise an ambition from an idea to something real or to raise a family and know what it is to love and be loved?

To own memories to christen your dying thoughts and supersede all past failures and mistakes. Memories which illuminate the darkness of solitude and gloom of loneliness, that are so tangible in its mental composition that not only can you hold them, but they embrace you.

However, in the absence of such significant achievements and moments that declare worth, there sits a void of unfulfilled dreams; a black hole left from a dying star. Upon our hearts, we feel the weight of wasted potential and the shards of life's broken promises. We hear our own silent resignation to mediocrity and the mocking victories of the minority that question our value. We indulge in denial and the playing of hide and seek with the truth. During the day we mourn the death of opportunity and at night are haunted by its ghost "What if..."

All persons are born equal, but somewhere along the line, we convince ourselves otherwise. We accept the notion that only one in one hundred can win, can be successful, can truly live as we would want, and in accepting those odds, we accept that we will lose; and here is the great paradox, we find comfort in losing, because there we are not alone, in fact, we reside with the majority. And there we lay, along the side-lines of life, hopelessly feeding off of each other's desperation.

We all know the price of our dreams but fear we cannot afford them, believing they can only be bought with the currency of worthiness. So, we decide to no longer try, foolishly questioning the value of our own happiness.

I never knew how to love. To everyone else, it was like walking or breathing, but to me, it was a secret that I was never told.

Because of things I suffered, there were things I couldn't feel. I could never love my sister, my husband or my children in the way I wanted to. I never loved myself, so how could I ever be loved, or be happy.

Once upon a time, I wanted to be happy, I wanted to love and be loved. Now, I no longer have the inclination towards love, happiness, or life.

I fooled myself into thinking that I had time. That once 'this' was done or 'that' was finished, then I would try, then I would fight, and find that which has been missing and make it mine.

You won't see it coming, the day that it finally takes you. There are no warning signs, so don't wait to see them. All of a sudden, it will make all the sense in the world, and it will stop being a question.

To my Sister Claudine – You deserved more. You raised me well. But pains even you couldn't protect me from became too much. Please, care for my boys as you cared for me.

To my Husband Winston – You were a good provider. I respect that you wanted to wait until the children left University before you left the home. It wasn't that you were unlovable, I just didn't know how to love you, and everyday felt like failure.

To my Son Benjamin – You are the strongest person I've ever known. Follow your instincts my son, and they will always lead you true.

To my Son Joseph – I'm so sorry, I'm so, so sorry. When you see it coming my son, fight it. I see too much of myself in you to believe you won't feel it too. But your gift, is your ability to try and keep trying. That is how you will win.

I'm sorry I could not keep trying for you all.

This is my gift to you Aaron, to help guide you when you're older, in return for the gift that you have helped me grasp, the gift which so many, including my mother lost;
Hope.

Joseph Bogart

Reviews

"I started to read 'My Name Isn't Joe' by James Thomas, and at just three pages in I was totally invested in the character Joe and the authors infectious writing style. Right from the get-go I remained captivated and in awe of what was unfolding before my eyes. The authors compelling writing style had the ability to hold my attention continuously so much so that I set my alarm extra early so I could complete the book before work the next day! Through their compelling descriptions you are drawn into the characters emotions and their lives, they are so vivid you cannot help but feel 'present' within the story. I am completely blown away; I loved every inch of this book. I am an avid reader, but this book honestly blows all the other books I have read recently out of the water. This book is one I will be raving about to friends, family, and colleagues it is amazing." **Chantel-Hall Reid Publishing House Executive**

"Wow! This story was incredible to read. It made me go through all the emotions possible and had me hooked on every word from beginning to end. I found the story emotionally moving, especially when your touch was light enough to let me make my own connections. You had me hooked on every word from beginning to end. It was a memorable story and it will definitely be a very popular book." — **Nadine Adened**

"I'm writing this with tears down my cheeks, this will be in my memory as long as I live. I see it the same way I would see a Pollock. At first glance, abstract expressionism is chaos, it might chase away some people, but if you keep looking, it unveils the internal chaos of the beholder, and it is exactly what this Novel did to me. I would definitely reread the book, and it is a book that I would definitely recommend." **Salma El Ghaib**

"I enjoyed the way you worked the narrative to help speed up or slow down the pacing. The details you do have in this narrative are beautiful! I loved the way you described emotions, and I also thought the way you described ethnicity without stereotyping characters was a brilliant move—I wish other authors would write skin tones out that way. Joseph is such a deep, complex character and I loved learning about him. Beautiful job on that ending!" **Maddy D.**

"The charm of the story resided in the fact that every single word was so well written that even the simplest things raised the highest interest, creating and keeping the pleasure of reading through the whole book. I enjoyed every single word of the story, and I think it was masterfully told. I loved the irony that left space for joy and hope even in the gloomiest moments. This is the best book I have read in a long time!" **Andrea Padurean Reader**

About The Author

James Thomas, a born and bred Londoner of Jamaican descent, is an author and screenwriter.

Across his career he has written short films and feature length screenplays for several independent directors, producers, and independent production companies, as well as working in Los Angeles as a script editor.

Coming out soon: The Other Side of Love – a collection of short stories and poems on the unspoken aspects of life's most potent emotion.

To find out more about James Thomas go to: www.jamesthomaswrites.co.uk

www.marciampublishing.com